# The Dastardly Debutante

### HELEN GOLTZ

Atlas Productions

The Dastardly Debutante – The Lady Mortician's Visions, book 3.

PUBLISHED BY: Atlas Productions

First published 2023.

Cover design by Karri Klawiter, Art by Karri.

**PLEASE NOTE: This book is written in British-Australian English.**

*Chapter 1*

*M*ONDAY 1 SEPTEMBER 1890. *Brisbane, Australia. Overcast skies, rain threatening, wind variable, 25 degrees daytime.*

Phoebe Astin expected a busy Monday morning. Not because more people died on the first day of Spring as if pleased to have survived Winter and then declared the game over. But rather because her brother Julius insisted Phoebe and all the staff enjoyed time for personal pursuits, and Sunday was the day Phoebe spent in nature and not in her workroom. This resulted in somewhat of a stockpile as the unfortunate mortals who did turn up their toes on Sunday were often held at the hospital or morgue and invariably found their way – with some assistance – to the office of *The Economic Undertaker* on Monday, where they were welcomed like the many dearly departed before them. Two souls had already arrived – Miss Daisy Dorchester and Mr James Voss – and Phoebe was yet to read her notes to determine who took precedence for preparation.

From her large room in the basement where Phoebe plied her skills, she could hear the voices of her two brothers, Julius and Ambrose, drifting downstairs as they prepared for the day, discussing the roster of collections and booked funerals with the business frontman, their grandfather, Randolph. The comforting hum of their voices and the recognisable and impatient shuffle of Ambrose, the younger of the two brothers, was distinct. She could also distinguish the light shuffling on the floorboards overhead of dear Mrs Dobbs, who managed the kitchen, keeping the family and customers supplied with tea, biscuits and cake – a great consolation for the bereaved or, in Ambrose's case, the perpetually hungry.

Phoebe was alone; how long that would last was uncertain, but she had enjoyed a couple of months' reprieve from troubled souls lingering and asking her for help. The only visitor of late had been her Uncle Reggie, who had yet to move on for reasons he had not made clear to her, but she anticipated he would do so when he was good and ready. Most of her visitors did in good time. Some just popped in to thank her for her work, presenting them at their best, while others wanted messages passed to the living or, in a number of cases, justice served for their death. To see and hear them was an odd skill she had inherited from her mother's side of the family, and she suspected Julius also saw the dead, but he would not own to it.

'I like your dress,' a voice said, making Phoebe jump. She turned to see a young lady who would be described as beautiful by even the harshest of critics. Her glossy chestnut hair fell in waves to her shoulders, framing her heart-shaped face, and her bright sea-blue eyes, uniquely almond-shaped, made her quite exquisite.

'Thank you,' Phoebe said, smiling at the lady of similar age and running her hand down her dress.

'It's different, your dress.'

'Yes, it is more flowing than some of the fashions.'

'You're different.'

Phoebe flushed a little. 'Because I can see you?'

'What do you mean? I can see you too.' The young woman tipped her head to the side, curiously studying Phoebe. 'I meant you are unconventional in your style. I like it. I met an artist recently who dressed and wore her hair free as you do. I don't think that style would suit me, though. My aunt says my figure is one to envy and should be flattered by my dresses.'

Phoebe's eyes widened, unused to such displays of vanity and uncomfortable with compliments, even veiled ones, she moved to the two covered bodies lying in wait and looked at the name tag on each one.

'Would you be Miss Daisy Dorchester?' she asked without lifting the sheet to check for herself.

'I am, and I don't believe we have been introduced. I don't recognise you as one of the debutantes this year,' the young woman said, her eyes travelling over Phoebe and looking around to determine where she might be.

'No, I confess to having no interest in making my debut.' The startled expression on her visitor's face told Phoebe that such a concept was utterly foreign to her young guest. She continued, 'My name is Phoebe Astin, and I am the mortician here at *The Economic Undertaker*.'

'Oh,' Daisy said and looked around, 'I am at a funeral parlour; I thought I was dead but did not want to think too much about it. It is extremely inconvenient.' Her voice finished on a rise with a touch of annoyance.

'You are in respectful hands, Miss Dorchester, I assure you.' Phoebe adopted a pacifying voice.

'Is that me?' Daisy nodded to the sheeted body.

'Yes, you arrived early this morning. I would say I am pleased to meet your acquaintance, but usually, I meet people under sad circumstances, and I assume, as you have not yet had your debutante ball, you are quite upset?'

'Indeed, especially as it was widely known that I was to be the belle of the ball, and it was heralded to be one of the grandest balls of the season, with the finest of music and gay dancing.' Daisy drew in a deep breath as if for fortitude and wandered around the room, her hand trailing over Phoebe's desk and the furniture. Phoebe had learnt not to rush her guests as they were usually singularly focused and sometimes needed a moment to gather themselves to the shock of being deceased.

Daisy started again, 'It was meant to be this Saturday, but I shan't be attending now, obviously.' She looked around and threw her hands up in the air in despair. With great melancholy, she announced, 'I am dead.'

Phoebe gave her a sympathetic look. 'I am afraid so, Miss Dorchester. I am sorry. Aside from your debut, did you have great plans?'

'I had great prospects,' she said haughtily. 'As you may be my last earthly friend, please call me Daisy, and I shall call you Phoebe.'

'Let's do so,' Phoebe agreed. 'Can I assist you, Daisy, or did you wish to advise me on how you would like your hair and make-up to be done should you have an open casket?'

'Oh, I want to look my best naturally and look like myself, not some ghoul.'

Phoebe hid a smile. 'Of course. No one wants to look ghoulish.'

'But yes, I need help... please,' she added the latter, reluctantly realising that Phoebe need not do her bidding.

Phoebe gently lifted the sheet covering Daisy and studied the young lady before her. She had seen enough injuries to know that

Daisy had received a fatal blow to her head; how it came about was from a fall, or so Phoebe had been informed.

'You appear to have taken a nasty fall and struck your head. How can I assist you? Would you like me to deliver a message to your family, perhaps, or to someone special? They would need to be receptive to it. Or is there something you have not completed to your satisfaction?' Phoebe looked up from the body to the lady present in spirit.

'No,' Daisy said with impatience. 'I did not fall. Someone hit me. I felt their presence, but when I turned, all I could see was a hand and a rock, and then, I don't remember anything. But I am sure I was struck, and I want them punished! '

# Chapter 2

PROFESSIONAL PHOTOGRAPHER, MISS KATE Kirby, did not like to look a gift horse in the mouth, but she would be very happy when the horse bolted. Kate was tired of debutantes and their mothers, although some were very sweet, others were terrible prima donnas – the young lady, Miss Daisy Dorchester, who was in the studio last week, came instantly to mind. Kate refocused her attention on the young woman sitting before her.

'Isn't she the most beautiful debutante you have ever photographed, Miss Kirby,' the neatly presented mother standing nearby Kate asked.

'Oh, indeed,' Kate responded automatically, even though her subject was best described as plain. She smiled at the fair-haired debutante who had the good grace not to scowl, but the expression directed at her mother was pained.

'Really, Mama, Miss Kirby does not care what I look like. I am sure she has photographed many beautiful people, and she cannot improve on what nature has given me,' Miss Melanie Bains said. She was too tall to be considered dainty, her expression too practical to be considered whimsical, and Miss Bains would no doubt appeal to a no-nonsense man seeking a woman to support him in his home and business.

'Nevertheless, Miss Bains, the camera can assist presentation with lighting and a little touch-up as needed,' Kate said, sharing a conspiratorial smile with Melanie Bains.

'Ooh, can we pay extra to enhance my daughter's natural beauty?' Mrs Bains said. Kate recognised that Mrs Bains was one of those mothers who never missed an opportunity to push their daughters forward with whatever advantage presented itself.

'No need to pay a shilling more, Mrs Bains. I assure you of my best work for the price you are paying,' Kate said, restraining a groan.

'It was a recommendation that brought us to you,' Mrs Bains said.

'How kind,' Kate added. 'I've met a number of ladies making their debuts this season, and all very excited by the prospect of the ball ahead.'

'The sooner it is over, the better,' Melanie muttered, revealing the excitement had not reached her as yet.

'It should be the time of your life,' her mother remonstrated with a frown and slight shake of her head. 'You've met some lovely young ladies, and those contacts will serve you well in the future.'

Kate moved back to her camera after repositioning Melanie, and Mrs Bains moved out of the area of the framed image in Kate's lens.

'That is true,' Melanie said, 'and I have met some horrid young ladies.'

'Melanie!' her mother declared, and Kate laughed.

'It is quite all right, Mrs Bains. I have photographed a few ladies that fit that description, but I will keep your sentiments secret if you keep mine.'

Melanie laughed. 'Agreed. Did they tell you how to photograph them?'

'Several have made helpful suggestions.'

Melanie laughed again. 'Very diplomatic of you, Miss Kirby. Fortunately, I was not blessed with beauty, so you cannot make a silk purse out of a sow's ear, or so Miss Daisy Dorchester, one of the debutantes, felt she needed to tell me last week.'

'That young lady has a terrible, nasty streak,' Mrs Bains agreed. 'I heard her berating a young lady who laughed too loudly.' She hurriedly added, 'Remember not to do that, Melanie; it is most ungainly.'

'I shall do my best not to laugh aloud, share opinions unless asked, swing my arms when walking, and all those characteristics that made me who I am and were drilled out of me at deportment class.' Melanie raised an eyebrow in Kate's direction as her mother thanked her for being considerate.

'Miss Bains, regardless of what one debutante had the audacity to say to you, I believe you are mistaken. You are a handsome, well-presented woman, and I hope you will be happy with my work.' Kate stood back from her camera equipment. 'We are finished. If you would like to call back on Wednesday afternoon, the images will be ready for you, Mrs Bains and Miss Baines.

'Excellent, thank you, Miss Kirby. Come, Melanie, we have a fitting to attend,' Mrs Bains ushered her daughter to the door.

'My best wishes for your debut, Miss Bains.'

'Thank you, Miss Kirby. It shall be done this time next week, and hopefully, life will return to normal.'

The women exchanged smiles as Melanie and her mother departed, and Kate locked the door behind them. As one of the few female photographers in the state, she was delighted with recommendations and any work that came her way, but if only she could photograph some gentlemen. Handsome, single gentlemen, preferably. Why don't they seek to get calling cards or even business portraits done? So frustrating, she sighed.

A quick rap on the door startled Kate, and she opened it slightly to see a lady she vaguely recognised dressed in a black mourning gown.

'Hello, may I help you?'

'Good morning. I was here last week with my niece, a debutante.'

'Oh, of course.' Kate recalled the woman, although she was not in black last week; she had hoped their business was over. If memory served, the woman in the doorway had been bossy and snappy – a trait several mothers and chaperones displayed. 'Please come in.' She moved aside, and the thin, well-groomed lady entered.

'My niece came to have her debut photograph taken by you. Her mother is down south, and I am her sponsor, Mrs Audrey Stewart.'

'Mrs Stewart, of course, but I can't recall which young lady was your niece. I have taken a dozen or more portraits in the past week.'

'Miss Dorchester, Daisy, is my niece.'

Kate nodded, recognising the name of the obnoxious young lady in question immediately – the very Miss Dorchester that they had just spoken about. But Kate did not interrupt the woman who, despite her small stature, had a strong presence about her.

'I'm afraid there has been an accident... a death.' Her voice hitched, a white lace handkerchief was retrieved from her sleeve, and her eyes dabbed.

Kate closed her mouth, realising she was staring, shocked and surprised. 'I am very sorry to hear that, Mrs Stewart, but I don't do death portraits. I can recommend another photographer to you.'

The woman shook her head. 'No. I am not after a death portrait,' she said with an impatient wave of her handkerchief. 'It's Daisy. I want the portrait of Daisy. Can you give it your immediate attention before all others? I would like to collect it tomorrow.'

Kate looked confused. 'Are you saying Miss Dorchester has passed away, Mrs Stewart?'

'Of course, that is what I am saying. The portrait, I need it immediately.'

Kate leant back against the table in her office, gathering herself from the unexpected news and trying not to react to Mrs Stewart's rudeness. She took a deep breath.

"My sincere condolences, Mrs Stewart. It is quite a shock,' Kate said, hand upon her heart. 'All the young ladies want their portraits early, but may I ask why you wish for it so urgently now?'

The lady's lips thinned, and her gaze turned steely. 'I intend to press charges, Miss Kirby.'

'Oh? What has happened? Oh, you mean against me, whatever for?' Kate asked, stunned.

Mrs Stewart pointed a bony finger at Kate and then to the camera apparatus. 'You, that thing, you stole her soul. I warned her of the evil and vanity of having her image captured, and look what happened.'

'But Mrs Stewart, if that was the case, all the debutantes would be dead, would they not?'

Kate could see that logic did little to persuade Mrs Stewart, who looked at the camera and sneered.

'No doubt it only wanted the most beautiful of the girls. I want all the images it took for my peace of mind.'

'I will make it a priority, Mrs Stewart, but believe me, if you think Miss Dorchester's death is at all suspicious, I suggest you speak with the constabulary to investigate wider than the photograph and its photographer,' she said with a raised eyebrow. Kate softened, 'I imagine, however, Miss Dorchester's mother will treasure her daughter's last portrait. It would give me great comfort to have it were I Mrs Dorchester.'

Mrs Stewart gave the briefest of nods.

'Might there have been some other cause of death, Mrs Stewart? Was she ill?' Kate knew very well that was unlikely. Miss Daisy Dorchester had been full of her own importance and boasted of the match she would make and the suitors she already had. Not to mention, she had wrinkled her nose and loudly proclaimed how happy she was not to have auburn hair like Kate and be prone to freckles.

'The police officer on duty said it was an accident,' Mrs Stewart said, making a tsk-tsk sound in frustration. 'Daisy was visiting her father's grave, and the officer claims she must have tripped on the hem of her dress or slipped on the damp grass, falling and striking her head on a headstone. Incompetent fool he was.'

Kate gasped. 'How dreadful.'

Mrs Stewart nodded. 'Don't think for a moment your sympathy lets you off the hook, Miss Kirby, I am sure you know what this machine is capable of doing.' She waved a hand in the direction of the apparatus. 'I intend to speak with my contact at the police station about my suspicions.'

'Of course. I am at the disposal of the constabulary should they wish to investigate,' Kate acquiesced. She had heard the accusation before when items had gone missing, or an illness befell the subject of a portrait. 'However, may I suggest if the police do not wish to investigate – they are very busy – you could hire the services of a private investigator. I recently met a competent gentleman, Mr Bennet Martin of South Brisbane.'

'Goodness, how much would that cost me?' Mrs Stewart exclaimed.

'I cannot say. My apologies; I was not aware of your financial situation.'

'There is no situation,' she said tight-lipped, and Kate let the matter drop.

Mrs Stewart sighed. 'I can only imagine how devastated the other debutantes will be to hear the news of dear Daisy's passing. She was so popular and beautiful and bound to be crowned the debutante of the ball.'

'Yes,' Kate said, and her eyes narrowed. One hour in the presence of Miss Daisy Dorchester had not created any warm feelings towards the young lady, and she could well imagine how the other debutantes felt about her and how convenient her death was for the ambitious young ladies amongst them hoping to marry well.

One down, nineteen to go, she mused.

# Chapter 3

DETECTIVE HARLAND STONE RAN a hand over his face and let out a sigh usually expressed later in the day, and not in the freshness of the morning before the day's challenges presented themselves.

'I believe we have made a rod for our backs, but I can't say I regret it.' He placed a file on the desk and picked up another.

'It's more of a double-edged sword, Sir,' his young protégé, Gilbert Payne, with his dark, neatly parted hair, spotless attire, and enthusiastic appearance, mused as he sat opposite his superior, considering a file before him.

'Yes,' Harland said with a smile, 'you are right, Gilbert, it has both favourable and unfavourable consequences. We must be doing something right to be offered a choice of cases, even if they are the most difficult and the inspector would like us to manage them all, but I reminded him that as there were only two of us, at some point, we do need to sleep.'

Gilbert chuckled.

The unlikely duo had enjoyed great success on their first few cases together – cases that attracted significant public interest and seemed unsolvable, but Detective Harland Stone and Detective Gilbert Payne proved otherwise.

Harland imagined his colleagues were not quite as quick to mock him these days – not that he placed much stock in what his colleagues thought – but there was much amusement when he was saddled with the youngster who was accelerated due to Gilbert's father's connections more so than skill. Very few would mock Harland Stone to his face – he stood at six-foot-three and was a keen and capable boxer with the odd mix of rough edges and a sterling private school education. He had agreed to take Gilbert on as his protégé if, in return, he was given the new detective position in the city – a coveted position made possible by a death in office; Harland was one of the youngest applicants. The chance to return from a country post to the city, even if Brisbane was not his birth city, was too good to refuse.

Harland applied his mentor's teaching to his young protégé – *'Harness your strengths and play to them'* – and was surprised at how Gilbert's skills of fact gathering proved most useful. The neat and bright young man may succeed as a detective after all.

'I am struggling to categorise them, Sir,' Gilbert said, interrupting Harland's thoughts. 'Except to say that some seem most unsolvable and others appear somewhat unsolvable. But...'

'Yes?' Harland looked up from the file he was reading, hoping to have some direction to follow.

Gilbert waved a file in front of his superior. 'There might be a link between this file...' he tapped another next to him and underneath it, 'and these, Sir.'

'Excellent,' Harland said, sitting back. 'We may be able to kill two or rather three birds with one stone. It would be fortunate to wrap them up and close several at once. What have you then?'

Gilbert nodded, gathered his thoughts as Harland had been instilling in him to do before speaking, and began.

'In all three cases, the crimes themselves are different – a possible murder, death by misadventure, and an assault,' he tapped the three files, 'but there is a note in each of the files from the coroner saying further investigation warranted.' Gilbert hastened to add, 'I understand why the police officers might not have connected these three cases, Sir, given they are dissimilar in their manner of death.'

Harland nodded, biting back his impatience. He expected an obscure theory from the young detective, such as they all shared a similar middle name; he was not disappointed.

'They all had something out of character in their pocket, Sir, with the same sentiment expressed in all three cases.'

'I see.' Harland did not but indulged his young colleague further. 'Something significant? Was the item the same?'

'No,' Gilbert announced firmly. 'According to the list of items found on the deceased, the first victim had two locks of hair; the second victim had a hand-written verse of poetry, and the third had an engagement ring box but no ring inside.'

Harland nodded as his mind ran over the significance of the items. 'They are all items related to matters of the heart, but I struggled to see how they could be linked. Tell me then, what is the shared sentiment, and why do you think the items are out of character for each victim?'

Gilbert opened the first file on the top of his group. 'A handwritten verse found in the pocket of a priest – Father Damien Horan, aged 28. It is dedicated to "D" from his "devoted admirer," and the paper has a slight scent of perfume, according to the coroner.'

'Is he a Catholic priest?'

'Yes, so he has no business carrying such an item,' Gilbert said most seriously. The young man was devout in his faith. 'Unless it is gifted and the feelings are not returned.'

'Yes, you are right, it is out of character indeed,' Harland agreed. 'But are the lines meant to convey love? Could it not be a prayer that the "devoted admirer" might have shared with the priest?'

Gilbert shook his head. 'I don't believe so, Sir. I have some knowledge of poetry and verse, and these are lines of love.' Gilbert read it from the file. 'It is a poem by Robert Browning. The lines are *"Grow old along with me! The best is yet to be"*,' Gilbert looked up from reading the poem.

'I believe you are right; that could not pass as a prayer. The next victim?'

'A young lady named Miss Daisy Dorchester, aged 18. She had two locks of hair in her possession, tied up as if to be gifted.'

'And it is her own hair, I assume?'

'The coroner believes so.' Gilbert consulted the file. 'The odd thing is that both locks are tied with a pink ribbon and feature a small gift tag reading the same lines of poetry. Written below that are the words "with my great affection" and her initials.'

'So, she is romancing two men then? We don't know if that is out of character,' Harland said, awaiting a further explanation and was not disappointed.

'Except that the file claims she is to be engaged after she makes her debut and lists her guardian and her betrothed as next of kin,' Gilbert said with a raised eyebrow. 'Why would she be giving her betrothed two locks of her hair?'

'It is odd,' Harland agreed. 'The final victim then?'

'Fortunately, he is still alive – a man by the name of Theodore Wright, aged 22, who had an engagement ring box in his pocket. He was attacked and found in time to be helped.'

'And why is he connected to our victims?'

Gilbert continued. 'In the engagement ring box that he had on his person are those very same two lines of verse scribbled on a scrap of paper.'

'*Grow old along with me! The best is yet to be,*' Harland said softly, running his hand over his jaw as he thought.

'One moment, if you will, Sir, while I check their next of kin and carers to see if they have any names in common.'

Harland exhaled and returned to the file before him, pleased to have Gilbert distracted on a short-term mission. The file in his hands was a suspected murder case, a missing wife... he closed it. Harland had experienced his share of the murdered fairer sex and had no desire to face another case of that nature just yet; he placed the file aside.

Gilbert confirmed, 'No, the files indicated no connection between the three, Sir, but that does not mean there isn't.'

Harland nodded and accepted the three files from Gilbert. He waded through each page, searching for something, then announced, 'They were all harmed within very close proximity. That, too, is odd and should have been considered by the constabulary.'

'True, Sir, although two more incidents in that area seem to have no connection to these cases – a robbery and another death by accident.'

'Hmm, I suspect the cliffs, the church, and the nearby cemetery are areas that attract walkers and the devoted in larger numbers than most,' Harland mused.

'Don't you think it is odd that all three had items in their possession featuring the same verse?'

Harland closed a file and gave Gilbert his full attention. 'It is indeed peculiar. Were the locks of hair destined for the young man and the priest? Did Miss Dorchester's betrothed find out and kill all three?'

Gilbert looked shocked.

'A wild hypothesis only, Gilbert, do not be alarmed. The victims might not be known to each other, the deaths might be accidental, or it could be a coincidence.'

'Yes, Sir. But I believe they are linked.'

'As do I.'

'You do?' Gilbert's expression revealed his surprise, and he quickly masked his reaction.

Harland grimaced, almost hesitant to ask. 'How are you familiar with the poetry? Was it something you were made to study at school or by your mother, perhaps?'

'Neither. Sir, I recently enjoyed a rigorous debate on this poem at the last Poetry Foundation meeting of which I am a member. It was not written as a poem to a lover, but as words of an older man advising a younger man about all that age has to offer.'

'But it serves very well as a love poem,' Harland said. 'Any chance the three victims are members of the Poetry Foundation?'

Gilbert looked at the names of the victims on the files.

'I do not recognise the names, Sir. I might know them by sight, but I think these three people suffered because of love.'

'This does not bode well,' Harland said, 'but it is as good a reason as any, Gilbert, to take the cases. Let's go through the remaining half dozen files, and if we can find any more connections, we shall select them.' He shut the file he was working on and reached for another, adding under his breath, 'Heaven help us.'

# Chapter 4

Ambrose Astin thundered down the stairs to Phoebe's workroom, making enough noise to wake the dead. She turned to give him a frustrated look.

'Goodness, you are like a herd of elephants; can you not descend quietly?' Phoebe scolded him playfully.

'Sorry, are you alone?' he asked, looking around and not seeing any visitors. 'I heard you talking.'

'Oh my, isn't he handsome?' Miss Daisy Dorchester said and began to twirl a long lock of her dark hair between her fingers. 'You look nothing alike, although you are attractive too, of course, but he is most dashing.'

'He is indeed,' Phoebe smiled, looking at her brother, 'but I'm afraid he can't see you.'

'Who can't I see?' Ambrose asked, stopping beside his sister and looking – she noted – particularly handsome in his dark suit, with his dark hair in need of a cut and his bright blue eyes expressive and kind.

'It's not fair,' Daisy wailed like a child, and Phoebe released a small sigh of exasperation.

'Miss Daisy Dorchester is in attendance and thinks you are most handsome,' Phoebe said, smiling at her brother.

'And on that account, she is correct. Thank you, Miss Dorchester, wherever you may be,' he said, giving a small bow and flicking his dark hair from his blue eyes on rising. 'A young lady of good taste and good sense.'

Daisy laughed, delighted. 'He is charming too, isn't he?'

'Ambrose!' Julius bellowed from upstairs, and Ambrose rolled his eyes.

'We are running late,' he explained. 'Julius got trapped by a young lady seeking directions outside the office. I suspect she knew where she was going, but then she asked for a glass of water, and he had to oblige. Mrs Dobbs took her in hand; she did depart quite quickly after that.'

'Well done to her. Ladies have many ploys at our disposal,' Daisy said, smiling.

'Perhaps she was genuinely lost,' Phoebe said.

'Well, she was asking for directions, and perhaps Julius was the only person nearby,' Ambrose conceded, 'but he does tend to attract the damsels in distress.'

'A clever move; I have done similar, I must confess.' Daisy said as if contributing to the conversation.

'Have you? Goodness,' Phoebe said, turning to look at her. 'The thought would never cross my mind.'

'Then you are not well versed in the art of flirting, my dear new friend,' Daisy said with a coy look as if she would instruct Phoebe in the finer skills.

'Have you what?' Ambrose asked, only hearing Phoebe's side of the discussion.

'Oh, sorry, I was responding to Daisy, who believed it was a ploy to engage Julius in conversation,' Phoebe said.

'I guess that is possible,' Ambrose said with a disinterested shrug. 'But, to business, Julius asks that you prepare the lady in your care first as her aunt wants to book a mourning room for friends and family to pay their respects. She anticipates a significant number of mourners.'

'The lady in my care is Daisy,' Phoebe said with a nod in the direction of the debutante, 'and yes, I will begin immediately. I have some new powders to choose from, Daisy.'

'Ooh,' she squealed as if attending a dress-up party. 'All my admirers and the debutantes will want to come and say goodbye; you will need a large room. Can you accommodate a large gathering?' Daisy uttered the words without a hint of self-consciousness, and Phoebe marvelled at her vanity. She could not imagine speaking so confidently and being so full of her own self-importance.

'I imagine we can,' Phoebe assured her.

'What do you imagine?' Ambrose asked.

'Sorry, I was replying to Daisy,' Phoebe said.

'Most confusing,' Ambrose said with a slight shake of his head. They both turned as Julius rushed down the stairs.

'Oh, my goodness, another one and even more handsome!' Daisy exclaimed.

'This is my eldest brother, Julius,' Phoebe said, studying her brother to see if he appeared to see the apparition of Miss Daisy Dorchester standing nearby her. He did not give the slightest indication of seeing or hearing the young woman in attendance.

'Come, Ambrose, what is taking so long?' he snapped.

'He is often grumpy,' Phoebe explained in a low voice.

'I heard that,' Julius replied.

'That's because Phoebe said it and not the ghost or rather the spirit of Miss Dorchester. Can you see Miss Dorchester, brother?' Ambrose stirred him.

'Let us go,' he snapped. 'Phoebe, can you do the lady first?'

'I've already asked her that,' Ambrose said, 'it's the reason I'm here, remember?'

'I will, Julius,' Phoebe assured him.

'Good, thank you.' He turned to leave and looked back. 'Are you coming, Ambrose?'

'So grumpy this morning. You need to visit next door and avail yourself of the sight of Miss Forrester. That will cheer you up for the rest of the morning, and we will all be grateful... well, the horses, me and the dead,' Ambrose said in jest with a wink to Phoebe as he took the stairs behind his brother. 'Good day, Miss Dorchester, I will collect you soon,' he called back.

'Does he have a beau?' Daisy asked. 'Your eldest brother. Oh, I imagine he has many with that handsome face.'

'He has one in particular, a most special lady. Come then, let's get you prepared.'

'But what of my murder?' Daisy insisted. 'I refuse to start my preparation until you call the police.'

'Then I will have to start without you,' Phoebe said, putting her foot down. Little did she realise just how destructive the indulged Miss Dorchester could be.

A cloud of cigar smoke seemed to hover above the head of *The Courier* editor, Alex Cowan, as he paused to consider the two young reporters before him. He grunted.

'You've done well. But don't get ahead of yourselves, Lewis, Griffith,' he said and looked back down at his notes on the desk, shuffling a few and pulling out the papers he wanted.

Reporter Lilly Lewis, whose ambition exceeded her 5ft 6 frame and belied her age of 22, glanced at her fellow writing partner, Fergus Griffiths, and grimaced. They were the two youngest reporters on the team and, until recently, Lilly had been consigned to writing the *Births, Deaths and Marriages* column and Fergus the *Shipping News*. Some believed that was where a lady reporter belonged, but a lucky break – namely Lilly's friendship with Miss Phoebe Astin, who tipped Lilly off about a possible crime story discovered from a dead client – gave Lilly a chance to barter with Mr Cowan, who admired gumption in his reporters. She also bartered to partner with Fergus, not the lecherous and well-known journalist Lawrence Hulmes. Surprisingly, Mr Cowan indulged her.

Lilly's last crime story captured the public's interest – a fake child, a wealthy family, and a historic kidnapping – and Lilly had no intention of letting the story slip through her fingers and be assigned to a male reporter. She coerced Mr Cowan with the promise of an advantageous agreement she had struck with the new detective in town, Detective Harland Stone, to share information and respect the detective's processes in return for the lead on the story. Lilly's editor let her have a go, and the young pair made a success of it. Lilly's nose for sniffing out a story got her the headline pages of the paper and earned her the respect of some of the journalists, or at least they admired her for her work and not just her appearance for that brief time.

Now, Lilly had no intention of going back on the *Births, Deaths and Marriages* column and every intention of continuing to do some real investigating and reporting. The softly-spoken but serious Fergus Griffith, with his mop of brown hair, intelligent dark eyes and a wife and child to support, shuffled beside her, and she could sense his dread at returning to his former role.

'Well, you've had two wins now with the success of your first story on the cemented bride,' Mr Cowan started, 'and, yes, you did a reasonable job on the fake missing child story,' he added, never one for excessive praise. 'But I need not remind you that you are only as good as your next story,' he huffed stopping long enough to inhale more of his tobacco. 'This time needs dictate, and all my other reporters are busy, so I've got a job for you.' As always, Mr Cowan finished his sentence in a tone that brooked no argument.

'Yes, Mr Cowan, what have you got for us?' Lilly asked, accepting temporary defeat; she had hoped to be invited to find their own story again.

'There's a dead debutante; the readers will want to know about it... a nice sympathetic piece with a beautiful portrait. Talk to the family, friends, beau, the usual lot. Needs a woman's touch.'

Lilly grimaced and then schooled her features. 'Debutante. Do we know how she died?'

'She slipped and struck her head on a gravestone in the cemetery, I believe,' he said, then chuckled seeing Lilly's face. 'Not every death will give you a murder to report, Lewis.'

'Yes, Sir,' she said with a small smile.

'Griffiths, two boats have been stolen. Your old contacts from your *Shipping News* days will be useful.' He handed Fergus the report, then sat back and webbed his fingers over his stomach. 'Get those in quick enough, and I'll consider anything else you want to throw at me.'

Lilly smiled. 'Yes, Sir.' She nudged Fergus, and they departed in haste as most did from Mr Cowan's office.

'Let's wrap these up in a couple of days and pitch something to him midweek... keep your ear to the ground when you are out and about for something we can investigate.'

'I'll see what I can sniff out. I thought my shipping days were behind me,' Fergus sighed.

'At least you don't have to write a puff story about a debutante and all the frippery that goes with it,' Lilly said, her disdain evident. She sighed, 'I'll start with the corpse.'

'Good as place as any, and if you're lucky, it will be at *The Economic Undertaker*,' Fergus teased and watched Lilly for her reaction.

'Whatever do you mean, Fergus Griffiths?' she asked, looking coy. It was no secret to her writing partner that she admired the senior Astin brother, even if she believed he was lost to another. Still, Julius Astin and Miss Violet Forrester weren't married yet.

# Chapter 5

Detective Harland Stone left his superior's office, pleased with the outcome, or rather, his superior was pleased to get only three of the six files back. Returning to his shared office, he grabbed his coat and hat and beckoned for his young partner to follow.

'And bring the priest's file with you,' Harland said. 'We shall start with the most peculiar of the three.'

Harland strode down the hallway, Gilbert following in his wake.

'As it has been a few days since the death occurred, I don't favour our chances of finding much now, Sir,' Gilbert said, catching up and juggling his jacket on his thin frame.

'Nor do I, but nevertheless, we will drop into the rectory first. I suspect any of the priest's possessions or any evidence may be lost to us. Then we'll see why the coroner believed it needed investigating.'

They entered a hansom cab that waited outside the police headquarters, sure of being of use given the comings and goings of the constabulary, and settled back for the short ride to New Farm. Gilbert flipped open the folder.

'Shall I summarise, Sir?'

'Please.'

Gilbert cleared his throat. 'Father Damien Horan, 28 years of age, was found at the bottom of the cliff at his presbytery. Father Horan had served at St Patrick's for three years.' Gilbert stopped, turned the page over and announced, 'That is the sum of Father Horan's life, Sir, according to this file.'

'Most unhelpful,' Harland said. 'And what of the coroner's report?'

Gilbert lifted the sheet of paper with the coroner's imprint and summarised, 'The coroner notes that the first police assessment of accidental fall or misadventure is inconsistent with subsequent autopsy results. He writes, "At midday, a 28-year-old male was found dead on the grounds of the St Patrick presbytery; his location would indicate a fall from approximately 16 feet. Because of the injury to his head, the police assumed a traumatic head injury by strike impact. The external examination revealed additional bruising to the neck, trauma of the thorax, and fractures of the pelvis were detected, the latter of which could be explained by the fall. The bruising on the neck did not appear consistent with the fall. Conclusion: On the basis of an external post-mortem examination and markings to the neck, death from foul play cannot be reliably excluded", and that is all that we have on Father Horan.' Gilbert closed the file.

'A priest grabbed by the neck. What was Father Horan up to?' Harland mumbled, 'or who had a grudge against him or the sentiments he was preaching? And why did he have a romantic verse in his pocket gifted to him and scented in perfume?'

Gilbert was learning not every question required an answer, and they sat in silence for a while, musing over the case until Harland turned to the younger detective. 'I wouldn't have picked you for a poet, Gilbert,' he said, studying his young partner. 'I thought matters of science might have been more your persuasion.'

'I like structure, Sir, in all things. A well-written verse can transport you to higher places, like science opens your mind. I enjoy them both. Should you ever need a verse written for a lady friend, Sir, I would be willing to try my hand at it for you.'

Harland smiled, constantly surprised by the young man. 'Thank you, Gilbert, most considerate. However, I am sure no self-respecting young lady would believe me capable of producing such words and would be sorely misled if she thought more were to follow.'

Gilbert smiled. 'My father once said the same about me being a detective, that I was incapable, yet I am here.'

The men alighted, and Harland realised that perhaps Gilbert did not know his father had a hand in accelerating him through the ranks. As if reading his mind, Gilbert hurriedly added, 'I know my father used his influence to further my career, Sir. I begged him not to, but he was wilful. But I don't think he expected me to be able to hold down the position and to have contributed a little to our recent successes.'

'Put it behind you, Gilbert. You won't be the first or the last to come with a recommendation of sorts; the onus is on you to prove yourself, and you are doing so. As for me reciting poetry...' he chuckled at the thought as they made their way to the rectory, '...for now, let us focus on our prayers.'

Phoebe was by far the most patient of the Astin family members and the most suited to her own company, but the deceased debutante, Miss Daisy Dorchester, was giving the young mortician plenty to vent about at the next meeting of the *Vexed Vixens* with her dearest girlfriends in attendance.

'Daisy, if you do not return my powder, I shall put a colour on you that will be most unbecoming, and I am quite certain you do not want your friends or family to see you looking anything but your best,' Phoebe said, standing with her hands firmly planted on her hips and assessing her work trolley and the space which once held the missing powder.

Daisy appeared on the other side of the table on which her body lay and made a face at Phoebe. 'It will reflect on you, not me. No one will want to use your business again!'

Phoebe knew Daisy was correct, but she anticipated the debutante's vanity would outweigh all else; she called Daisy's bluff.

'Ah, but they use our business because we are so economical that many will not care how they look in death. I'm sure it will be of little consideration to me,' Phoebe said with a slight shrug as she ran a finger over the top of her other powders before tapping on a jar and selecting it. 'This will do nicely. A little darker than you are used to, but everyone will assume you were not wearing your sun bonnet.'

Daisy gasped. 'I would never!' She turned away angrily. 'The powder is hidden beneath that pile of clothing.'

'Shrouds,' Phoebe advised her. 'That's what we wrap the bodies in.'

'Eew and I touched them,' Daisy squealed, wiping her hand on her dress and looking appalled.

Phoebe bit back a laugh and added, 'They are cleaned after each use, I assure you.'

The sound of the door opening upstairs and a young female voice had them both listening.

'I suspect this is someone enquiring after me,' Daisy said, tilting her head to the side and again, Phoebe was amazed at the debutante's conceitedness.

Behind them, light footsteps could be heard across the upstairs floorboards, and soon, the guest took the stairs to the room below, revealing Phoebe's dear friend and photographer, Miss Kate Kirby.

'Oh, it's her, the photographer. I didn't know you knew her.'

'Kate, what a lovely surprise,' Phoebe said, ignoring Daisy. She hastened to cover Daisy's face with the cloth that pooled around the deceased's neck.

'You have the debutante!' Kate said, seeing the flash of Daisy's face before it was covered. 'That ghastly girl is causing me trouble even in death.'

'Ghastly!' Daisy proclaimed, 'how dare she! I was so professional and offered a number of suggestions and poses for capturing me at my best advantage.'

Phoebe grimaced. 'I'm afraid Daisy is here as we speak.'

Kate's eyes widened. 'Oh, I am sorry. I don't like to speak ill of the dead, but she was... never mind.' Kate cleared her throat, slightly uncomfortable with not being able to see precisely where Miss Dorchester was or if the deceased intended to continue being ghastly.

'Is that what brings you here?' Phoebe prompted, 'Not that you need a reason to visit.'

'Thank you, dear Phoebe, but yes. Miss Dorchester's aunt has visited my studio demanding her niece's photograph and has accused my camera of killing Miss Dorchester by stealing her soul. Have you ever?' Kate gave a short laugh that was more hysterical than humorous. 'She intends to go to the police, so I suggested she look for the real killer if she believes her niece's death was not accidental.'

'Oh, that is good news. Thank you, my dear aunt,' Daisy exclaimed, clapping her hands together. 'See! I told you, Phoebe, that it was so, and now I like Miss Kirby even better for her advice.'

'I can imagine why someone would want to bump her off,' Kate continued, and Phoebe nearly choked with a laugh.

'Um, she is still here.'

'Oh, of course,' Kate said with a slight shake of her head as if to clear her thoughts. 'My apologies again, although I do feel hypocritical for offering them when I have obviously said what I meant.'

'I don't care what you think, Kate Kirby, my aunt is right. I was murdered, struck with force; someone needs to do something about it with haste.'

Phoebe tried to ignore Daisy and converse with Kate. She heard a small bell ring upstairs.

'Ah, perfect timing. That is Mrs Dobbs saying there are no customers in the house and morning tea is ready. Kate, do stay for a cup of tea and a slice of cake? We can talk in private,' she added in a hushed voice.

'It's not fair,' Daisy's voice wailed as the two young women took to the stairs to depart.

'I will be back soon, Daisy,' Phoebe assured her.

'Is she following us?' Kate whispered.

'No, and I doubt she will come where she is not welcome.' Phoebe added at the top of the stairs, 'But I suspect you might be right. She can be rather self-indulgent.' The two ladies exchanged a small guilty smile and went to join Randolph and Mrs Dobbs in the kitchen, where Phoebe's grandfather pulled out a chair at the table for both ladies.

'Do join us, won't you, Miss Kirby,' Randolph said in his usual charming manner.

'I would be delighted, thank you, Mr Astin,' Kate said and looked hungrily at the apple upside-down cake in the middle of the table. 'I did time my visit well.'

Mrs Dobbs smiled, and wiping her hands, she took her seat at the table, a slicing knife in hand. 'The more to enjoy my cooking the better, my dear, and you appeared to be most flustered on arrival. I suspect you need a good cup of tea and something sweet.'

'The dead debutante's aunt is causing Kate trouble,' Phoebe informed the party.

'Oh dear, don't tell me the soul-catching camera has struck again,' Randolph said, most amused.

'Yes, I believe so,' Mr Astin,' Kate said with a grin and lowering her voice added, 'And it couldn't have chosen a better subject to steal.'

'Although Daisy does claim to be murdered, but not by you, dear Kate.' Everyone at the table stilled, and Phoebe continued. 'She claims she was struck as she turned around on hearing someone behind her, then fell onto the tombstone. She did not slip on grass or the hem of her skirt and hit her head as stated by the police.'

Mrs Dobbs blessed herself, which she frequently did in her employ at *The Economic Undertaker*.

'Will you share the information with Detective Stone?' Randolph asked.

'Oh do, he's so handsome,' Kate said, 'and then he will have a chance to visit you.'

Phoebe blushed lightly.

'It's as good excuse as any,' Mrs Dobbs agreed with an encouraging nod of her head.

Phoebe shook her head at them but could not help but smile. 'Best save him a slice then, Mrs Dobbs; I do believe he was very taken with your cake last visit.'

'I shall send a message once tea is done,' Randolph said.

'Until then, you will just have to put up with her,' Kate said, 'oh, how uncharitable that sounds.'

'But true,' Phoebe agreed. 'I am afraid Miss Dorchester is most spoilt and might be our guest for longer than we planned.'

# Chapter 6

J ULIUS COULD FEEL AMBROSE studying him as they went through the motions of burying the dead. They were both well-practised at maintaining a sombre expression, keeping the procession moving along, and ensuring dignity prevailed even when challenged, like today. Sometimes, it was just not possible to remain solemn if the mourners were not prepared to mourn, or human oddity prevailed – like the dear old girl fondly referred to as Aunty Myrtle at today's funeral. Myrtle was not only a little loopy but hard of hearing and had told Ambrose several times that he reminded her of her dearly departed husband. She elaborated to add that he was a most handsome man, and her sister had her way with him outside in the garden near the flowering Hibiscus bush – to Ambrose's great amusement.

'Myrtle, if I were fortunate to marry a beauty such as yourself, there would be no liaisons near the Hibiscus bush or near any shrubbery for that matter,' Ambrose assured her.

She laughed and slapped his arm. 'Get away with you, you young charmer, and your brother so serious. Is he always so?'

Julius grimaced, overhearing the conversation as he did his best to appear indifferent.

'Oh yes,' Ambrose assured her. 'Except when he's waltzing with his belle.'

A hiss escaped his lips at Ambrose's impertinence. The shenanigans were at least distracting, given Julius had not slept well and was – as Ambrose described – grumpy. He was positioned to hear the conversations from the back of the gathering whether he wished to or not.

'Why isn't Val here?' A male voice could be heard asking from the back row of chairs set up for the elderly who could not stand for any great length of time at the graveside.

'She died last year, Walter. You went to her funeral,' a random voice responded.

'Shh, the priest is trying to talk,' another added.

'I don't remember it,' Walter grumbled.

'You do,' Aunty Myrtle said, 'they served that fruit cake you like at the wake. I hope they have it today.'

'Oh yes! The one with the brandy in it,' Walter brightened.

The priest momentarily stopped, all voices hushed before he continued: 'As we bury here the body of our brother, we ask the Lord to deliver his soul from every bond of sin...'

'About time,' Walter muttered, starting Ambrose off on a fresh round of chuckles as Julius gave the priest a sympathetic look; sometimes their work was not appreciated, but it was part of the process of putting the dead to rest.

Julius's mind wandered as the priest's words he knew so well washed over him. It had been two months since he last enjoyed feeling the small hand of Miss Violet Forrester in his own. It was the night of the Hospital Ball that Phoebe coaxed family and friends to support. Julius had attended because Miss Violet Forrester was invited and hastily secured the three waltzes in Violet's dance card. But since that night, Miss Forrester constantly found an excuse not to accept his invitation for an evening out, or that is how he had started to read the situation. Initially, her aunt was visiting from interstate and staying three weeks, the longest three weeks of Julius's life. Still, he understood family responsibility, and Violet and her brother, Tom, had so little family left now that the elderly Aunty must be attended to, as Violet explained.

When he could find an excuse, he enjoyed the occasional visit to the mourning wear dressmaking store next door that he had opened some months back, placing Violet as manageress after meeting her at her grandmother's funeral. The brief visits to see

45

Violet on the pretence of business were short-lived, and Violet's staff were usually in attendance – young Miss Mary Pollard, who seemed terrified of him, and the mature Mrs Nellie Shaw, whose intentions to match-make the pair, Julius found himself welcoming in his current dilemma.

No sooner had Violet's aunty departed than another family member arrived – Violet's late grandfather's brother, Uncle Bertram, who felt it was his duty to call on Violet and Tom. He was not a young man himself – in fact, his ill health had Julius wondering if they might be of service before Bertram's visit was up.

Bertram Forrester considered himself a man of business and inspected Violet and Tom's workplaces to her mortification. Finding it satisfactory, he took charge of the young pair and, calculating Violet and Tom's salaries, declared they must move up in the world and out of the depressed housing area that had served them well to this day. Uncle Bertram sourced new accommodation befitting a manageress and apprentice carpenter and moved his young relations – a task Julius had hoped to achieve and preferably into his abode.

The uncle's final pearl of business wisdom did not serve Julius well at all – Uncle Bertram did not think it was wise for Violet to date her employer, not that Julius had heard that directly from Violet, but Mrs Shaw had taken it upon herself to become a confidant of sorts to Phoebe, who dutifully warned Julius. Uncle

Bertram was leaving this very weekend to return home, and not a moment too soon. Julius hoped and prayed there were no more relations to come calling and he could care for Violet and Tom. But he felt a cooling between him and the lady he admired; perhaps her uncle's words had caused her to be cautionary with Julius again, as she was initially in the early days of their acquaintance. He was nudged out of his thoughts by Ambrose.

'What is the matter with you today?' Ambrose sidled up to him. 'I would have thought you would be on top of the world with Bertram leaving this weekend and the prospect of resuming your friendship with the delightful Miss Forrester.'

Julian frowned at Ambrose. 'Shh, we're at a funeral.'

Ambrose shrugged. 'It is where we spend half of our days. Doesn't it make you want to live life to the fullest?' He gave his brother a slight smile, mindful that one could not look too joyous at a funeral, although it had happened amongst the mourners before when a particularly unlikeable relative had departed this earth.

A small sigh escaped from Julius – a rarity as he was usually the picture of all that was dignified in the work environment – and when he was sure the family were distracted by the priest's words, he said, 'I fear she has heeded her uncle's warning that it is not wise to form an attachment with the manager.' He uttered some rare words of vulnerability, adding, 'I must be cautious but not leave Miss Forrester uncertain of my feelings.'

Ambrose's eyebrows could not have risen any higher without flying from his forehead.

'Surely, she will not be swayed by her uncle. You are both so suited and enamoured by each other. It would be best if you acted fast; invite Miss Forrester on an outing. She will be expecting it.'

Julius turned to look at Ambrose, about to question how he might know this, and then remembered himself and resumed his position. 'Will this ever be over?' he muttered.

Again, Ambrose looked like he could have been knocked over with a feather, his mouth dropping over. 'I cannot recall you ever saying that before. You do have a case of love-itis.'

Julius groaned. 'Do shut up,' he hissed, and Ambrose restrained a grin.

'Amen,' the priest said, and all joined in.

'We shall discuss it further on our journey home,' Ambrose added.

'No, we won't,' Julius said.

'Oh yes, brother, we will. You clearly need my advice in matters of love.' Ambrose cleared his throat and conceded, 'Although I may not have won the heart of the woman I want – the beautiful Miss Lilly Lewis,' he sighed, conceding defeat, 'but Lucian and I are frequently successful in seeking female companionship,' he said of his cousin.

'You should not give up on Miss Lewis so easily.'

'Well, if you take your own advice, brother, I might as well.'

Julius grimaced, his lips drawn in a thin line, and on hearing the last words of blessing over the deceased, he nudged Ambrose forward so they could lower the dead into the ground and conclude the drawn-out event.

Unfortunately, the elderly deceased man's young wife took that moment to throw herself over the casket and wail loudly.

'Oh, for the love of all that is holy,' the deceased's sister said, rolling her eyes skyward. 'There's no need for the theatrics, Florence. It will not change the will.'

'How dare you,' Florence responded, and Julius stepped in, offering Florence his hand to assist with raising her from the coffin.

'Thank you,' she said, batting her eyelashes at him, which had several guests rolling their eyes.

'I heard he left everything to the church and his bag pipes club,' Aunt Myrtle said and was shushed just as quickly and escorted to a waiting carriage, but not before she added. 'They are both good-looking young men. Florence could catch herself another husband while she is here.'

Ambrose chuckled again, disguised it as a cough and ignored Julius's admonishment.

As he went through the motions of lowering the deceased, Julius thanked the priest and wished the departing family well. He then concluded that Ambrose was right – a conclusion he rarely drew. He did need advice in matters of the heart, and there was only one person he could seek it from. Uncle Reggie.

# Chapter 7

WITHOUT HESITATION, KATE ACCEPTED a second slice of moist apple upside-down cake from Mrs Dobbs.

'Clearly, I have no regard for my figure,' she said with a small laugh and began to eat it immediately.

'I like a young lady who enjoys her food,' Mrs Dobbs said with an indulgent smile, enjoying the response to her much-loved cake.

'You are lucky the boys aren't here, Kate, or you might struggle to get a second piece,' Randolph said with a smile, having polished off his own slice.

Kate stopped. 'Oh dear, have I eaten their share?'

'Absolutely not,' Randolph assured her. 'Please do eat on. Those boys want for nothing.'

Mrs Dobbs smiled. 'I made two cakes, do not give it a second thought.'

Kate smiled and resumed eating. 'It is the best cake I think I have ever tasted.' She swallowed a mouthful and concluded the subject she started during her first slice of cake, 'So that is my story. One dead debutante, an aunt who intends to hand me in to the police, and yet another person who believes my camera captures a person's soul. If that were the case, I assure you, I would be pointing it around town at anyone who vexed me.'

Phoebe laughed. 'People seem to be most superstitious about anything new. I was asked recently if I embalmed a lady's husband, could he be brought back to life at another date.'

'Goodness,' Mrs Dobbs exclaimed. 'What a frightening thought.'

'Indeed! While Kate is dealing with the aunt, I have the young lady herself in my workroom, and she is very demanding. With her beauty, I imagine she is quite used to being indulged.'

'Does she wish to oversee your work?' Randolph asked.

'I suspect she will have plenty to say about it, but we haven't got too far along yet. Daisy – that is, Miss Dorchester – hid my powder and refused to return it until I helped her prove she was murdered.'

Mrs Dobbs blessed herself, saying, 'What a state of affairs.'

Kate frowned. 'If the coroner and police department have released her to your care, then it is unlikely they believe so.'

'My thoughts too, Kate. But she is quite insistent, and I do not believe I will have any peace until I act upon her request.' Phoebe sought her grandfather's advice. 'I am not sure how truthful

Daisy's claim might be, and I don't want to waste the detectives' time. What do you think I should do, Grandpa?'

Randolph pursed his lips and thought for a moment. 'I hesitate to call in our detective friend when, as you say, the young lady is petulant, and this might just be attention-seeking.'

Mrs Dobbs shook her head. 'Even in death, goodness, such behaviour.'

'So it seems,' Phoebe said. 'I have never seen such confidence.'

'What if I ask Julius to speak to his coroner friend?' Randolph asked. 'At least we will know if he had any suspicions on first sighting the young lady's corpse.'

'That is the perfect solution,' Phoebe brightened. 'Thank you, Grandpa.'

'It would suit me if Miss Dorchester were found to have been murdered,' Kate said. 'Then surely they can't suspect my camera of stealing her soul.'

Phoebe teased. 'Who knows what that beastly machine is capable of doing.'

'Then the employees of *The Economic Undertaker* should come in for a staff portrait and see for yourselves,' Kate said.

'That is a fine idea,' Randolph brightened. 'We have never done so, and it would be good for business to show the faces behind our family business and extended family,' he said with a nod towards the mourning clothing shop in one direction and the stables out the back where the stable hands worked. 'I shall suggest it to Julius.'

'No charge, of course,' Kate added. 'With your permission, if I can display a copy on my wall, it might inspire other businesses to do the same and open up more work for me.'

'That is too generous, young lady, and you are most welcome to display the image, but we will insist on paying,' Randolph said. 'You are a business lady and must charge for your professional services, and this will be a professional portrait.'

'But you can do us a special rate,' Phoebe said, nudging her.

'It's a deal,' Kate grinned. 'Just hold on to your souls!'

The distinguished Father Morris – clean-shaven, light hair smattered with grey, and kind eyes – stood on the edge of the worn-out stone steps that led down to the cliff, with his hands clasped before him. Wearing his long black cassock with the small white collar, to a passer-by, he might look as if he were about to bless the ground and the men who stood before him.

'God has called the good young man to him and gone too soon. I suspect, in my case, I will lead a long life,' he said with good humour.

Harland smiled. 'You won't be alone, Father; I'll be lingering as well if only the good die young.'

Father Morris chuckled. 'Well, the company will be good then. Are you young men practising your faith?'

'Ah, the inevitable and expected question,' Harland said, making the priest laugh. 'No. You might call me lapsed, but a better definition would be astray.'

Father Morris gave a solemn nod, his expression non-judgemental. 'I am sorry to hear that. I imagine you see the worst and best of people in your role... that must challenge your beliefs. And you, Detective Payne?'

Gilbert swallowed. 'I am with the... other lot, Sir.'

Father Morris put his head back and laughed. 'Ah, that Church of England mob, then?'

Gilbert smiled. 'Yes, but I do try to attend church regularly. My mother insists on me accompanying her when I am not called to work.'

Father Morris tapped his nose as if about to impart a great secret. 'Between you and me, Detective, we should both be fine. I believe we are both praying to the same God.'

'Well, that's a relief,' Gilbert said with a grin.

Harland brought the matter to a head. 'Father Morris, do you believe Father Damien Horan's death was accidental?'

Father Morris hesitated long enough to tell Harland what he needed to know. 'I am torn,' he said, looking to the steep fall below. 'Damien was a capable, sure-footed young man who walked this path regularly. He enjoyed his walks and was no stranger to this path. According to our parish secretary, it wasn't wet that day, nor was he distracted. But the thought that he might have been harmed deliberately... well, I can't imagine who would do that and why.'

'Was Father Horan or the parish the receiver of any threats you are aware of?' Harland asked.

'No. Quite the opposite. We try to provide comfort, not engender ill-feeling. I don't know why anyone would want to harm him unless it were a random attack, but this path is on church property and doesn't attract a general thoroughfare. One would have to be coming here with a purpose.' Father Morris sighed. 'He was a very personable young man.'

'Then you will forgive the impertinent question, I hope,' Harland said. 'Might he have attracted the attention of a lady?'

Father Morris raised his chin and studied Harland as if anticipating the question. 'Sadly, we cannot take a wife, as our colleagues in the Church of England can, but Damien was very devoted. His compassion for the dying was what set him apart. I believe the death of his parents in the last few years taught him a great deal about suffering and forbearance and made him a better man for it. But to answer your question directly, I have no knowledge of a liaison, but it may have been concealed from me.'

Harland took in the information, pleased that Gilbert asked a question as he filed the priest's words in his mind. Gilbert had also been furiously taking notes, and Harland was keen to hear his interpretation of the meeting.

'Reverend... sorry, Father,' Gilbert corrected himself, 'Father Horan had an item in his pocket which was surprising. Maybe you can help.'

'I'll do my best.'

'It was a handwritten verse on scented paper – a couple of lines from a poem by Robert Browning,' Gilbert said and recited the lines. Both detectives watched the priest for his reaction.

Father Morris's eyes widened in surprise, and his mouth opened slightly. Harland assumed he knew nothing of it or its significance.

'I can't imagine. Was it signed?' Father Morris asked.

'Not in a manner of speaking, just initialled,' Gilbert said. 'It was dedicated to "D" with devotion.'

Father Morris shook his head. 'Well, that does not bode well, but in all honesty, I have no idea who might have given Damien the verse or why he might be carrying it.' He opened his mouth to say something further and changed his mind.

Harland studied him. 'Something bothering you, Father?'

Father Morris looked to Harland. 'We both read people for a living,' he said with a smile, understanding why Harland was pushing him. 'It's a silly thing, most likely means nothing, or so I thought at the time, but now I am not so sure. I don't wish to waste your time.'

'You won't be, quite the opposite, Father,' Gilbert said. 'You would be amazed how often a throw-away line or a strange little coincidence helps us. In our last case, a nursery rhyme turned out to be very significant.'

'Is that so?' Father Morris mused. He swallowed and said, 'I stepped in to take one of Father Horan's masses recently when he was called to give the last rites – it was an unexpected death. I found a love poem inside his bible that I used for the mass. It was beautifully written, and naturally, I worried that he might be questioning his devotion to his faith if he had fallen in love.'

'Did you ask him about it?' Harland asked.

Father Morris nodded. 'Of course. I hoped he might confide in me if he needed support or counsel. But he laughed and said he enjoyed poetry and had met a like-minded group of poets who often challenged each other to write and recite verse.'

Gilbert snapped to look at Harland, who retained a poker face as the priest continued.

'Damien explained that their challenge that week had been to write a romantic poem, and the members thought it amusing that he would be tested to do so, but he said it would be a love poem to nature and the universe.' Father Morris frowned. 'He was very convincing, and I never thought about it again. But now, I wonder if there was passion involved which contributed to his death.'

'Where might we find this bible as the good father might have other verses in his possession and we can compare the writing?' Harland asked.

'Ah, I believe the parish secretary packed all of Father Horan's worldly goods, which, mind you, would not amount to much – we give up our earthly possessions before we enter the priesthood. They will be returned to his family. I shall see if his bible is still here, and if so, drop it at the station should I find it.' He gave a wave to a young lady bearing flowers who entered the church. 'That is Miss Melanie Bains, a devout young lady. Soon to make her debut and not quite as excited about it as her mother,' he said with a smile.

'Debut? Do you know Miss Daisy Dorchester?' Harland asked.

'Why yes, but only fleetingly. I know her aunt, Mrs Stewart. Miss Dorchester joined the parish after I left, so she has been in Damien's pastoral care.' He sighed on mentioning his former ecclesiastical colleague's name. 'I also know Miss Dorchester's intended, Mr Eldon Foster. He has been a devout member of this parish since he was a child, as has Miss Bain, our flower arranger. I believe they are good friends.'

Harland looked to Gilbert, who noted the names and nodded to his superior.

'Thank you, Father,' Harland said. 'That is more helpful than you know.'

'Anytime. Do call by if I can be of any assistance or even if you wish to seek some solace.' He looked at Harland and added, 'I promise not to preach, and I have a fine port in stock.'

Harland laughed. 'You might just bring me back to the flock with that promise.'

The men departed, but not before Harland tentatively made his way down the path in the footsteps of Father Damien Horan.

It would be very easy to give someone a nudge to their death on such a cliff, Harland mused. Just what was Father Horan involved in, and with whom?

# Chapter 8

I N HIS USUAL POSITION at the front desk of *The Economic Undertaker*, the distinguished Randolph Astin heard the horse and cart – the hearse – returning at the back of the premises where the stable lads would now strip and clean it. A stalwart of the business, customers preferred to deal with the mature, silver-haired Randolph Astin when it came to matters of death, and being handsome and well-presented added to his charm. Fortunately, he was a happily married man, as no shortage of widows had set their caps, or rather, their hats, at the head of the Astin family.

'The boys are back,' Mrs Dobbs said from the nearby kitchen, 'I shall put the kettle on.'

Ambrose came through the back door at his usual fast pace, flinging his hat onto the rack; Julius followed purposefully, his actions measured.

'Did everything go to plan, lads?' Randolph asked.

'All is well, Grandpa. The dead are buried, and Julius is still grumpy,' Ambrose said with a smile to his brother, who grunted and passed him to wash up.

Randolph was well familiar with their routines; Ambrose was happy to brush himself down and do a quick buff of his shoes to remove the dust from the cemetery and travel, while Julius removed his jacket, rolled up his sleeves and did a full wash of his hands and face as if he feared the collected dust over time would be enough to bury him. His eldest grandson soon joined him at the desk where Ambrose sported a cup of tea while dipping one of Mrs Dobbs' generous home-baked biscuits into it.

'Where is Phoebe?' Julius asked, thanking Mrs Dobbs and accepting the same.

'Her order of powders is due to arrive today, and she was too excited to wait for my post office run, so she has ventured out to collect it,' Randolph said. 'I do encourage that, I confess. I don't like her being in the workroom all day, not seeing light or people.'

'Has she said as much?' Julius asked, concerned he might be working his little sister too hard and she would be the last to tell him.

'No, not at all, not for a minute. Phoebe loves her work and would never surface if we did not force her up for morning or afternoon tea,' Randolph assured him. 'She does have a request of you, though.'

'To cheer up?' Ambrose suggested and chuckled at Julius's grimace.

'We all hope for that,' Randolph teased Julius.

'I'll do my best,' he promised. 'What does she need?'

'A trip to the coroner to enquire about an unwelcomed guest.' Randolph explained about the debutante's insistence that she had been struck and murdered and how she was hindering Phoebe in her work until something was done.

'What a hide,' he said of the young woman. 'Am I free now?'

'For several hours,' Randolph said with a glance at the book. He handed Julius a slip of paper with the young lady's name, date of birth and death for the coroner to cross-check.

'I shall go now then,' Julius said, taking a large gulp of tea and an equally large bite of biscuit.

'Before you do, Phoebe's friend, Miss Kirby, dropped in this morning. She only recently photographed the deceased debutant and is being accused of stealing her soul,' Randolph said, and Ambrose chuckled.

'I would buy one of those cameras immediately if I thought it so effective,' Ambrose said. 'Then we could finish off our most troublesome clients and benefit from their funeral.'

Julius made a scoffing sound. 'Very entrepreneurial of you, brother.' He turned to his grandfather. 'And what of Miss Kirby?'

'She suggested a business portrait of all of our staff, including the dressmaking business and—'

'—an excellent idea,' Julius said, surprising his grandfather. 'Phoebe mentioned similar a few months ago, but I have not had the time to orchestrate it. It could be good for our advertising, and we could have one portrait here and another next door. It will have to wait, though.'

'Allow me to coordinate it, brother,' Ambrose said, finishing his tea. 'I shall negotiate a rate with Miss Kirby, organise a time with Grandpa and all parties for a shoot before work or just after perhaps, or if Miss Kirby can take a photograph here, we need not close up shop entirely.'

Julius's expression relayed his surprise. 'Thank you, Ambrose, that would be most helpful.'

Ambrose momentarily sobered. 'Julius, I am not unsympathetic to your plight. It has not been easy—'

Julius cut him off. 'Ambrose, do not start, I insist.'

'I shall go now then,' Ambrose said, delighted to have got out of a meaningful discussion and to have the chance to venture into town. His grandfather gave him a smile, pleased with his support for Julius and amused at Ambrose's delight in not having to bear his emotions any more than necessary.

The door opened, and a client – a young couple – stepped in. Randolph stepped up, Ambrose slipped out, and Julius took the stairs down to Phoebe's room, Randolph's eyes watching his grandson's descent with curiosity.

Julius was pleased Phoebe was out for a brief time and that his grandfather and brother were occupied. He rarely had a moment to himself in the business and did not wish to stay after hours as his grandfather always offered to remain and assist.

He looked around, hoping the young debutante would not be there so he did not have to ignore Miss Daisy Dorchester or send her on her way. The room was empty.

'Uncle Reggie,' he said in a whisper, enough to call the dead but not attract attention elsewhere and then he waited. He spent every moment in this room ignoring the spirits who appeared, but now he felt that needs must.

Julius walked to the window at eye level, which was too high for Phoebe given the depth of her office in the basement; she had to stand on a chair to see out. From there, he could see Ambrose organising to take the small trap and the lads cleaning out the hearse and brushing down the horses from this morning's ceremony.

'Julius.'

He turned sharply to see his uncle standing nearby. Reggie's hands were clasped behind his back, and his clothing – a riding outfit of nearly thirty years ago – spoke of quality and wealth. Reginald and Randolph were the closest brothers; his untimely death at age 40 in a horse accident shattered the family. To see Reggie with his nephew – the shared dark features, tall frame, and square-cut jaw – was to see a physical version of Julius in the coming years, although they were most dissimilar by nature.

'Uncle. Thank you for coming.'

'I must say, this is a surprise. You work so hard at ignoring my presence.'

Julius gave a slight nod of his head. 'It is not personal, it is—'

'I understand,' Reggie cut him off with a wave. 'Not everyone wants to reveal they can see spirits, even entertaining ones. What is wrong, nephew?'

Julius gave his uncle a small smile. 'Nothing catastrophic. I hoped to ask for your advice, and I don't know who else to speak with... it is a matter of the heart,' he added uncomfortably.

'Ah,' Reggie said and smiled. 'Then I'm delighted to be at your service, even though I died a single man.'

'You are rather well known for your liaisons, Uncle.'

'One must have a legacy,' Reggie smiled and, sobering, asked, 'What is troubling you to such a degree that you deign to call on me?'

'I think I am losing the lady I have feelings for, and I don't know what my next step should be.'

'Miss Forrester, the beautiful Violet. Tell me what has happened.'

For fear of Phoebe's return, Julius hurriedly recounted his last meeting with Violet, her hesitation to be beholden to him as her employer and the visiting relatives, the uncle, in particular, warning her off.

'Ambrose has suggested I devise a memorable outing and do my utmost to impress her,' he finished, requesting his uncle's advice.

Reggie thought a moment. 'Your greatest strength, my nephew, will serve you well. Don't be tempted to do grandiose gestures. I believe Miss Forrester, like yourself, is conservative and sensible, and that will only make her uncomfortable.'

'She is,' Julius agreed.

Reggie shook his head. 'My advice would be not to do that, so you must determine whose advice you will follow or ignore us both.' He gave a small smile, and then his countenance saddened. 'I misread a lady once whom I held great affection for and hoped to marry. I wooed her so I could stand out from the other competitors seeking her hand. It was too much; she was uncomfortable with my gifts and showy displays of love. The man who won her hand understood her. Be direct, be kind and do not make her uncomfortable, Julius. If you are meant to be together, you will be.'

'Are you saying you were never meant to be with this other woman then?' Julius asked curiously.

'Yes, it would have been an ill-fitting match in the long term. But you and Miss Forrester are most suited; I am convinced of it.'

'As am I. Did you not find anyone you wished to wed?' Julius asked and saw his uncle's shift in emotions.

Reggie cleared his throat. 'I only ever truly loved one woman, but she wasn't mine to have.'

'Why, may I ask?'

'Oh, I thought we would be together. We were great friends, and I intended to court her, and then she met my brother.'

'Grandpa?' Julius asked, surprised.

Reggie nodded. 'The better man. My handsome, conservative and kind brother, and Maria was happy to consider me her charming brother-in-law and friend.'

'I had no idea,' Julius said. 'Did Grandpa?'

'I suspect he did, but we never spoke of it. Maria's heart was his from the moment she set eyes on him.' Reggie sighed. 'How I loved her until the day I died. Imagine if your Violet loved Ambrose?'

Julius winced at the thought. 'I couldn't bear to be near them.'

'Nor could I. That is why I travelled and worked away as much as possible.' Reggie gathered himself. 'So, if I were in your shoes, knowing you still have a real chance at love, I would be quick about it. Be forthright, sincere and frank; no elaborate gestures. That is the best I can do. I hope that is of some help?'

Julius inhaled and nodded. 'It is, and I understand you perfectly, Uncle Reggie. Thank you.'

'Anytime, my dear nephew. When might you come out and confess of seeing the spirits Phoebe sees?'

'I am not ready yet. I am not sure I will ever be.'

Reggie nodded, and with a smile and a slight bow, he faded. Julius gathered himself and raced up the stairs, slowing as he saw his grandfather at the desk but no sign of the young couple. Panic took hold of him.

'That was a quick client meeting,' he said, hoping his grandfather did not hear the murmur of his voice from downstairs.

'The young lady was calling on behalf of her mother, who sought a written quote to bury a relative in the throes of death. Her mother also requires some mourning clothes but is too unwell to travel, and she does not have a dressmaker she trusts.'

'Did you offer our services?' Julius asked. 'I am sure one of the ladies next door could make a house call to measure the lady in question and deliver the appropriate clothing.'

'I did indeed on both counts.'

'Of course, sorry, Grandpa,' Julius said with a slight shake of his head.

'A natural question, but you might forewarn the ladies next door after your return from the coroner.'

I will,' Julius agreed, knowing his grandfather constantly found reasons for him to go next door and consult with Miss Forrester.

'I shall head off to see the coroner now.'

As Julius grabbed his hat, his grandfather said, 'You know you can always talk with me if you think I can be of any assistance, Julius. I have some life experience,' he said with a small smile.

Julius turned to look at his grandfather, surprised and slightly confused. Had he guessed what Julius was doing downstairs talking to "himself"? He mumbled his thanks.

'How I miss him,' Randolph said in a voice so low that Julius barely heard him. 'Did Reggie have a message for me?'

Julius froze, his hand on the doorknob. To deny he did would admit he saw and spoke to Reggie, but to deny all knowledge would be a blatant lie. Phoebe pushed on the door from the other side, relieving him of answering, and Julius bid them both farewell, departing in a hurry.

# Chapter 9

C HEERFUL SCOTTISH CORONER DR Tavish McGregor grinned at the gentlemen in his presence.

'I have never felt so popular,' he said, stroking his short ginger beard. 'The only thing that would make it better is if you had brought a fine drop with you.'

'Sorry about that, Tavish, we're on duty,' Harland said with a smile as his young partner, Gilbert, appeared apologetic for not bearing the requested spirits.

'If Ambrose had come instead of me, you might have been in luck,' Julius added, having arrived at the same time as his detective friend.

'Now, what are the odds you are enquiring after the same body?' Tavish mused. The men answered in unison.

'—Miss Daisy Dorchester,' Julius said.

'—Father Damien Horan,' Harland responded.

Julius gasped. 'Father Horan is dead?'

Harland looked surprised and then regretful. 'I am sorry, Julius, yes. Were you friends?'

'Of sorts. He officiated many funerals that we were booked to do. I saw him only last week,' Julius said, bewildered. 'What has befallen him?'

'That is what we are trying to discover too, Mr Astin,' Gilbert said, addressing Julius more formerly as their relationship was not as familiar as his superior. 'The constabulary believed he fell to his death on the cliff stairs, but we are not so sure.'

'Good Lord,' Julius said, shocked. 'I cannot believe he is gone.'

'I am sorry to have delivered the news to you so bluntly,' Harland grimaced.

'I did point out the marks around his neck,' Tavish said, shaking his head. 'Worth considering, but his death resulted from the fall.'

Harland cocked his head to the side as he considered Julius. 'What of the young miss you mentioned? She is also one of our files. Why are you enquiring about her, may I ask?'

'Miss Daisy Dorchester. She is a debutante delivered to us for burial,' Julius said, gathering himself from the shock of Father Horan's death.

Tavish made a knowing sound. 'Poor young lady. According to the police officer who reported the death, that was a fall most likely from slipping on damp grass or tripping on her hem, resulting in a savage strike to the head on a tombstone. Very hard to prove otherwise, but an assailant may have also struck her.'

Julius gave the two detectives a look, implying he had information that might prove the contrary, but as the coroner did not know of Phoebe's unique skills, Julius did not elaborate. Harland gave a brief nod, and Gilbert sealed his lips to show his understanding.

Julius added, 'Miss Dorchester's aunt is most insistent that the death was foul play, although at this stage the aunt is blaming Phoebe's friend, Miss Kirby, who took the photograph of the debutantes and thus stole the young lady's soul.' The party smiled at the strange superstition. 'I promised Phoebe, who is concerned for Miss Kirby's reputation, that I would discuss it with you, Harland.' He embellished the truth slightly to hide the real reason for his enquiry – that the young woman had appeared to Phoebe demanding action.

'And you thought it best to check with me first in case there is nothing suspicious about Miss Dorchester's death?' Tavish finished for him.

'Precisely so.'

'Well, let us dig out both files and see what we can discover,' Tavish said, smiling, as if he was happy for the company regardless of any extra workload it might create.

'Is the priest's body still here?' Harland asked.

'It is, but he is due to be buried. Miss Dorchester is gone.'

'She is with us,' Julius said, 'the aunt is organising a viewing so all her young debutant friends may come to pay their respects. Heaven help us,' he muttered under his breath and noted the amusement of the gentlemen present.

'It is a season for falls, is it not?' Gilbert said. 'Everyone seems to be slipping and sliding.'

'Or they've been assisted with a good push,' Harland said, and Tavish did not rule it out.

He flicked through the pages of each file to the page where he wrote his conclusions. 'You are correct, Harland. Both parties may have been assisted to their death; I could not rule it out. Father Horan had fresh bruising around his neck that was not caused by the fall, but his death resulted from his tumble. Miss Dorchester's wound may have been the result of contact with the sharp edge of the tombstone or from a blow inflicted from this angle.' He indicated the direction using Gilbert as his model.

Harland frowned. 'I know this is an odd question, but did Miss Dorchester have any possessions on her person at the time of death that were not recorded?'

Gilbert elaborated for Julius's benefit, 'Father Horan had a verse of poetry and the same verse appeared on a gift tag in Miss Dorchester's possession.'

'How odd,' Julius said with a frown. 'Was it a prayer verse?'

'No, a verse of... ah, affection,' Gilbert said discretely.

'Here it is,' Tavish said, scanning the notes on Miss Daisy Dorchester's attire and belongings. 'The two locks of hair are listed, and I found another item when folding away her clothing that was not written here – a small item in her pocket, which is not what you would expect.'

'So not a handkerchief, a fan or a small purse?' Harland asked.

'No. Miss Dorchester had a folded-up portrait. It has not been collected yet by her family.' Tavish handed the folded card to the senior detective, who unfolded it for all to see.

It was a most peculiar item for Daisy Dorchester to have in her possession – a handsome and formal portrait of the deceased Father Damien Horan.

'I think there might be more to the death of these two victims than first realised,' Harland concluded. 'The other victim whose file we have retained as he too had the verse upon his person, was...' he turned to Gilbert.

'Theodore Wright, Sir,' Gilbert answered without having to consult his notes.

'I did not hear of him as he survived,' Tavish said, and added in jest, 'they haven't started bringing me the living yet.'

The gentlemen laughed.

'Why is he a victim? What has befallen him?' Tavish asked as he gathered his files and closed them.

'He was brutally assaulted with a severe blow to the head, enough to leave him unconscious. It was an unfortunate incident for a young man, with an engagement ring or at least its box, in his pocket. I hope she accepted whomever she might be,' Harland said.

Gilbert added, 'He had the verse in his pocket too. The very same that was in the possession of the other two victims.'

'Well, I hope the bump to his head has not taken his memory,' Julius said.

A loud knock on the door got their attention before the doors opened, and a couple of large men wheeled in a trolley.

'Another one, Doc,' one of the men said, and as Tavish was distracted directing the delivery, Harland turned to Julius and spoke quietly.

'Do tell, what is Miss Dorchester saying to Miss Astin?'

'That she did strike her head on the headstone but as a result of being struck from behind. She claims she will not rest until it is proven so,' Julius said under his breath.

'The spirit is still present?' Harland asked.

'Yes, visit in if you wish.'

Harland nodded and stepped back as Tavish re-joined them. After a brief summary, the party dispersed, and Tavish looked around his workroom. With a sigh, he returned to keeping company with the dead.

# Chapter 10

HARLAND DID HIS BEST not to grimace as Gilbert announced, 'Why, there is Miss Lewis coming out of Mr Foster's house. At least we know he is in residence.'

Sure enough, the young journalist, Miss Lily Lewis, emerged, looking lovely in a pale blue gown that brought out her blue eyes. Her chestnut hair was a little loose, no doubt from being out and about. She closed the small front gate behind her and grinned at the detectives as she joined them on the footpath.

'Hello Detective Stone, Detective Payne, what a lovely surprise,' she teased. 'I saw that grimace, Detective Stone.'

'Merely a reaction to the bright light on exiting the cab,' he said with a small smile, and she laughed at his audacity.

'I am no stranger to that expression,' Lilly assured him, 'and I believe I am one step ahead of you.'

'Then Mr Eldon Foster is at home?' Gilbert asked with a glance at the door.

'Yes, in mourning.'

'And is he?' Harland lowered his voice, interested in Lilly's perspective.

'I think it is fair to say he is not despairing. However, for my feature article on the untimely death of the beautiful debutante, Miss Daisy Dorchester, he will be the man who intended to propose once she debuted and is now inconsolable.' She sighed. 'It offends my journalistic sensibilities to apply gloss where it is not.'

'I can imagine so, Miss Lewis, when your stories are so well researched,' Gilbert said.

'Well, thank you, Detective Payne.'

Harland brought the topic back to the man in residence. 'Did Mr Foster say anything of particular interest?' He saw Lilly's surprised expression and anticipated she would understand exactly what he was asking; Harland was not disappointed.

'Ah,' she studied the senior detective. 'You are asking me because you are suspicious Miss Dorchester has been murdered. That is a good story if it is true. You believe so?'

'No—

'It is possible—'

Both gentlemen spoke at once, Harland in denial, Gilbert not so, and Lilly laughed at the grimace Harland now transferred to Detective Payne, who swallowed and looked somewhat remorseful.

She looked skyward for a moment, saying, 'Now let me see, what might he have said to me that he would not say to two detectives,' she mused.

'Don't mean to hurry you along, Miss, but do you want the cab or not?' the hansom driver interrupted them.

'Yes, please, I am coming right this minute.' She turned back to the detectives, 'I am off to see the organisers of the debut ball to ask for their favourable reminisces about Daisy Dorchester. I hope they can find some.'

'Oh, has it been difficult to write your article, Miss Lewis?' Gilbert asked, no doubt storing away the fact that their victim was unpopular.

'To say the least, Detective Payne.'

'Perhaps Gilbert, you could also accompany Miss Lewis to speak with the organisers.' Harland suggested. 'You might then elaborate on your observations of Mr Eldon Foster during the journey, Miss Lewis?'

Lilly nodded. 'I'd be delighted to have the company.'

'Yes, Sir,' Gilbert said and offered a hand to Miss Lewis before following her into the cab. 'Sorry, Sir,' he added for Detective Stone's ears only.

'It is not important. We shall meet back at the office and discuss what we have learnt later today.' He saw them off, opened the gate and moved up the path, rapping on the front door. Harland's eyes surveyed the home and garden; while not ostentatious, it spoke of money and was well maintained. The door opened promptly.

'Can I help you?' the worn-looking man in residence asked.

'Mr Eldon Foster?'

'Yes.'

'Forgive the intrusion in your time of grief, Mr Foster. Detective Harland Stone, may I have a word?'

Eldon Foster frowned and then nodded, moving inside. Harland followed him down the hallway, glancing in at rooms as they passed – a nicely appointed lounge room with a fireplace that most likely was never used in the warm climate, a large bedroom, and a sitting room; then they arrived in a sunny, timber kitchen. Eldon waved to a chair at the table opposite where he sat.

'The tea is still warm; I made it for the lady reporter. Would you like a cup? I am going to have a second,' he said.

'Thank you, yes,' Harland took the offered seat.

'Unusual to see a lady reporter, but she seemed most competent,' Eldon continued.

Harland was pleased he was talkative; it boded well for the interview. He accepted the cup of tea with thanks. 'Can you tell me about your relationship with Miss Daisy Dorchester, the deceased?'

Eldon sighed and sat back in his kitchen chair. 'Our fathers started a shipping business together; our mothers were pregnant at the same time with us. We grew up together. Everyone wanted the happy, family merger.'

'Did you and Miss Dorchester?'

'Once upon a time,' Eldon answered honestly. Harland nodded, assuming the young man would fill the silence, and he did. 'She's beautiful, she was, there's no denying that. But she was spoilt and indulged, and Daisy was not always nice except to those that mattered. My parents adore her.'

'I see. And if you wanted to renege on your intentions?'

Eldon looked horrified. 'I could never do that.'

'Why? If neither of you professed to be in love or wished for the union?'

Eldon's eyes narrowed with a look Harland attested to bitterness. 'My father would disown me. This house was to be our wedding gift from my father, and Daisy was entering the union with a sizeable gift from her father. It would set me up, set us both up for the future. So, as you can surmise, it was not in my best interest to do Daisy harm, at least until we were married.'

Harland nodded. 'True, and your candour convinces me there was little real feeling left between you.'

Eldon looked a little ashamed. 'I had thought of playing the grieved potential husband, but I could not do so sincerely. However, if I think about the young Daisy, the adventures we had as children...' His voice trailed off.

'My condolences. You no doubt knew the real Miss Dorchester above all others.'

Eldon looked surprised at the Detective's empathy.

'Yes, I believe you are correct.' Eldon took a deep breath and said, 'I will deny this should you ever repeat it, Detective, but it is a blessing in disguise for me. My father gifted me this house yesterday; my mother made him do so. She believed I had lost enough without that which would have rightfully been mine by doing their bidding. Now I might find real love, not love that has long since tarnished with familiarity.'

'Some might say familiarity could strengthen a bond,' Harland suggested.

'Not when you realise you do not like your intended in the slightest, Detective. Nothing I did was good enough for her. I am not handsome enough, gentlemanly enough, dashing enough, witty enough, I am not enough of anything.'

Harland did not speak. He sipped from his teacup and observed the young man, interested in whether he might rise to anger... enough to kill his potential betrothed. But his temperament remained the same.

Eldon spoke again. 'I just need to get through the viewing and funeral, and then I will begin anew. I feel like my future has been returned to me.'

'Where were you on the day of Miss Dorchester's death, Mr Foster?' Harland asked.

Eldon paused, then laughed with surprise. 'Nowhere near her or where the debutantes were rehearsing, I assure you.'

'Who informed you of Miss Dorchester's place of death?'

Eldon paled and sputtered. 'I do not know, the police who came to advise of her death perhaps, or did Daisy's aunty tell me? I can't recall. You must understand it was quite a shock.'

Harland nodded, satisfied but not ruling Eldon Foster out of misadventure, given his sense of entrapment. 'Have you another lady you are interested in?'

Eldon hesitated. 'Ah, you think we conspired, and she might have felled Daisy? Good theory.'

Harland refrained from sighing. Thank goodness for the public and their endorsement, he thought. 'Do you?'

'There is a lady I am holding a flame for, but I do not believe she knows of my interest yet.' Eldon gave a small shrug. 'There was no point in pursuing it as I could not offer her anything. But now, I am better positioned to tell her my intentions.'

'Miss Melanie Bains? I believe you are old friends?'

Eldon looked surprised. 'No. I mean, yes, we are old friends, but not her.' He looked slightly embarrassed. 'Her friend, Miss Hilda Dickinson. She has the voice of an angel and a wonderful laugh.'

Harland knew Eldon to be genuine as he smiled at the thought of her laugh.

'What do you know of the verse, "Grow old along with me, the best is yet to be". Does it mean anything to you?'

Harland rolled his eyes. 'Daisy and her poetry. I was not poetic enough for her either, Detective. After the debut, I was to propose to her, and she told me of her expectations for a romantic proposal. Truly, I am sure no man could live up to it, but Daisy did give me a book of verse, highlighting poems that she thought were particularly romantic. I had those lines inscribed in the engagement ring I was to present.'

Harland frowned, an unsavoury thought stirring within him.

'What is it, Detective? You have thought of something?'

'Yes. Was Daisy faithful to you?'

Eldon scoffed and then paused, not quite as confident given the line of questioning. 'I could not say. She was flirtatious even in my presence. It was, on occasion, humiliating, especially when people looked at me with pity. But I cannot say if she was in a relationship. Surely not.' He hesitated and added without looking Harland in the eyes, 'I once hoped she would be unfaithful and call off our agreement, then the shame would not be mine to bear.'

'Yes, unless she had a sister and you had to offer for her?' Harland said in jest, which he rarely did with interview subjects.

Harland laughed, caught unaware. 'No, fortunately not.'

They both sobered.

'We have another gentleman – the victim of an attack – who had in his possession an empty engagement ring box and a note bearing the verse I just mentioned. I am curious whether there is a connection between you or Miss Dorchester to this man.'

Eldon paled, and he gaped. 'My best friend, who would have been my best man once the proposal was done. Surely not? He took the ring to have it engraved.' Eldon rose quickly. 'I have not seen him for several days, but he has been busy, and I have been mourning.'

'I see.'

'Can you tell me the victim's name, Detective?'

'Yes. Theodore Wright.'

Eldon cried out with shock and lowered himself back into his chair. His emotion was real, his pain evident. 'Theo... harmed.'

'I am sorry, Mr Foster, but fear not, I believe he was taken to the hospital and is recovering. As the ring box was still in his possession, but the ring gone, we assumed he proposed to a lady before the assault, and she accepted.'

Eldon shook his head. 'No, the ring in the box was mine, and I care nothing for it, only for Theo's health. I shall go to him immediately.'

'As will I now.' Harland added, 'Before you, if I may?'

Eldon nodded. 'Yes, of course. Please tell him I will be there to see him post haste.'

Harland nodded. 'Would he have met with Miss Dorchester for a rendezvous? Or do you know why anyone might wish to harm two people who were very close to you?'

'No,' he said, his eyes wide with shock at the inference. 'No, I can't imagine. Theo would never betray me, and in fact, he did not like Daisy at all. He always said we were unsuited, and she had airs and graces. I can't imagine... but you say he was attacked?'

'Yes.'

'It is a strange coincidence.'

Harland rose. 'Thank you, Mr Foster. You have been most helpful, and I am sorry to have brought you more distressing news. I shall see myself out.'

And so he did. But Detective Stone did not rule the young husband-to-be out entirely as a suspect, nor the integrity of his best friend, but Harland felt Eldon Foster had been punished enough, for now.

Detective Gilbert Payne was often uncomfortable in the presence of ladies; he found them rather baffling, and as a man of facts, rhyme and reason, sometimes, he could not follow their reactions. His mother was a direct woman, his grandmother and aunt the same, and he had little experience with the theatrics he heard that Miss Daisy Dorchester displayed. Heaven forbid he should find himself tied to such a woman. Gilbert felt very relaxed with the kind and logical Miss Phoebe Astin, and now, in the company of reporter Miss Lilly Lewis, Gilbert felt quite at home. Not because he found Miss Lewis a calming force, quite the opposite. Her energy levels and non-stop conversation required little from him and allowed him to relax and contribute only when she drew a breath.

'And so, I don't think Mr Foster is heartbroken, but I don't think he had the constitution to kill a person,' she concluded.

'That is very helpful, thank you, Miss Lewis. I will be sure to pass your observations on to Detective Stone.'

'Do you like him?' Lilly asked, and Gilbert's expression reflected his surprise at her directness.

'Detective Stone, I mean. Do you like him?'

'Yes. Yes, I admire him a great deal and respect him. He has been accommodating and kind to me.'

'Then you are lucky,' she said, bracing as they went over a bump. 'I can't say I like my boss, but I do not dislike him. He is a complex man; managing him takes some work.'

'Detective Stone manages me rather than the other way around, and he has been most patient.'

'I am sure you do not give yourself enough credit, Detective.'

Gilbert looked to the passing traffic, at a loss as to what to say and was relieved to see the building in sight. 'I believe we are here.' The cab stopped, the pair alighted, and Gilbert paid.

On entering the premises of the large and impressive building where the debutantes would make their debut and dance the night away, they could hear a rehearsal in process.

'Left girls, left! Left is the direction opposite to your right!' an impatient female voice snapped at a couple of the girls, causing laughter to titter through the lines of ladies.

'Goodness, so many ladies. I imagine you are feeling quite outnumbered, Detective,' Lilly joked.

'I was raised in a predominantly female household and often stepped up as a dance partner, but I do hope they don't ask me to do so today.' He watched two gentlemen amongst the dozens of ladies escorting the ladies as needed for the rehearsal.

'Duty, Detective, if it is required...' she teased. 'Oh, there is Emily; you remember her from the hospital ball?'

Gilbert glanced in the direction where Lilly was waving and saw the attractive and stately Miss Emily Yalden of the *Miss Emily Yalden School of Deportment* assisting the rehearsal. A tap to her chin, or standing taller, was all she needed to do to get her charges to improve their posture.

He smiled. 'Yes, of course. I believe we even had a dance that evening,' Gilbert said and readied himself as Emily approached. Gilbert had admired her composure, lady-like manners, sparkling eyes and neat dress and style, not unlike his own appearance, but he did not make that connection.

'Hello, Detective Payne, hello, Lilly,' Emily whispered, her dark eyes alight with the pleasure of seeing them. 'How nice to see some friendly faces.'

'Good day, Miss Yalden. Has the atmosphere been less than friendly?' Gilbert asked, leaning closer to keep his voice low.

'Yes. It is fair to say the debutante organisers are rather bossy, Detective, and I thought I was tough on my girls, but they are positively harsh. My girls will think me a kitten after these tigers.'

'Are your students faring well?' Gilbert asked, observing some ladies who seemed most at ease while others were awkward.

'Of course they are,' Lilly ribbed him.

'Oh, my apologies,' Gilbert stammered. 'I have no experience in these matters, but naturally, your charges would reflect your decorum, Miss Yalden.'

'Ignore her, Detective. Lilly is just teasing you,' Emily assured him and gave Lilly a stern look, making her friend laugh. 'I am pleased to say they are rarely criticised, but I will be glad when it is over.'

'A ridiculous tradition,' Lilly scoffed.

Gilbert spoke again without thinking of the consequences given the ladies surrounding him.

'If it serves the purpose of introducing a young lady to other friends and, should she wish, to a potential husband, I see no harm as long as she enjoys it.'

'Nor I, Detective,' Emily said with a firm nod. 'It is always beneficial to practice our manners and our conduct in society, and this is a safe introduction for many young ladies.'

'I imagine so,' Gilbert said, feeling more confident having found an ally in Miss Yalden. 'I have several friends, myself included, who would no doubt benefit from a similar polish-up for chaps.'

Emily smiled at his humility, and Lilly made a face at the pair.

'Oh phooey, you two. So, what have you observed, Emily, and can you say some kind words about your student for my article, given you were her instructor?'

Emily drew in a slow breath and exhaled. 'Now you are testing me, Lilly.'

Gilbert's eyebrows shot up. 'It appears quite a few share your sentiment, Miss Yalden.'

Emily winced. 'I try to speak kindly of my students, but some can be quite challenging. I confess the *Vexed Vixens* have heard their share of my complaining.'

'Ah, I have heard of your small group. It is no doubt good for your constitution to have a release for the tension your business may cause,' Gilbert said. 'My mother is always trying to get me to take up painting, walking, or some hobby, as she fears I may implode with the daily anxieties of work life. Having someone to share your day with, no doubt, releases that tension.'

'Exactly so, Detective. 'Thank you for your understanding,' Emily said, looking at him with great satisfaction, to Gilbert's immense pleasure. He straightened as if Emily's endorsement made him ten feet tall. 'Do you have a talent for painting?'

'None whatsoever, Miss Yalden,' he said honestly, and she laughed at his honesty.

They exchanged looks as given by those agreeing on life matters and its pleasures, and Lilly rolled her eyes at the pair of them.

'Well, I am not so charitable as you, Emily. I believe Miss Dorchester was a nasty young lady – not that I shall say that in my article – but I prefer to call a spade a spade, as does my editor.'

'Which is why you are well suited to your career, Lilly,' Emily said. 'I can say that Miss Dorchester enthusiastically took to her training.'

'Oh, that is good,' Lilly wrote down the comment.

'She was a young lady with great potential. Will that suffice?'

Lilly smiled, 'It will, thank you. Potential for what, may I ask?'

'Not to be included in your article, but the potential for causing havoc,' Emily said with a wry look, making them both laugh.

'May I ask, concerning my investigation, did she speak of having an admirer or a pending betrothal, Miss Yalden?' Gilbert asked.

Emily nodded and looked at Lilly. 'Can I speak without being quoted?'

'Consider our interview done,' Lilly confirmed, closing her pad. 'I will make you sound professional and mention your business name.'

'Thank you, dear Lilly,' Emily said with a smile and returned her attention to the detective after a glance around to ensure they were not overhead. 'She did not speak directly to me, but I overheard her boasting a few times to the other young ladies. Miss Dorchester claimed she had many admirers but did not intend to marry the man her family expected her to marry. Supposedly, she had a forbidden love.'

'Ah, that is most interesting,' Gilbert said.

'Is it? I hope I have been useful,' Emily said sincerely.

'You have, Miss Yalden, very much so.'

Emily continued. 'I heard her boast of that forbidden love several times, but she did not mention a name. Miss Dorchester did—' Emily hesitated mid-sentence, 'no, that is too petty to tell.'

'Every bit of information may help,' Lilly said. 'Isn't that so, Detective?'

'Certainly, and I assure you of my discretion. I will not sit in judgement.'

Emily pursed her lips and continued, 'Miss Dorchester was to have her hair cut and styled for the evening but insisted that she was keeping all of her locks so she could make gifts of the locks of her hair. That would imply that perhaps she intended or hoped to receive more than one offer.'

Gilbert nodded, his eyes narrowing.

'You know something about that, don't you?' Lilly pounced on him.

He hesitated. 'I imagine Detective Stone would not mind you knowing if you do not report the information without his permission.'

'Agreed.'

'Two locks of hair were found in Miss Dorchester's possession, each tied with a ribbon and bearing the same verse, "*Grow old along with me...*", a beautiful verse.' He stopped short of saying both lines.

'The best is yet to be,' Emily finished and smiled.

'Never heard of it,' Lilly said frankly.

'By Robert Browning,' Emily said.

'Indeed it is,' Gilbert smiled at her as they shared another moment of collusion.

'You three, do be quiet!' A loud voice barked in their direction, making all three jump. 'Oh, never mind, take a break, girls.' The coordinator thundered towards them. 'This is not a social occasion.'

'Detective Gilbert Payne, Madame, apologies for the interruption, and Miss Lilly Lewis from *The Courier*.'

Emily excused herself to speak with her girls during their break.

'Ah, right, my apologies,' the coordinator stammered. 'Is this about the dead debutante?'

Gilbert noted that tact was not one of the coordinator's skills. 'It is,' he replied.

'I can't tell you much; they are all the same to me. I just need to get the ladies moving, herd them along as gracefully as possible, and get them to supper once they have all come out. One less girl, however, is frustrating as my numbers are out now.'

Gilbert restrained a sigh. The coordinator would not be anywhere near as helpful as Miss Emily Yalden, and as Lilly asked her questions, he glanced in the direction of Emily only to find her glancing at him. Both hastily looked away.

Arriving at the hospital bed of Theodore Wright, Detective Harland Stone was surprised to see the young man sitting up, reading a book and looking well enough to leave.

'They will release me tonight,' Theodore informed him after introductions. The patient touched the bandage around his head gingerly. 'Will you find out who did this, Detective?'

'I hope so, but that implies you have no idea who struck you then?'

'No, the blows came from behind me and slightly to the side.'

Harland moved to the window and lowered himself to sit on the wide edge of the windowsill. He noted the man was slim in appearance, most likely under six foot in height given where his feet ended in the bed, whereas Harland's would have been overhanging, and Theodore was more likely to be found in a library than a brawl. Harland also noted the young man looked similar to Mr Eldon Foster. Perhaps that is why they were friends; they were both thin, nervous-looking young men who were probably at the mercy of more brutal boys in their schooling years.

'What exactly were you doing when you were struck, Mr Wright?'

'I was just returning from the jeweller with my best friend's ring. I'm to be the best man and had it engraved for him.' He closed his eyes momentarily and then opened them, adopting a mournful expression. 'That is to say, I was to be the best man.'

'You were struck near the church grounds; that's a fair distance from the trade strip where you might find an engraver.'

Harland could tell Theodore Wright was thinking on his feet from the quick movement of his eyes and the slight furrowing of his brow.

'I enjoy the walk home along the cliffs, past the church.'

'The ring was not in the box when you were found and taken to the hospital, according to our constable's report.'

'No. I can only assume the blackguard who struck me stole the ring. It featured several sizeable gems and was a good quality gold band.'

Harland nodded, storing this information. 'Did you see Miss Dorchester in your travels? Your best friend's fiancée?'

'No. Why would I have seen her?'

He was defensive, and Harland suspected Mr Wright was hiding something and would reveal more with very little pressure.

'I have just come from your friend, Mr Foster's house. He had no idea you were harmed but will visit immediately.'

A stricken look crossed Theodore's face. Harland took a gamble. 'However, he was quite distressed... I believe he knows,' Harland said, hoping the ambiguous statement would result in an admission of what was happening and the connection between all parties.

'What might he know... how...' he swallowed and leant back on the pillow, the book falling to the floor beside him.

'You loved her,' Harland said, taking a safe gamble.

'I have been such a fool.'

'Perhaps start at the top,' Harland said with a moderate voice displaying no judgement. 'Provide me with your side of the story.'

Theodore shook his head and winced with the pain it caused him. 'There is not much to tell. I fell in love with my best friend's intended, and I declared my love to her. I am the worst of friends.'

'Mr Foster does not know?'

'No!' he proclaimed, alarmed. 'He does not. And I am a fool. She teased and flattered me, but I realise now that Miss Dorchester wants to be admired by everyone. She had no feelings for me. And I found that verse just for her.'

'The verse on the ring... "*Grow old along with me*", you selected it?'

'Yes. Eldon does not have a romantic bone in his body, and he complained that Miss Dorchester wanted poetry from him. I gave him several verses from books in my possession, and she loved that one. So, I told him I would engrave it on the ring for him.'

'And you were struck a blow on returning from collecting it?' Harland asked, trying to get a timeline in his head.

'Yes. I knew where Miss Dorchester would be; she was seeing the priest. Eldon told me she was becoming quite devout of late. So, I ensured we crossed paths.' He looked ashamed. 'I did that often, I confess. She always seemed pleased to see me.'

'And you professed your love to her?'

'I know it was wrong and that I would lose Eldon's friendship, but I was so in love with her that it consumed me, and if I could have Daisy, Miss Dorchester, as my wife for life, it was worth it. Now, I realise it was not worth anything.'

'What did Miss Dorchester say at your proclamation?' Harland moved Theodore Wright's recounting along.

Theodore's eyes narrowed, and his jaw locked. 'She laughed and called me a "silly man" and that we were just friends. She told me Eldon had admitted the verse he selected for the ring came from me and that she liked it so much she put it on the lock of hair for him. She was particularly cruel,' Theodore said, his lips thinning. 'And then she said, "Wait until I tell Eldon, how he will laugh" and I knew she would.'

'That is particularly cruel. Were you angry enough to kill Miss Dorchester? She shunned you and then was likely to tell your best friend of your betrayal?'

'No!' he said with great conviction. 'I could never do that. Never. But I hated her in that moment.'

Harland did not speak, allowing Theodore to calm himself and slow his breathing. Eventually, the young man added, 'She got what she deserved. I left hurriedly, and some petty thief most likely felled me as I passed the cathedral.'

They both glanced to the door, where a movement caught their eye, and Eldon Foster moved out of the shadows and into the room. How long he had been standing there was anyone's guess.

'I shall leave you gentlemen to talk then,' Harland said. 'But we will speak again, Mr Wright.'

Theodore nodded, and Harland left the men to their unpleasant discussion, but he had not ruled out either man as a suspect in the murder of Miss Dorchester. Eldon Foster may have found out about his friend's betrayal, killed his soon-to-be-fiancée, then attacked his friend, or once slighted, Theodore Wright may have killed Miss Dorchester, but she struggled and struck him in self-defence. He may have left injured, collapsing near the church. Why the priest was killed was another mystery, but Harland had no doubt it was all part of a storm created by Miss Daisy Dorchester.

# Chapter 11

P HOEBE THANKED HER BROTHER, Ambrose, for the ride
as he deposited her out the front of Miss Violet Forrester's
home and departed with a wave, not daring to enter the
premises when a *Vexed Vixens* gathering was soon to be in
progress. Violet's brother, Tom, had also made other plans
for the evening. As the newest member of the *Vexed Vixens*
group, Miss Violet Forrester – manageress of *In Mourning –
Attire for the Family* dress store – was hosting the gathering
for the first time. Along with Violet, the members – mortician
Phoebe, reporter Lilly, photographer Kate, and proprietor of
the *Miss Emily Yalden School of Deportment*, Emily – did not
seek to grow the circle unless another young lady of the same
inclination should cross their paths; they were, after all, all
unique in their outlooks and occupations.

Violet had prepared a simple supper, and once all ladies were in attendance, she gave them a tour of her cottage, which took little time, given the smallness of the abode. Phoebe wandered through admiring Violet's touches and aware that Julius had hoped to 'rescue' Violet from her previous lifestyle and move her and Tom into his home as his wife and ward; the uncle had derailed his plans, but Phoebe still held high hopes that Violet would one day soon be her sister-in-law.

Once seated, Lilly spoke. 'I must start with something that is vexing me more than I have been vexed in a long time. I am sorry, Violet, to usurp the gathering.'

'Not at all. Please do tell what has you so vexed,' Violet invited Lilly to speak as she filled the ladies' glasses with a fresh batch of her lemon drink, and the ladies served themselves from the pots and platters on the table.

'This article about debutantes,' Lilly said, waving a sheet of newspaper at them. 'Not from *The Courier,* I am pleased to say, but allow me to read from *The Australian Town and Country.*[1]

### Bringing Out the Buds.

'Can you believe that title?' she asked before even reaching the article's first line. Lilly cleared her throat and continued.

The presentation of debutantes is an important
feature of the season's first ball. To people who take

society seriously – and there are a good many of them – the debutantes are of the most enormous importance. They decide the future of society.

The opinions of younger men are not worth a button; they only know what they like; they are no criterion of the taste of the great world. They are apt to fall foolishly in love with a girl. But the veterans never make such mistakes – their feelings never carry them away. They note when a young lady is "very neat" or is "going to be as fine a woman as her grandmother".

The lot of the debutantes is not as rosy as outsiders might suppose. They must combat tremendous rivalry. Great things are expected of her, and, from the first, a sense of fear and possible failure oppresses her. She contends against severe odds – other girls as handsome as she, much wealthier or cleverer. But once plunged in, she must go forward; to retreat is to confess defeat.

'It is a load of rubbish,' Lilly said as she tossed the newspaper article onto the table in front of the other *Vexed Vixens* and helped herself to a piece of egg and bacon pie.

'Goodness, it sounds so competitive,' Phoebe said, 'like a business transaction, and heaven forbid love should prevail.'

'It makes me very pleased and relieved I did not make my debut,' Lilly said.

'Well, I made my debut,' Emily said. 'I must say I enjoyed it. It was not as pompous or silly as that article makes out, but I'm sure such rivalry exists.'

'It does,' Kate said, touching a strand of her red hair and straightening a curl at the thought of the preening involved. 'But as I am not a classic beauty, I was never a threat to anyone when I made my debut.'

'Fiddlesticks, Kate,' Emily declared. 'You are very attractive and, dare I say, a contradiction. You appear demure of nature, but I am sure those blue eyes, fair complexion, and wonderfully wild hair, not to mention your unique profession for a lady, make you quite fascinating to the male species.'

'Thank you, dear Emily,' Kate said, appearing quite pleased at how her friend regarded her.

'And you have attracted a number of suitors willing to discover the true young lady behind the camera, including the coroner, Dr Tavish McGregor,' Phoebe reminded her.

'Oh, that could never be. Both of us with red hair, goodness, our temperaments would get in the way.' Kate continued, 'As for the debutants this season, I have met quite a few in my studio, and several have grand ambitions of finding themselves a wealthy suitor.'

'I am sure,' Lilly mused. 'It is strange that we all seem to have some connection to the debutantes. I am required to write a piece on the death of Miss Daisy Dorchester and hope to visit you tomorrow, Phoebe, if I may, as I believe she is in your care?'

'Indeed, I have the honour of preparing her, and please do call in,' Phoebe said, clearing her throat slightly at the small lie. 'In truth, she is a bit of a nuisance.'

The girls tried not to laugh, given the seriousness of the situation.

'So, she is visiting you?' Lilly asked, delighted at the prospect.

'Yes, pestering would be a more accurate description. If you prefer, she will be having a viewing the day after. It might be a good chance to speak with some of the other debutants if you want comments for your column.'

'Excellent, thank you, Phoebe,' Lilly beamed. 'I shall visit the family and the accident scene first, then finish with the viewing and her debutant friends last.'

'And I am preparing some of those girls for their debuts,' Emily said with an eye roll. 'Heaven help me.'

'Oddly, I am preparing Miss Dorchester's aunt's mourning dress,' Violet said. 'We are all connected.'

'Yes, and that would be the very same aunt I suspect who accused me of killing Miss Dorchester with my camera by stealing the spoilt girl's soul,' Kate scoffed. 'I am so sick of debutantes; I can't remember being so silly when I made my debut.'

The ladies exchanged smiles, knowing that Kate most likely would have been one of the silliest when fussing over dresses, her hairstyle and the gentlemen attending.

'I saw that look, all of you,' Kate said with a small smile. 'Perhaps I was, but having photographed a recent batch of the ladies, I can honestly say there are also many clever and presentable ladies amongst them. There is, of course, always one or two who are real misses, as my grandmother would call them.'

Phoebe nodded. 'Like Miss Daisy Dorchester, although one should not speak ill of the dead. This chicken hot pot is delicious, Violet.'

'Thank you, Phoebe. It is from *Mrs Lance Rawson's Cookery Book*, that was left to me amongst Grandma's possessions,' Violet said. 'As for speaking ill of the dead, I believe that is held sacred because they cannot respond or defend themselves, but in your case, they often can,' she teased.

Phoebe laughed. 'Too true, that gives me some licence to speak freely then. I do feel sorry for Daisy; it is sad to see someone young depart the world before they have truly tasted life.'

'I read of her death in the newspaper,' Violet added with a small shake of her head. 'Terrible. But I am increasingly convinced that not all of us are meant to lead full lives, and her life was not cut short but predetermined before she arrived. Her time is done.'

'I have often dwelled on the same theory,' Kate agreed, 'especially if I have been asked to do one of those ghastly death portraits or called in to photograph a crime scene if the police photographer is unavailable.'

'But that would mean a murderer was always predetermined to kill,' Phoebe mused. 'Goodness, an interesting topic. It is good that we do not know how many years we have on the earth; we might all live our lives differently.'

'Let us change the subject,' Violet said, 'I don't wish to be the hostess with the most morbid *Vexen Vixens* gathering.'

The ladies laughed at the thought, and Violet referred to the article before them. Tapping the story, she said, 'I cannot imagine a man – whether he is a veteran or young man – saying a young lady is "very neat". Goodness me. On overhearing Tom and his friends speak, neatness would not occur to them when a lady enamours them.'

The amused vixens agreed.

'I am disappointed,' Phoebe joked. 'I would so love to be considered neat.' The thought set them off in peals of laughter again.

'You are the epitome of neat,' Emily teased. 'I, for one, am very pleased for the debut balls, as ladies preparing for such events make up a sizeable amount of my clientele, even if they vex me no end with their questions.'

'Do tell, such as?' Lilly asked, interested as she gathered material for her piece on the deceased Miss Dorchester.'

'Well, let's see,' Emily said, sitting back in her chair and dabbing her napkin to her lips before placing it on her lap. She was a young lady of independent means since inheriting her aunt's townhouse in Bowen Hills on Montpelier Hill, enabling her to start the deportment school. With her dark hair, dark eyes, olive skin and slim build, Emily was the epitome of elegance and the perfect role model for young ladies needing to refine their social skills. A certain detective thought so, too.

'Well, one of my students, a young lady who I very much admire, asked how she could talk about the weather when it held no interest for her, and she feared if she had to discuss it with every gentleman on her dance card, she might impale one of them on her pencil.'

'Oh, I like her,' Lilly agreed. 'Pray tell, what did Miss Yalden of the *Miss Emily Yalden School of Deportment* advise?'

'It is difficult because we are always told not to discuss subjects such as politics or finances. I told her to get on the front foot early before the gentleman could open his mouth and lead with a question completely off-tangent, such as, "Sir, time is very unkind, and I have so little in your company this evening, but I so wish to hear of your travels. Have you visited anywhere of great interest recently?" or similar.'

'Oh, Emily, that is wonderful advice,' Phoebe said.

'Unless they haven't been anywhere,' Kate pointed out the obvious.

'Then they can discuss where they aspire to travel,' Emily suggested. 'I have never known a gentleman who will not readily talk about himself.'

'My brother, Julius, says the same of us ladies,' Phoebe grinned and then realised she should not have said that in front of Violet, who may now choose to share less of herself.

Lilly rescued her. 'That is because most ladies in your brother's company gush and don't realise for some time that he has not said a word.'

'Or plot, like the lady asking Julius for directions and a glass of water,' Kate said and added in case Violet thought she was in Julius's confidence, 'I arrived to see Phoebe when Ambrose told us this directionless lady had delayed them.'

Phoebe knew Violet was considering all that was said. She inwardly sighed – life sometimes was fraught with complications when talking with people.

'So, what does Miss Dorchester want, may I ask?' Emily addressed Phoebe, moving the conversation along.

Phoebe looked around as if ensuring they were alone before dropping her voice. 'Daisy says she did not slip and strike her head, but rather she was attacked. She is convinced that with herself out of the way, other debutantes will have a much better chance of succeeding at the ball, and she believes that is why she was murdered. She wants me to instigate the investigation.'

'I would not be surprised if she was struck,' Kate huffed. 'She was quite nasty at her photographic sitting. I can only imagine what she might have been like at the rehearsals.'

'Oh dear,' Emily said, 'perhaps there is something in that then, Phoebe. When Detective Gilbert Payne arrived with Lilly today at the rehearsal, I thought it might just be procedural to ask a few questions, but perhaps she was bumped off, so to speak.'

'I fear as much, and if I do not help her, she may never depart my workroom – a fate worse than death,' Phoebe added with a smile. 'Julius was to speak with the coroner this very afternoon.'

'Dr McGregor was such fun at the dance, wasn't he?' Kate said, distracted as often was the case. 'Such a big personality and with that lovely Scottish accent.'

'A similar heritage to your own then?' Violet asked.

'I think we might be more Irish than Scottish, but both accents are so lovely. I wish I had a trace of one,' Kate said, sighing dramatically.

The ladies agreed. Phoebe continued. 'I left before Julius returned from seeing Dr McGregor, so I do not know the outcome. If the coroner thinks there are grounds for a review, we will ask the detective to take a look.'

'The handsome Detective Harland Stone?' Kate teased. 'He was watching you all evening at the dance.'

'No,' Phoebe said, surprised and delighted.

'He was,' Emily agreed, 'and I believe he was quite envious of Mr Martin for having so many dances with you.'

'Then why did he not ask for a dance?' Phoebe said, annoyed. 'I cannot believe he holds any interest in me whatsoever. Perhaps he is studying me like a specimen, wondering what oddity he beholds.'

The ladies mocked her idea.

'I doubt that very much,' Violet said. 'I imagine it is a matter of honour. If he believes Mr Martin is enamoured with you, he is likely too honourable to approach since they are acquaintances. Have you seen Mr Martin recently?'

Phoebe shook her head at the thought of Bennet Martin – the artist and Julius's close friend, who also ran a private investigation agency.

'No. Perhaps Julius has told him I am not interested in receiving his courtship. It would be better coming from him than me, and hopefully then, if we encounter each other in work situations, it is not too awkward.'

'Perhaps he has had no grounds to call legitimately,' Emily said. 'Although men always manage to find a reason.'

'I think it will always be uncomfortable until the other party loses their heart to another,' Lilly said and sighed.

'Is this an opinion from personal experience or research?' Phoebe asked, curiously studying her friend.

'Both, sadly. But to cheerier matters, I may have found my next story if it proves to be true that Miss Daisy Dorchester was murdered,' Lilly said and looked far too cheery for one broaching such morbid subject matter. 'I cannot wait to pitch that to the editor!'

# Chapter 12

A BEAUTIFUL SPRING DAY in Brisbane guaranteed the good mood of many citizens going about their daily toil. In the office of *In Mourning – Attire for the Family* dressmaking business, Miss Violet Forrester, the manageress, felt lighter and not only because the weather was lovely, but her uncle had departed. While she was burdened with indecision about her future with Mr Julius Astin, her morning had been pleasantly distracted with the good company of her staff and plenty of work to starve off idleness.

But mid-afternoon, the feeling soon turned to one of anxiousness; she knew Julius was approaching before her young assistant announced it. Maybe she sensed his presence, or perhaps she was always vigilant for a glimpse at him, torn as she was by her uncle's insistence that she should not accept the advances of her employer. His words haunted her.

'He has set you up very nicely, my dear. What does he expect in return?'

'What if he tires of you? He is a successful businessman and will expect a woman with accomplishments. I am not saying you are unaccomplished, on the contrary. But can you move in circles that would support his success and rise? Any businessman worth his salt would expect it.'

Violet knew she could not, but she had not thought Julius was particularly ambitious to socialise and move within the top echelons of society. He seemed to dislike every moment of having to spend time with the business sector at the recent dance they attended and only did so at his grandmother's insistence. Then her uncle's question shocked her; that he would question her honour seemed to overstep the mark.

'If you lose yourself to him, he will tire of you and then will you keep your position? He may not wish to lay eyes on you every day. Do tell me you have not given yourself?'

'Goodness, no, Uncle,' Violet had proclaimed, embarrassed at the question and having her honour questioned.

'Good, good, I thought as much,' her uncle had said with a nod and a wobble of his chin.

At first, Violet could easily dismiss her uncle's ramblings – he was of a different generation with different expectations. She was sure of Julius's affection and caught up in the romance of their evening at the dance. But her uncle's badgering continued evening after evening.

*'I have done some private research on your employer, my dear. A most interesting man is Mr Astin. He was once dating the mayor's daughter but did not offer for her hand.'*

Maybe he was ambitious to move in the right circles, after all, Violet thought with a rising feeling of dread. Her uncle continued.

*'He also dated a teacher, but she left when she received no offer. It does not bode well if you are hoping for the same.'*

It did seem odd that he had two ladies he was associated with and offered for neither unless they declined him, but on what grounds? Whom could she ask? Perhaps the man himself, but they were not that intimate.

*'What work would you do if you lost your position, Violet? Would the Astin family give you a reference? You have more rent to pay now than before. Remember that.'*

The thought infuriated Violet. She was quite happy in her small house in the lowly neighbourhood where she had lived with her family for many years. They did not have much, but the people around her were caring and hard-working, like herself and Tom, and she would not have moved if her uncle had not taken charge.

Her plan before the move – and Violet always had one – was to remain where she was and save as much as she could so that she might put a roof over her head if need be or start a small business should circumstances dictate. Of course, Violet had considered that she might move from the neighbourhood if she married. But Uncle Bertram would not hear of her plan or her and Tom remaining. He believed the area unsafe for a woman living with a young brother and no senior male protector. She bowed to her uncle's wishes in memory of her departed grandfather. Now, it put her in a position of financial insecurity.

The last two months with the visiting relatives had been nothing short of torture, and now, ensconced in her new home, away from the friends who supported them during the difficult years, Violet felt lonely. Slowly, surely, she became a little more insecure in her position both at work and in Julius's thoughts and heart.

She had no one to speak with about the situation, no close friend who did not have a connection with Julius, and no mother or grandmother to ask their opinion. Tom would say to ignore their uncle and believe in Julius; he had great affection for the man he believed rescued them with his offer of work and trade. The nearest she came was her senior seamstress, Mrs Nellie Shaw, whom Violet regarded as a friend. But she feared Mrs Shaw was a little biased and taken with Julius, not to mention invested in the prospect of Violet and Julius as a couple.

'Violet! He is coming, Mr Astin is coming,' Miss Mary Pollard said, scissors frozen mid-air and her eyes wide with alarm.

'Do not worry, my dear,' Mrs Nellie Shaw soothed her. 'Mr Astin can visit his business anytime he chooses, and I am sure there is no reason for concern.'

Violet nodded and smiled at Mary. 'Mrs Shaw is right. I promise you, Mary, if there are ever grounds for concern about our employment or the quality of our work, I will inform you. You will not hear it from Mr Astin; I understand he is very happy with us and this new business.'

Mary breathed out and lowered her hand, returning the scissors to the fabric.

'It's just that he is rather scary,' she said under her breath.

Mrs Shaw chuckled, and Violet added with a small smile, 'Yes, I suspect he can appear very stern.' She did not fear the tall, handsome, and impressive Julius Astin, but Violet did feel anxious.

He appeared in the doorframe of the shop and opened it slowly, sticking his head in to check for customers and, finding it empty, entered.

'Good afternoon, ladies. Is now convenient for a visit?' he asked.

'Mr Astin, you are the proprietor; any time is convenient,' Mrs Shaw said with a smile as all three ladies rose. Julius waved them back to their seats.

'Thank you and good afternoon, Mrs Shaw, Miss Pollard, Miss Forrester,' he added, greeting the three ladies.

'Sir,' Mary said, standing again to drop a quick courtesy from behind her work table.

'I hope you are well, Mr Astin?' Violet addressed him formally in front of the staff, even though they agreed to call each other by their Christian names in private.

'You look particularly well,' Mrs Shaw said, and Julius smiled at her compliment. 'Is that a new suit?'

'A new shirt,' he added with a glance at Violet.

Knowing he intended to visit, Violet wondered if he wore his best suit, polished his shoes, and donned a crisp new shirt on this occasion. She just as quickly scolded herself for being presumptuous.

'A new shirt not made by us,' Violet said, looking at him with wide eyes as if slighted.

Julius looked surprised. 'I would not dream of interrupting your work to produce my wardrobe, Miss Forrester,' he said and relaxed as she began to smile.

'And who would take measurements?' Mary asked, then blushed profusely. She looked away on realising what she had said, making all three senior people in the room exchange smiles.

'Very good point, Miss Pollard,' Julius said, relaxing her. 'Forgive the interruption, ladies; I hoped for a word with Miss Forrester.'

'Of course, Mr Astin, perhaps in the meeting room?' Violet said, rising and leading the way, leaving the door slightly ajar for propriety. His presence in the room seemed overwhelming, as it was the first time he visited her home bearing gifts on the pretence of ensuring she was satisfied with her grandmother's burial the day before and with the offer of work. It seemed like such a long time ago now, when it was only some short months ago.

She could smell a light scent of soap on him and imagine he had scrubbed since she heard the hearse departing earlier for a funeral mid-morning. They sat around the table, Julius waiting for Violet to sit first before settling himself.

'Your uncle has departed?' he began.

'Yes,' Violet said with a small sigh of relief. 'I confess it is very hard to live with strangers, and I never thought I would look forward to some solitude, but I am.'

He smiled. 'I felt the same when I moved into my home. Bennet offered to move in, but I quickly got used to my space. I am not sure I could live with anyone now.' He hurriedly added, 'Except if I were married, that would be different.'

'Oh yes, for me too,' she added and then the room seemed even smaller.

Julius cleared his throat. 'A young lady visited this morning seeking services for her mother, who cannot leave the house at present.' He explained and gave Violet the details.

'We would be happy to call on her. I know you are very busy, Julius; you are welcome to put a note in the daily messages that

Mr Astin senior brings back and forth and not trouble yourself to visit,' she offered. 'I assure you we will attend to all matters.'

She realised how her words sounded, and while the intent of cooling matters between them was very much on her mind, she had not meant to be so forthwith. Julius blinked a couple of times rapidly, moved slightly back as if she had struck him and then rose to his feet at a great pace, looking embarrassed for the intrusion.

'Of course, I am sorry to have taken up your time.'

'But you didn't,' she rose just as quickly. 'I just meant to say—'

'I understand perfectly, Miss Forrester. Thank you for taking care of that matter. Good day then.'

Violet could see by his countenance that Julius's emotions and thoughts were as overpowering as her own, and he was out of the room before Violet could utter another word. Julius recovered himself in order to bid the ladies a quick farewell, return his hat to his head and depart.

Violet had no idea she could wound his confidence so carelessly and she was filled with alarm and regret. Her uncle would be pleased; Violet was not, and the pain in her heart was swift and brutal. When Mrs Shaw came to see what had caused Mr Astin's abrupt exit, Violet could not hold back her tears. What had she done?

Julius felt the humiliation burning him. What a fool he had been; she had dismissed him for wasting his time and hers. He could not remember a time ever when a woman had rejected him so out of hand. The funeral industry was not a profession that every woman wanted their husband to work in, but his success had made that undesirable element of his career choice somewhat obsolete. Was she ashamed to be seen with him? Julius's heartache was worse than his humiliation. He walked past the office of *The Economic Undertaker* but did not enter. He kept walking.

In her company, Julius had seen the future for the past few months. He was of the age to wed, but no one had ever captured his heart like beautiful Miss Violet Forrester. Prior, he had dedicated himself to business and ensuring his family was established and his grandparents comfortable after their years of sacrifice. But she interrupted his life and changed how he saw himself. Julius believed he and Miss Forrester were kindred souls – reserved, hard-working, caring deeply for their family, and he hoped for each other. He held her hand while they waltzed; he was sure of her feelings then. Had her family persuaded her otherwise? Now, with one brutal delivery by the woman who held his heart, he could no longer see what lay ahead.

What if he had not offered Violet the job but requested to court her instead? Ah, the very mention of her name was painful. But how could he spend time courting her and watching her struggle to pay the rent, knowing she needed to sew daily hour-upon-hour to make enough money to survive? No, that was unconscionable, but now he had placed himself in the role of employer, and her integrity was at risk, or so her relatives believed. There was nothing to be done.

Julius did not see the people passing by or hear the street noises around him. All he could hear were her words, her rebuke – *'You are welcome to put a note in the daily messages that Mr Astin senior brings back and forth, and not trouble yourself to visit'.* He had made a fool of himself, and even the conversation was painful to recall.

Julius strode without thinking where he was going but soon realised he was heading to South Brisbane, to the home of his friend, Bennet Martin. For the first time in all his working years – and Julius had started working during his school years on a paper run, giving his earnings to his grandmother – he had no intention of returning to work that afternoon.

# Chapter 13

E NSCONCED UNDERNEATH A BLACK curtain and standing behind the tripod where her Thorton Pickard camera was propped, Miss Kate Kirby called out to her subject.

'Now do give me your loveliest expression and pose, Miss Dickinson. Imagine you are declared the debutante of the season! That is it; please hold that pose for me.'

To Kate's delight, Miss Dickinson lit up; she radiated her natural attractiveness; her poise improved, and she looked toward Kate as if she had spent her life in front of the camera.

'That is perfect, just a little longer, if you will please.' A few moments later, Kate announced, 'And we have it, just lovely, thank you, Miss Dickinson.' She appeared from behind her curtain and saw the debutante was still preening.

Kate turned to see the subject of the young lady's attention. She found the very debonair Ambrose Astin leaning against the doorway, looking particularly handsome in his dark suit, with slightly ruffled dark hair, blue eyes that relayed a hint of mischief and a smile upon his face.

'Mr Astin, well, this is a surprise,' Kate said, colouring slightly at the sight of Phoebe's brother in the doorway and no Phoebe to be seen.

'Miss Kirby. Forgive the interruption when you are in the throes of capturing an image for posterity.'

'Well, technically, you did not interrupt, so thank you. Do come in.' Kate did her best to preen a little – straightening her pale blue gown and patting a few strands of her auburn hair back where they belonged; the curtain over the camera played havoc with her hair.

Ambrose moved out of the doorway and entered the store.

'May I present Miss Hilda Dickinson, debutante,' Kate said, remembering the young lady in attendance.

'Good afternoon, Miss Dickinson,' he said with a polite nod. 'You were quite the picture.'

Miss Dickinson smiled with delight. 'Thank you, Sir, and thank you, Miss Kirby, that was fascinating. I'd best meet my mother then. One week, you say?'

'Yes, they will be ready then,' Kate assured the neat, young woman, who gathered her belongings and departed with a special smile for Ambrose.

'Well, I am grateful for your appearance.'

'You are?' Ambrose asked, surprised.

'Yes, Miss Dickinson was quite wooden until you arrived, and then I caught a lovely twinkle in her eyes.'

'Yes, I have that effect on people,' he said and laughed when he saw Kate's grimace. 'Well, on my grandmother. Julius and Phoebe find me quite annoying.'

'I can't imagine why,' Kate said, giving him a look of all innocence, and he narrowed his eyes suspiciously at her, making Kate laugh. 'I am only teasing. You have been of great service. Perhaps if I get a difficult client in future, I could send word, and should you be passing by in the hearse, you might be of assistance.'

'The sight of the hearse should give them something to smile about. It says, "Cheer up; you are not dead." Now, there is a good lesson.' He wandered around, looking at the images Kate had taken that were framed on the wall as she hurriedly cleaned up after her last client.

'This is a lovely studio you have here and an impressive piece of equipment.' He looked at the camera but did not approach it – it looked expensive.

'Oh, Thornton is a delight. Strong and dependable, and as biased as I may be, handsome, I would say,' she said in jest, looking at the camera mounted on the tripod nearby.

'Thornton, is it? So, this is the competition a man must aim to outdo in order to secure your attention.' He rubbed his chin and sized up the camera, making her laugh again. He was such a light-hearted soul, she thought, and very comfortable to talk with and share a laugh.

'Would you like a portrait while you are here?' Kate offered.

'Now?'

'Why not?'

'Well, that is what I have come to see you about. We – that is, *The Economic Undertaker* – would very much like to hire you to take a photograph of our business and staff.'

'Ooh,' she squealed and clapped her hands, her blue eyes wide with delight. 'How lovely. Mr Astin senior expressed interest, but I thought he was being polite.'

'He is that, but Grandpa and Julius believe it to be a very good idea for the business. They hope to feature it in our advertising.'

'That would be wonderful for both of us,' Kate marvelled. 'We could do the photograph out the front of the store with your staff in their best dress, the hearse and horses wearing the plumes,' she said, waving her hand around as if framing the shot. 'I can see it now, most dignified.'

'Perfect. And the ladies at the *In Mourning* dressmaking store next door? They too will need a professional image taken.'

'Of course, that would be my pleasure.' Kate put her head to the side as she thought. 'Perhaps a photograph of them within the business, standing around one of their most modern sewing machines with a mannequin in the background fashioned in appropriate mourning wear.'

'Excellent. Now all we need do is arrive at a mutual date and time, and our business is concluded.' He looked at the camera. 'I would love a photograph if you were in it with me. Can you take it and be in the image at the same time?'

'Indeed I can,' she said enthusiastically. 'Something fun or serious?'

'No one would believe the two of us could be serious,' he teased. 'With your twinkling Irish eyes and my boyish charm, could we pull it off?'

'It would be a challenge.' Kate laughed, folding her arms across her chest; she mused on a suitable pose. 'What if we sit formally beside each other, trying not to laugh? Or we could sit back-to-back sipping tea, except we cannot move for fear of blurring the photograph, so you will have to hold your tea cup and be very still.'

'That could work,' Ambrose said and looked around, spying on Kate's hat stand an umbrella and hats of all different shapes and sizes.

Kate followed his gaze. 'Ah, they either get left behind or guests decide their hat wear is inappropriate and want to change it. I keep a few in stock.'

'Perfect, let's try this.'

Ambrose grabbed some props while Kate set up the photo. Dressed, ready and laughing before they did their best to look sober, Kate snapped the image.

In later years, when she looked back on that amusing photograph of herself in a man's top hat with Ambrose hatless and holding an umbrella over her head, his expression most serious, she would remember with great fondness that day – the beginning.

# Chapter 14

J ULIUS ASTIN STARTLED DANIEL Dutton – the studious and impertinent clerk of the artist and private investigator, Bennet Martin, and nephew of housekeeper, Mrs Clarke. It was apparent the young clerk got quite a fright when the door swung open late afternoon, and Julius entered with intent.

'Mr Astin, my, how you startled me,' he said, hand on his heart.

Julius took stock, drew a deep breath, and apologised. 'Forgive me, Mr Dutton, I forgot myself. Is Bennet in?'

'No apology necessary, Mr Astin. It was not your fault – the room was too quiet, and I was deep in contemplation and accounts,' he said with his customary light humour. He adjusted his spectacles and offered, 'Bennet is in his studio painting. Not that he normally paints at this hour of the day,' Daniel felt the need to explain, 'but since earning a considerable income from the last two cases he worked upon, he prefers to indulge in his art than seek more work.'

'Admirable, I am sure,' Julius said in a voice that appeared to think quite the opposite. He was, after all, a man driven by ambition.

'I shall let him know you are here,' Daniel started towards the stairs.

'No need, but thank you. I know the way,' Julius said, taking off up the stairs before Daniel could warn his boss.

Julius rapped on the door and heard Bennet grumble.

'Do not interrupt me, Daniel, unless it is on the threat of death, feast or famine.'

Julius entered. 'It is all of those things,' he said and smiled.

'Julius!' Bennet's eyes flicked around the room, his face flushed with embarrassment, and he moved away from the canvas he was working on – a beautiful scene of the river with small boats floating upon it at twilight.

'I am sorry to intrude.'

'You are always welcome,' Bennet assured him. 'This is a surprise. I can't remember the last time you visited rather than met me at the club, or for that matter when I saw you socially at this hour. Is it a social visit?'

'Of sorts.' Julius joined Bennet at the easel and admired the canvas. 'Ah, you have a talent. I am constantly amazed by anyone who can apply such skill to a canvas.' Then Julius froze. In his peripheral vision, he saw painting upon painting of his sister, Phoebe. Close-up portraits, landscape gardens featuring Phoebe, even paintings of Phoebe in attire her brother had never seen.

'I can explain,' Bennet started.

'Tell me she did not pose for these portraits,' he said, aghast. Phoebe had confided in him that she was not interested in Bennet romantically, which would imply otherwise.

'Of course not! She does not know they exist,' Bennet insisted, and Julius relaxed. He moved towards them, studying each one slowly. Bennet did not speak, remaining instead by the easel. Julius was impossible to read – his stance was stiff, and he might have been silently seething or disgusted. Might he swing a punch the way of Bennet? Could it mean the end of their friendship?

'Are there more?' Julius asked when he reached the end of the paintings on display.

Bennet winced and gave a small nod.

'I understand.'

Bennet opened and closed his mouth before saying, 'You do?' Frowning, he put his brush down and ran a hand through his blonde hair, adding a few colour highlights as he often did when painting.

Julius nodded. He might not have understood yesterday, but with the agony of loss he was suffering, he understood better than most.

'You love her, my sister.'

Bennet lowered his head and released a shaky breath before facing Julius. He swallowed and said with raw honesty, 'Her and her alone. I have wanted to tell her so many times... I thought you knew.'

'I did, but you never acted upon it.'

'I was working up to speaking with you and your grandfather, and then I would talk myself out of it by remembering Phoebe is a modern woman, and I wondered if she would be offended if I did so without talking with her first. I have been going around in circles for far too long.'

'She knows,' Julius said.

'Ah, so she does. I had wondered if I was obvious in my affection.' Bennet rose and began to clean his brushes, turning away from Julius so his emotions could not be witnessed. 'It is unrequited love, is it not?'

Julius took a breath and slowly released it before answering, measuring his words. 'It is not for me to ruin any hope you—'

Bennet turned sharply to face him. 'You are my closest friend, Julius. Please honour me with honesty.'

Julius hesitated and nodded. He saw his friend's chest deflate, his expression fall and added, 'It is why I, too, am out walking and despairing at this hour of the day.'

'No!' Bennet's head shot up, and he stared at Julius. 'No. Not Miss Forrester? She seemed so... I thought...' his words drifted away.

'As did I. But I believe her uncle has persuaded her that it is not wise to encourage her manager's interest. I am convinced there is no one else for me. I had started to believe... well, you know.' Julius returned his attention to the paintings, not seeing them, while he gathered his emotions and swallowed.

'I do know. I dreamed as much but with no evidence of returned feeling, but Miss Forrester danced with you and seemed so...' again, his voice trailed off. 'Julius, what sorry souls we are.'

'Indeed.'

'Best we drink to our sorrows then,' Bennet said, and Julius did not object on this occasion. A rap on the door had both gentlemen turning.

'Sorry to interrupt, gents,' Daniel said, 'but there is a lady here – a Mrs Audrey Stewart – wishing to hire you, Bennet, regarding the death of her niece, Miss Daisy Dorchester. She has no appointment, but her niece is the debutante we read about in the paper who fell and struck her head, causing her death.'

'We have her body, and Phoebe is preparing her now,' Julius added and flashed Bennet a look of apology for mentioning his sister so soon after Bennet's confession.

'Will you stay a moment?' Bennet asked Julius. 'That is, join in the meeting?'

'If you like.'

Bennet nodded to Daniel. 'Thank you, show her to the meeting room, and we will be right down.'

'Shall do. I'll have Aunty ply Mrs Stewart with tea.' Daniel departed, his footsteps echoing down the timber staircase.

'You might have your hands full,' Julius warned. 'The young lady has been visiting our rooms and proclaiming she was struck, but I believe Mrs Stewart has already accused Miss Kirby and her camera of stealing the debutante's soul and killing her.'

'For the love of all that is holy,' Bennet said, rolling his eyes. 'Poor Kate.'

'Kate?' Julius asked, amused.

'She insisted at the dance that we not be so formal, but I think she said that to everyone she met that evening,' he huffed. 'Come then, let's see what Mrs Stewart has to say to support her claim. Please add your thoughts as you see fit, given that you have a few insights from the victim herself, and then we can drown our sorrows as need be.'

Once introductions were done between the two gentlemen and Mrs Stewart, the party was seated, and her purpose for visiting was established, Mrs Stewart would tolerate no arguments nor be convinced that Daisy died of natural causes.

'Daisy is a very capable young lady... I am her sponsor, and I have spent a great deal on her education and deportment. I assure you, she is not a reckless or clumsy type who trips on her hem or wet grass. She went to see Father Horan about her pending nuptials and then to visit her father's grave. Someone has followed her into the cemetery, or she has encountered a ne'er-do-well there. I am telling you, there is something very wrong about her—'

She stopped, unable to say the word 'death' and instead placed a white handkerchief over her mouth as if catching the word and removing it from her lips. 'I believe you must also consider that photographer woman and her contraption.'

Bennet ignored her suggestion. 'Assuming it was not a random attack, but someone was following Miss Dorchester, could the assailant be known to her, Mrs Stewart? Do you have a suspect in mind?'

'Suspect? Well, Daisy is, was, a very beautiful and very popular young lady, perhaps some jealous upstart did this to remove the jewel from the crown.'

'Did she ever mention she felt threatened?' Bennet asked, his lack of interest in the case apparent to those who might know his usual style, and his voice flattened from the blow he received to his heart just minutes earlier.

'No, I cannot recall her saying she feared or disliked anyone. She was like a bright light that everyone flocked to be near.' Mrs Stewart gathered herself and continued, 'But I am sure every young lady looking to make a good match found her a threat,' the small and determined woman said, her sentences sharp and clipped.

'Had she set her heart on a gentleman?' Julius asked. 'My reason for asking is to determine if the said gentleman might have had a jealous young lady vying for his attention or if he was beset with jealousy if Miss Dorchester spoke with another man.'

Mrs Stewart gasped. 'Goodness. Yes, perhaps a jealous young woman saw an opportunity and struck Daisy when she was alone in that cemetery... I can't bear to think of it, Mr Astin. A very good point, but as for a jealous suitor, Daisy was promised to Mr Eldon Foster, who is a man of reason.'

'If she is spoken for, why would Miss Dorchester be a threat to the other ladies?' Bennet asked, weary now and wishing to leave and imbibe with Julius as soon as possible. 'Was she enamoured with Mr Foster, or perhaps, was she attracting the attention of other gentlemen that might normally be in the company of the other debutants?'

Mrs Stewart's lips pursed, and her expression soured. 'I concede that Daisy was not treating Mr Foster with the appropriate respect afforded to a beau. I believe she wanted to...' she stumbled for the appropriate words.

'Meet other ladies and gentlemen and enjoy all the opportunities afforded the young?' Julius added diplomatically and paraphrased his grandfather, who always told him to get out more and work less.

'Exactly so, Mr Astin, thank you.'

The men exchanged looks that spoke of sympathy for another poor man fighting the good fight for love but who had fallen by the wayside.

'Did Miss Dorchester agree to this union with Mr Eldon Foster?' Bennet asked, reading the body language of the shrewd woman before him and assuming the arrangement was thrust upon the debutante.

'It was an unspoken agreement since they were children, and Mr Foster was very much prepared to honour the expectation that they would become engaged and marry.'

'So, he would not have wanted Miss Dorchester to come to any harm to free him of obligation?' Julius asked, and Mrs Stewart gasped.

'That's outrageous.'

'Mrs Stewart, we need to ask these questions, even if they seem outlandish, to eliminate and refine your suspect list. Should we embark on this case, you would not want to pay me to investigate unnecessary leads.'

She nodded. 'I understand. No, Mr Foster was in awe of Daisy and very much looking forward to courting her after she made her debut.'

'Did she often visit the church and cemetery? Would someone know her routine?' Bennet asked.

'I would not say it was a regular practice. She had been visiting her father's grave more often of late, which I put down to sentimentality, but I have not found Daisy to be particularly interested in her faith.'

Bennet nodded. 'Mrs Stewart, where is Miss Dorchester's mother, if I may ask?'

'Mr Martin, Daisy's mother is a gentle woman, weak, one might say.' Mrs Stewart said it with a slight grimace of distaste as if she could not imagine any woman being so pathetic. 'She has left Daisy in my care to ensure the young lady has, that is, had, every advantage.' She gathered her shawl and stood, concluding the meeting. The men rose quickly to their feet.

'Will you take the case for my niece's sake? Somebody must stand for her.'

Bennet sighed. 'I have not been accepting cases for the last few months, but perhaps the distraction of throwing myself into a new situation might be for the best.'

'Excellent,' Mrs Stewart began taking his response as confirmation; she was not a woman denied. 'Your clerk has provided your rates. Will you start immediately?'

Bennet held up his hand. 'Let us be realistic, Mrs Stewart. There might not be a case here at all.'

'I have full confidence in you, Mr Martin. There is a viewing tomorrow for Daisy so her friends may privately bid her farewell,' she said, looking to Julius for confirmation.

'That is correct.'

'I shall see you both then, shall I?'

And Bennet realised he would have to face Phoebe tomorrow and accept defeat. He would be in mourning, but not for the debutante.

# Chapter 15

PHOEBE MOVED THE CURTAIN slightly and glanced out the front window of *The Economic Undertaker* premises, her eyes seeking Julius amongst the passing parade of people. Ambrose moved behind her, and Daisy moved in front, not that anyone present except Phoebe could see the beautiful young debutante looking out at the world of which she was no longer a part.

'Whom are you looking for?' she asked.

'Julius, we think something might be wrong,' Phoebe said, then glanced at her grandfather and Ambrose. 'I am just responding to Daisy.'

'And he just walked on past?' Ambrose asked his grandfather again.

'Yes, he did not even glance in.'

'Did he look upset?' Phoebe asked.

'How can you tell?' Ambrose gave a huff and moved away from the window. 'Julius is never one to wear his heart on his sleeve, but if his mood of the last few weeks is any indication, he is in turmoil.'

'I agree, lad,' Randolph said, concern etched on his brow. 'He was walking with purpose. I am disheartened to see him go from being so happy just a few months ago to the prospect of losing Miss Forrester.'

'There is plenty of fish in the sea,' Daisy chirped. 'That's what my aunty always says despite the fact she insists I must be betrothed to Eldon.' She pulled a face at the thought without realising she no longer had to commit to that promise.

'But how has that come about?' Phoebe asked, moving away from the window.

'We were promised to each other at birth,' Daisy said, 'ridiculous!'

'Sorry, Daisy dear,' Phoebe said kindly, 'I meant Julius and Violet's cooling. Could you wait for me downstairs, perhaps?'

Daisy showed no great interest in doing so and remained hovering near the window as if her contribution to the discussion was paramount.

'They seemed so devoted,' Randolph agreed. He and Ambrose were quite accustomed to Phoebe's side conversations.

'It is those relatives of hers interfering,' Ambrose said with a shake of his head. 'Tom told Lucian at work that his uncle was

138

ordering them around and having too much to say in Violet's future.'

'I imagine he has her best interests at heart,' Randolph said generously.

'Marrying your handsome brother, Phoebe, would be in any woman's best interest. He owns this business, does he not?' Daisy asked, and Phoebe gave her a brief nod.

Randolph continued with a glance at his diary before addressing his youngest grandson. 'We only have collections this afternoon; one of the stable lads can assist you. Then, perhaps Ambrose, you should drop into Julius's residence; he is more likely to confide in you than me if he needs someone to lean on. Phoebe, would you be comfortable going next door and seeking answers?'

'That will only serve to make Julius angry,' Ambrose said. 'I think we should let it be for now. Lucian and I will go out this evening and keep an eye out for him. If I do not see him, I will drop into his home at the end of the evening.'

'That's probably best,' Randolph agreed. 'I fear he has had his heart broken.' He held up his hand. 'I know he won't be the first or last to go through it, but... he is so deserving of happiness. His grandmother and I had hoped, well, you know.'

Ambrose nodded.

'Violet must be terribly upset too,' Phoebe said, 'I've no doubt her affection was real.'

'It's not fair,' Daisy said, 'we should all be allowed to be with the ones we love without our older relatives interfering. What would they know of love?'

'Do you have a beau, Daisy, besides your intended?' Phoebe asked and saw the coy expression on the young lady's face.

The door swung open before Daisy answered, and everyone turned as if caught in the spotlight. Randolph adopted a sober, ready-to-console expression; Ambrose straightened to appear forthright, and Phoebe glanced at the staircase as if seeking a quick escape.

Detective Harland Stone's face appeared around the door, and the Astins visibly relaxed.

'Ooh, who is this then?' Daisy asked, assuming her most flirtatious look.

'Am I interrupting?' he asked, stepping in with Detective Gilbert Payne behind him.

'The other one is not that handsome,' Daisy said, and Phoebe gave her a scolding look.

'Not at all, you are always welcome, Detectives,' Randolph said. 'Please do come in.'

Phoebe blushed slightly. 'Hello, Detective Stone, Detective Payne.'

'Mr Astin, Ambrose, Miss Astin,' Harland said formerly, 'please forgive the intrusion to your workday.'

'We are always happy to see the living,' Ambrose joked, and Daisy giggled, oblivious that she was not seen.

'It is lovely to see you again, Miss Astin,' Gilbert said with a smile. 'I enjoyed our problem-solving session on our last case.'

'As did I, very much,' Phoebe said with a grin.

'We are always happy to have her out of the dungeon,' Ambrose joked and got a tap on the arm from Phoebe for his trouble.

'Speaking of which, I best get back to my room unless you need me?' she asked.

'Actually, we do if that is convenient?' Harland asked.

'Who would have believed a mortician would have so many handsome men around her,' Daisy said, quite delighted with the new company. 'I bet they are here about me!'

'Is Julius not here?' Harland asked.

'Ah, no, that is whom we were looking for,' Ambrose said. 'He may not be back today.'

'Oh. Is he all right?' Harland asked, quick to pick up on the tension.

'We cannot say,' Ambrose said.

'He might be upset, that is all. Hopefully, he is not missing or your next case, Detective,' Phoebe clarified.

'I see,' Harland said, confused.

'How can Phoebe assist you today?' Randolph asked, getting to the point. Phoebe knew her grandfather would be keen to clear the waiting area should customers arrive.

'I hoped to see the body of the debutant, Miss Daisy Dorchester and Julius suggested you might have some insights?' Harland said to Phoebe.

'I told you so,' Daisy clapped her hands in delight and grinned. 'See, I was murdered!'

'Why don't you all head to Phoebe's workroom then, and I'm sure Mrs Dobbs will have the kettle on already,' Randolph suggested, concern still etched on his face about Julius.

Phoebe nodded and led the way, Ambrose followed acting as an escort or guardian of which he was unsuited for both and likely to forget his mission, and the detectives followed Miss Daisy Dorchester down the stairs without even knowing it.

Detective Harland Stone was not himself in the company of Phoebe Astin. He was not nervous about the spirits she may have around or intimidated by her beauty. He was, however, enamoured by her, which interfered with his concentration, especially when she turned her gaze upon him. But Phoebe was not his to admire when Julius's closest friend, Bennet Martin, had set his cap for her first. That would not bode well amongst their friendship group, of which he was a newcomer and had been made to feel so welcome since arriving in Brisbane to take up the detective role. Still, he was disconcerted by her presence and working hard to appear normal, so his feelings were not evident to his partner, Gilbert, Phoebe's brother Ambrose or Miss Astin herself.

Phoebe moved to Daisy's body, laid out and prepared for her viewing tomorrow.

'Did you wish to see the body, Detectives?'

'Yes, thank you,' Harland said, and as Gilbert moved ahead, the only logical space that remained to view the deceased was right beside Miss Astin. It was as if a spark ran between them; could she feel it, too? Harland did not dare glance at Phoebe in case he forgot himself.

'He's handsome, rugged, I like a strong man,' Daisy said, 'but your brother is much more appealing.' Phoebe did not take her eyes off the body but knew Daisy stood beside her brother, looking up at Ambrose with admiration; Ambrose was oblivious to her presence.

'It must be hard to prove a slip is a murder,' Ambrose mused.

Harland was never so grateful for Ambrose's words and the distraction at that moment. 'Very difficult unless there are injuries inconsistent with what we expect.' Harland looked up, 'of which there are not in this case.'

'But I was struck!' Daisy blurted out.

'She is a strikingly attractive young lady. Is Miss Dorchester here now, Miss Astin?' Gilbert asked, looking around.

'Ooh, I like him better now; what a kind thing to say,' Daisy said, admiring Detective Gilbert Payne.

'Yes,' Phoebe said, 'standing between Ambrose and the chair.'

Her brother's head whipped to the left, and he involuntarily moved slightly away.

'I was hit, struck with something, tell the detectives, Phoebe.'

Phoebe nodded. 'She would like you to know that she was struck and fell; she did not fall, causing the injury.' She continued, telling the detectives what Daisy was relaying. 'She felt a hand on her back, a sharp pain and was shoved forward with great force. She barely had time to register what had happened before she struck the grave, but she was very frightened in her state of confusion.'

Harland nodded. 'I can imagine so. Can Miss Dorchester tell us if she has any idea who might have been behind her at the time?'

Phoebe paused, waited for Daisy to respond, and answered, 'No, unfortunately, Daisy said it happened very fast and was unexpected, so she was not being cautious or aware.'

Gilbert asked a question, neither of the detectives dubious of Miss Astin's vision. 'Does Miss Dorchester know anyone who might wish to cause her harm?'

Phoebe's restrained expression did not relay the dramatic response by Daisy, who believed herself to be universally admired. Phoebe shook her head and said to Detective Payne, 'Daisy believes a number of debutants were jealous of her and may have wished her harm in order to secure the spot of belle of the ball.'

The small look of understanding and slight amusement that passed between Phoebe and Harland was not witnessed by all parties, but it was enough to give Harland hope that, perhaps, he and Miss Astin were forming an attachment. He cleared his throat and asked, 'Could Miss Dorchester explain why she had two locks of hair upon her, both with a gift tag attached and to whom she intended to gift them, please?'

Phoebe looked around and then sighed. 'Daisy, if you wish the detectives to believe you were murdered and to find your murderer, then you need to answer some questions, even if they may be unpleasant.'

'She has gone then?' Harland asked.

'No, she is back,' Phoebe smiled and appeared to listen before saying, 'Daisy does not want you to think ill of her.'

'She is dead,' Ambrose said with a shrug. 'I don't care what anyone thinks of me now, so I am sure after death, I couldn't give a hoot.'

'But you are not a lady who has been raised to believe our name, standing and reputation is important,' Phoebe reminded him.

'Please assure Miss Dorchester we would never sit in judgment,' Harland said.

Phoebe nodded and, after a moment, answered on behalf of Daisy, 'The two locks of hair were for two beaus. Mr Eldon Foster because her aunt saw her preparing one and assumed it was for him... Daisy says she was pressured to marry him.' She paused, waiting for Daisy to speak, 'And the other was for her true love.'

'Might we ask for the name of this love?' Gilbert enquired. 'Is it the same man whose portrait Miss Dorchester had in her pocket?'

Phoebe looked to Daisy, and all eyes turned to the space beside Ambrose. Phoebe listened and then gave a small gasp. 'Damien Horan. Daisy said her true love was Father Damien Horan.'

# Chapter 16

VIOLET HAD PREPARED A simple dinner and sat with her brother, Tom, to partake. She had no appetite but relished the time they spent together. It had been several months since their grandmother's passing, and while she had adapted to the silence of her home, the empty chairs around the table were always a sad reminder, even in their new abode where fewer memories were stored in the nooks and crannies of the house.

It was evident Violet's heart had been injured from today's brief encounter with Julius. The effort to hide her emotions frequently moved her from the present – from Tom's tale about the carriage he was helping to build – back to that scene in the meeting room, which she had repeatedly played in her head.

'What is wrong?' he asked, and she snapped to look at her brother.

'I was listening, I promise,' she said, feeling guilty at giving only half an ear to Tom's story.

He swallowed a mouthful of stew and said, 'You're quiet. Has someone upset you?'

'No,' she said hesitantly.

'It's this place, isn't it?' Tom looked around. 'Can I tell you something without you getting really mad?'

She gave him a wry look. 'When have I ever got mad at you? Except for maybe that time when—'

He cut her off. 'Lots of time, but I might have been an idiot.'

Violet laughed, enjoying the feeling after a gloomy day. 'There is truth in that. I won't get mad. Tell me anything.'

'I was catching up with the boys in our old neighbourhood today and saw Mrs Harridon. She said she missed us both, and she, too, is moving out.'

'Oh dear, is she all right?' Violet asked, pausing, knife and fork suspended. 'The dear old thing, she was always so kind to us and a good friend to Grandma.'

'She's well enough but is moving in with her daughter. Mrs Harridon said it was time and that she needed a hand now, so her house is available.' He hurried on, hoping to get more words in, expecting Violet to say no. 'Mrs Harridon said everyone would love to see us back, and she said we could take her house if we liked; she would talk to the agent. It has two bedrooms, smaller than our last one and cheaper. So, we could save more and be back with our friends and neighbours again. I miss living there.'

'Yes.'

'We can borrow a wagon from work, and I'm sure the boys from our old neighbourhood will help us move; they'll be happy to have us back; they all said so.'

Violet watched as her brother realised what she said and stopped talking just as he was about to launch into more detail to persuade her; Tom stared.

'You mean, yes, we can take it and move back to our old street?' His expression was one of hope.

'Yes.' She reached across the table and took her brother's hand. 'I would really like that. I am not at home here.'

He laughed. 'That is great, Sis. I hate it here; it's not us,' he said passionately. 'I told Mrs Harridon I would help her move.' He grinned. 'I can't believe you agreed.'

'I didn't want to move here, but Uncle was so insistent. Let us hope he doesn't visit again, or we will find ourselves in a very awkward situation.'

Tom scoffed. 'We've never met him before, so if he takes that long to visit us again, we'll be middle-aged.'

Violet laughed at the thought and then sighed with relief as she looked around. 'It will cost us a little to move again, even with help, but we will soon make up for that with the cheaper rent. And then, we can start saving for a rainy day again.'

Tom finished his last bite and put down his cutlery. 'You might not need to worry about that for long.' He shrugged, 'You know if you and Julius get married, then you can move in with him, or we both can. I bet his house is amazing.'

Violet did not meet his eyes. 'Tom, Julius and I have, well—' she could not finish the sentence. Saying the words out loud made it too real.

'Oh no, what has happened? You didn't—' he stopped as Violet raised her head and gave a small nod.

'I did.'

'Sis, why? That's ridiculous.' He became less sympathetic and angrier, asking, 'Uncle persuaded you, didn't he?'

Violet pushed back slightly and wrung her hands, resting them on the table. 'What he said was true, Tom. What will people think?'

'About what? A respectable romance? And who cares anyway? They'll probably be jealous.'

'And what if Julius tires of me?'

'Then you find someone else to love.'

Violet huffed. 'What if I lose my job because he doesn't want to see my face every day? What then, Tom, what will become of us?'

Tom's eyes narrowed. 'I don't believe the Astin family would ever dismiss you for that, Sis. They seem like good people. Julius's family struggled, too, and look what they've got now. It's not like he's looking down his nose at us and thinks he's too good for you.'

'I know that's true,' she admitted.

'Besides, I would support us. You don't need to look after me anymore. I am the man of this family and earn lots. Besides, I suspect it is much harder to find love than it is to find a job.'

Violet cocked her head to the side and studied her brother, who was no longer a boy, not yet a man. The planes of his face were sharpening, the stubble appearing darker, and the gangly look of youth was receding. Her feelings of pride in him threaten to set her crying.

'When did you start getting so wise?' she said affectionately

'I'm not sure I am,' he scoffed, 'but Julius says I have street smarts like him, which will go a long way.' He thought for a moment. 'I know he is book-smart too, and I am not, but I can support you if needed.'

'Thank you, my darling, Tom,' Violet said, blinking away tears and busying herself by reaching for the pot to pour them a cup of tea. 'You are right; Julius is a very successful businessman and very caring. Mrs Dobbs said he would not charge a widow last week for her husband's funeral because she would struggle to pay. Mrs Dobbs was singing his praises when she brought in some baking for our morning tea,' Violet said quietly. The pain of speaking of Julius was raw and hard on her heart. 'But Uncle was just looking after my reputation.'

'Uncle is a hundred years old. When he married in the old days, he probably wasn't even allowed to kiss the bride beforehand. Julius has always been good to us, and his cousin, Lucian, told me at work that Julius wants to make you his wife. He really loves you, Sis.'

Violet's breath hitched, and she swallowed a small cry of pain. 'It is too late, Tom.'

'It can't be. We will move, and we will fix this situation with Julius. Leave it to me.'

Violet hesitated and then surrendered. 'I will, Tom,' she said, appreciating her little brother stepping up. 'I will.'

Ambrose departed another venue in search of his brother. 'If he could just stay in one place for more than ten minutes,' he grumbled.

Lucian chuckled, following him out of a club. 'Bennet looked worse for wear; perhaps we should see him home.'

'Tavish and Max will see to it, I'm sure. Maybe Harland saw Julius home if he was as sozzled as Bennet. I'll try there now.'

'I will walk with you, it's on my way,' Lucian offered.

Ambrose thanked him as he slowed, put his hands in his pockets, and inhaled the cool night air. Most houses were in darkness, and the streets were empty at the late hour. 'None of us have had much luck in love,' he mused, comfortable in the company of his cousin. They were the same age and had grown up in each other's company, but while Lucian was an Astin, he took after his mother's side of the family and was fair to the Astin offspring's darker features.

'Have you given up on the delectable Miss Lilly Lewis?'

'Miss Lewis barely knows I am alive. Even when we were dancing, her eyes were scanning the party guests for Julius. Perhaps with Miss Forrester out of his life, Miss Lewis might set her sights on him again.'

'I am sorry, Ambrose.'

He shrugged. 'I have met someone else who I rather like,' he said with an involuntary smile.

'You dark horse,' Lucian grinned. 'When were you going to tell me?'

'When I told her,' Ambrose said in jest. 'It is Miss Kirby... Kate.'

'The photographer? She is lovely and talented. So, she does not know of your affection for her?'

'I suspect she does. We spent a little time in each other's company this week,' Ambrose said. 'Kate is going to take a portrait of our office and staff, and after that, I shall ask her to accompany me somewhere special. I am working on where that might be.'

'Good for you,' Lucian slapped his cousin on the back.

They arrived at Julius's house and saw it was in complete darkness: no lamp burned, no sign of life.

'I know where a key is; let's check.'

Ambrose retrieved the key, and it took but a few minutes to determine Julius was not home.

'For the love of God, if he left the club but twenty minutes ago, how far could he have gone,' Lucian said, throwing up his hands and now displaying the same impatience as Ambrose.

'I bet I know where he is,' Ambrose said. 'The cemetery.'

'Now? At this hour of the night? Does he never leave his work behind?'

'It is not about work, he will be visiting our parents,' Ambrose said. 'It is too far to walk; I'll find a hansom cab and leave you to head home.'

'Do you wish me to come with you? I don't mind.'

Ambrose shook his head in the negative. 'No, but thank you, cousin. Would you drop in on my grandparents on your way if a light is on? Tell them I am with Julius so they do not spend the night awake and worrying, which they will. It's just that it is out of character for him.'

'I will be passing right by. Let's get you a cab then.'

Ambrose saw him from afar, his brother's white shirt visible in the moonlight, a beacon in the dark. Julius had removed his jacket and laid it out on their father's grave. He was lying full length as if resting, his arms behind his head and looking at the dark sky. It was strewn with stars, and the early Spring night was crisp and comfortable.

Ambrose did not panic. He knew Julius would not take his own life; he would never do that to the family, and at the worst time of their life – when Julius, aged twelve, had seen his parents struck down by a horse and wagon going too fast, he did not resort to that. After Julius's small period of rebellion, he stepped up, and they were all the better for it.

'Brother,' Ambrose said, announcing himself before sitting on his mother's grave beside him.

'Ambrose.'

'Just resting?'

'I was.'

Ambrose shrugged off his jacket and assumed the same position as his brother.

'Do you come here often?' he asked.

'Yes.'

'Really? And lay here like this?'

'Yes, but not so much during the day. I don't want to startle anyone.'

Ambrose glanced towards his brother in the dark, trying to read his expression.

'But why do you come here?'

'Peace. Advice. To remember,' Julius said, his voice low and quiet, with no slur from drinking. He must not have consumed the quantity his best friend did, or Julius handled it better, Ambrose mused.

Julius continued in a low voice. 'I used to lay with Dad in the backyard looking at the sky when I was young, and he'd make up stories about spacecraft and other planets.'

'I don't remember doing that,' Ambrose said.

'Maybe you didn't.'

'Sometimes I struggle to remember them at all,' Ambrose confessed. 'I try, and then I get worried my memories will be other people's that I've heard and created in my mind.'

'You were only nine when they... left,' Julius said. 'Sometimes it is the same for me. I can only remember flashes or stories.'

'Tell me one.'

Julius thought a moment. 'Dad told me when he first met Mum, he had to persuade her to date him. She had several beaus wanting her hand in marriage. So, he learnt as much about her as possible to use to his advantage.'

'We should take note of that,' Ambrose interrupted.

'True. Mum relied on her instincts a lot, I believe. Dad had said she was very much into classic mythology and signs if something was meant to be.'

'I didn't know that,' Ambrose said, fascinated.

'We are all named from mythology... Julius is related to the Roman god Jupiter, Ambrose from ambrosia – food or drink of the gods, and Phoebe is the sun god.'

'How can I not know this?' Ambrose exclaimed and heard his brother chuckle. 'Go on.'

'Well, Dad had a friend who was a keen astrologer and had seen a comet that remained visible for several days. Dad spun Mum a story about how if he was the one for her and their love was meant to be, they would see a sign in the sky. He took her to see the comet through a telescope. Dad's friend told her it was rare to see such a sight, and only four or so had been seen in just under a decade. It was enough for Mum.'

Ambrose laughed. 'Very clever, Dad,' he said to the headstone behind where Julius lay.

They were silent for a while, watching the sky, when Ambrose asked without saying Violet's name, 'What will you do now? Will you try and provide a sign?'

'No. It is done.'

'I am sorry.'

'As am I. Everything has shifted. I was content with my life before meeting Violet, and now, everything frustrates me.'

Ambrose sighed. 'I understand that feeling more than you know.'

Again, there was silence briefly as Ambrose thought about Miss Lilly Lewis and Julius gathered his emotions.

'Can I stay the night at your home?' Ambrose asked.

'Yes.'

'Let's go then.'

Julius exhaled and struggled to rise; Ambrose rose and offered his hand, pulling his brother to full height. The two men bid their parents good night, gathered their jackets and departed.

# Chapter 17

THE VERY PRACTICAL, FAIR-HAIRED, tall, and direct Miss Melanie Bains entered the premises of *The Economic Undertaker* with four ladies in tow to pay their respects at the viewing of Miss Daisy Dorchester. While two of her party spoke with the senior man on the desk, Melanie whispered to her friend, Hilda Dickinson. 'I feel so hypocritical being here. I do not even like Miss Dorchester, and her comment to the photographer to not waste time on finding the best angle for me because you cannot make a silk purse out of a sow's ear was most unkind.'

Hilda gasped. 'What front. I confess I do not like her either, but I met one of the funeral parlour business owners – a Mr Ambrose Astin – at the photographic studio on the day of my shoot, and he was most handsome. I thought I might see him here again today.'

Melanie chuckled. 'You are terrible. My mother made me come to keep up appearances. If she had known of Mr Astin, I am sure she would find more reasons for me to visit than paying my respects to a rude, departed debutante.'

The two other young ladies joined Miss Bains and Miss Dickinson.

'A rude debutante? Are you speaking of Miss Dorchester?' one of the girls asked but did not wait for a response. 'She told me I looked like a wilted vegetable in my lime gown. My mother made that for me, and I thought it was lovely.'

'I thought it was most becoming,' Hilda added kindly. 'Miss Dorchester told me I had a laugh like a donkey.'

'Dreadful,' Melanie muttered. 'Let's get this over with.'

They followed Mr Randolph Astin into a large room where a coffin was placed against the far wall, and Miss Daisy Dorchester lay as if resting. Ambrose greeted them.

'That is him,' Hilda said and elbowed Melanie. 'Isn't he lovely?'

'My, he certainly is if you like very handsome men,' Melanie teased. She then saw the body and stopped. 'Goodness, she does look beautiful,' her voice softened, appreciating the solemnness of the occasion.

'Yes, she was always that,' Hilda conceded. 'All that promise, gone.'

'Come in, girls, thank you for coming,' a thin woman in mourning clothes with a superior tone said. 'I am Mrs Audrey

Stewart, Daisy's aunt and sponsor. I am sure you miss her terribly. Please take your time; say a few words if you please.'

Melanie grimaced but opened her mouth to offer some words of comfort when a gentleman entered sporting a bandage.

'Mr Wright, how good of you to come and when you are not well,' Mrs Stewart said, rushing to his side.

'Mrs Stewart, I could not stay away. Your niece was to be betrothed to my best friend, Eldon. I had the great pleasure of speaking with her on many occasions.'

'Of course. Mr Foster is not here yet; you did not think to come together?'

Theodore Wright shook his head in the negative. 'He is suffering and will come along when his grief allows it.'

Melanie gasped, tears filling her eyes. 'Poor dear Eldon. Forgive me, Mr Wright, but I overheard your words, and as Eldon is such a dear friend, it pained me.'

Theodore pulled a handkerchief from his pocket and offered it to Miss Melanie Bains.

'So kind, thank you,' she said, dabbing her eyes. He waved it away as she tried to return it and, excusing himself from Mrs Stewart, joined Melanie and her friend, Hilda, at the side of the coffin. Moments later, another two young ladies entered, weeping, which increased in volume at the sight of Daisy.

'Oh, Daisy,' the prettiest of them wailed and ran to the coffin, flinging herself across the body to hold her.

Melanie immediately recognised them as part of Daisy's small circle of friends.

'Oh, you poor dear,' Mrs Stewart said, moving quickly to the young woman's side. 'Such a terrible loss for all of us.'

'Yes,' Melanie muttered, watching the drama unfold. 'A terrible loss.'

Phoebe came up the stairs and glanced into the mourning room, exchanging a small smile with her brother, Ambrose, who was in attendance, arms behind his back and looking as officious as possible. Julius was outside with Bennet, most likely discussing their previous evening antics, and was yet to enter the premises. The gathering was much smaller than anticipated, and Phoebe regretted using the larger room now, which made the mourners seem scarce. Perhaps more ladies will come, she hoped.

'Where is everyone?' Daisy demanded next to Phoebe. 'Do people know to attend?'

Phoebe could not answer for fear of anyone overhearing her but gave Daisy a sympathetic look.

'At least my closest friends are heartbroken,' Daisy said, watching the two girls leaning over her body and crying with great dramatics. 'Why would that Melanie Bains come? She is so plain, and her friend, Hilda, with the terrible laugh, is with her. I hope they don't stay long in case we need the space.'

Phoebe restrained a laugh; even in death, there was nothing humble about Daisy Dorchester. Phoebe returned to the reception area as the business's front door opened. She hoped more mourners were arriving, but Detectives Harland Stone and Gilbert Payne entered instead.

'I hope we are not late to speak with some mourners?' Harland asked after greeting the gathered party.

'No, there are only a handful of young ladies here at the moment,' Randolph told the detectives, 'And no one has left yet. However, the funeral is this afternoon, so more people may be at the graveyard.'

'I don't want to be buried yet!' Daisy exclaimed for Phoebe's ears only. 'My murder has not been solved. I refuse to be buried!'

The door opened, and reporter Lilly Lewis entered. 'Such good timing,' she said, seeing the detectives, and grimaced, lowering her voice. 'Forgive me, Mr Astin, I forgot there was a viewing session in progress.'

'Think nothing of it,' Randolph said as the door opened again, and Phoebe's friend, photographer Kate Kirby, entered.

'Goodness, it is a full house,' Kate greeted everyone.

'There are more of our living party than the mourning party,' Ambrose said, coming out of the room on hearing Kate's voice and giving her a special smile that did not go unnoticed by Phoebe.

'Where are my mourners?' Daisy wailed beside Phoebe as Julius and Bennet entered, officially crowding the area.

'Ah, I shall check on the hearse for this afternoon,' Julius said, greeting everyone and taking the opportunity to slip back out of the room, leaving Bennet most uncomfortable.

'Miss Dorchester's aunt has hired me,' he explained and caught Phoebe's eye. 'She believes a murder took place.'

'We are here for the same purpose but unconvinced as yet if a crime did occur,' Harland said and greeted the private investigator and friend, and as several private conversations broke out, he added. 'You look a little worse for wear.'

Phoebe heard the comment and glanced at Bennet, who shook his head. 'Never again.'

Harland grinned. 'I may hold you to that.'

'Perhaps I should return to my room and make way for more mourners,' Phoebe said, reading her grandfather's concerned expression.

'If you have time to stay, I would appreciate it, Miss Astin. I am keen to hear what thoughts the... um... you have on the matter,' Harland hesitated, not knowing who was aware of Phoebe's special skills.

'I understand,' Phoebe said quickly and nodded her consent. She noted that Bennet looked away from her and appeared most uncomfortable. Did Julius mention her disinterest last night in his own state of heartache?

'I do hope it was murder,' Lilly said, interrupting Phoebe's thoughts. 'Oh, forgive me. I did not mean that to sound as it did, but I do need a good story.'

Members of the party hid their smiles.

Lilly continued. 'May I speak with you, Detective Stone and accompany you for the interviews? I may have an insight or two for you as I've spent the day talking with Miss Dorchester's aunt and friends.'

Harland hesitated before giving a brief nod. 'As long as you honour our arrangement, I will do the same.'

Lilly smiled and added enthusiastically. 'Agreed, thank you.'

'Has Miss Dorchester's intended arrived yet, Mr Astin?' Harland asked Randolph.

'No, only a small group of lady friends and one gentleman by the name of...' Randolph consulted the guest book and said, 'Mr Theodore Wright.'

Harland looked surprised at the name and glanced into the room to see the man he last interviewed in the hospital bed.

'Most odd,' Gilbert said. 'One would think her intended would be here greeting people and accepting condolences on her behalf.'

'Perhaps we should set the detectives, Mr Martin and Lilly, up in the small room then?' Phoebe said.

'My thoughts exactly,' Randolph said and moved from behind his desk to open a small meeting room door for them. 'I shall ask the mourners to spare you a moment before they depart, and send them in if you like?'

'That is appreciated, Mr Astin, thank you,' Harland said, following Gilbert and Lilly into the room that featured a small table, six seats and a fresh vase of flowers in the window area – a comforting room for the bereaved.

'I shall stay in the mourning room rather than the interview room if permitted, Mr Astin?' Bennet asked Randolph, 'I would rather observe this afternoon.'

'Of course, as you please, Mr Martin,' Randolph said.

He departed with a glance at Phoebe and moved towards the room where Daisy's body lay.

'I shall go quickly and pay my respects, then leave,' Kate said, moving from the reception area toward the viewing room.

'Allow me to escort you,' Ambrose said.

'Well, thank you, Mr Astin,' she said coyly, even though they had agreed to call each other by their Christian names.

'My pleasure, Miss Kirby. I would hate to see you lose your way and end up in the fitting-for-a-coffin room.'

'Is there such a thing?' Kate looked alarmed.

'Not quite, but you can pick your own.'

'Goodness,' she said, taking his offered arm. 'Please lead on.'

Phoebe looked at her grandfather and said in a low voice, 'Daisy does not want to be buried this afternoon.'

'Unfortunately, she has no choice. We can preserve her no longer, and the family has made arrangements for her. I hope she is not overwrought and causing you distress, Phoebe dear, you look quite weary.'

'It's not fair,' Daisy said again.

Phoebe winced, and as only she and her grandfather were in the reception area, she said to the dearly departed debutante, 'Perhaps you should return to your viewing and hear what your friends say about you, Daisy. I'm sure it will be gratifying to hear their kind comments.'

Daisy trounced off, achieving the effect even in spirit form, and Phoebe sighed.

'She is exhausting, Grandpa, and very demanding. Most of our visitors are well-mannered and grateful for any help we can offer, but Daisy is very expectant of attention.'

'I wish I could protect you. You are very pale, my dear,' Randolph said, concerned. 'Why don't you head back to the quietness of your room, and I will let the detectives know that you are not well.'

'I will be all right, thank you, Grandpa. I know time is of the essence for them, and I would not like to let them down.' Phoebe sighed, 'Oh no, Daisy has gone in with the detectives instead of the mourners.' She rolled her eyes and followed.

# Chapter 18

THE GENTLEMEN STOOD AS Phoebe entered the room, and she took a seat near the door, thanking them. Detective Gilbert Payne sat beside her, and not that anyone present could see, but Daisy stood right behind Phoebe, uttering statements and complaining in general. As the interviews progressed, Phoebe relayed in a whisper to Gilbert anything relevant, as stated by Daisy, who insisted everything was relevant.

The first to be interviewed were more senior members of the group who had come to pay their respects and leave just as quickly – Daisy's dressmaker, the lady who did Daisy's hair, and the family's staff. Harland made short work of their testimonies as none had anything of significance to contribute to the young lady's manner of death or knew of the other parties – Father Damien Horan and Mr Theodore Wright.

Daisy's two closest friends entered. The two young ladies sat, full of their own importance, and Daisy smirked beside Phoebe.

*'These girls loved me and needed me; I was their inspiration. I am sure I taught them a great deal,'* she said, looking exceedingly pleased with herself.

Phoebe noticed the testimony of the debutantes required more forbearance, and Detective Harland Stone – who rarely displayed frustration – appeared short of patience. Phoebe was surprised to see the toll it was taking on him; she understood and felt the same, but the detective dealt with people all day. Perhaps he was out with Julius last evening and imbibed too much. He ran a hand over his face and inhaled deeply.

Next to her, Phoebe noted Gilbert was more stoic – collecting facts, making notes, and frowning when something did not sound right or surprised him. Phoebe was exhausted by the banter and prodding coming from Daisy as she listened to the friends' recollections.

'She was tough on everybody, so I am not surprised if she offended someone and they bumped her off.'

Phoebe looked to Daisy, whose eyes were wide open in shock.

*'That is outrageous,'* Daisy declared, quietening only because her "friend" continued talking.

'She said I would never find a man unless I ignored our deportment teacher, Miss Yalden's instructions, and stopped gliding and started sashaying. Miss Yalden is so elegant.'

'So elegant,' her friend agreed and sighed.

'Daisy told me to imitate Hilda Dickinson's laugh, and I did because I was scared to get on her bad side, but I felt bad for Hilda.'

'She is so lovely and such a good singer.'

'Daisy did say she had a secret lover. Perhaps he did it. But she never told us who it was or what he looked like or did. I wondered if she made him up.'

*'I did not. And you are supposed to be my friend. They are all just jealous. Tell the detectives, Phoebe, tell them that my friends are lying.'*

Phoebe winced with the barrage of words and quietly relayed the message to Gilbert, firmly believing the truth in what was said. The look he exchanged said he felt the same.

Realising there was little to be gained but gossip, Harland thanked them and sent them on their way. The detectives excused Mr Theodore Wright as Harland had spoken with him in his hospital bed, thus next to enter were the disapproving Miss Melanie Banks and the pretty and quieter Miss Hilda Dickinson, the former quick to speak up.

'Detectives, I am not surprised that Miss Dorchester met her end. Her behaviour was destructive.'

'How could she say that? Phoebe, tell her to shut up!' Daisy prodded Phoebe in the shoulder.

'Could you please explain what you mean by destructive, Miss Dickinson?' Harland asked.

'Well, she already had a lovely suitor, Mr Eldon Foster, who is a good and kind soul and part of my church group, but she flirted terribly with every man. It was shameful.'

'I can't help it if they notice me; what am I supposed to do?' Phoebe wailed.

Melanie Bains added unprompted, 'If one of the ladies mentioned they hoped for the attentions of a particular gentleman, Daisy Dorchester went out of her way to capture his eye, and then, of course, they were smitten with her.'

'Of course.' Daisy smiled. 'It's not my fault you are too plain to attract a man, Melanie Bains.'

'She was disrespectful to everyone, from our teacher to the photographer. Her mother could not bear her and left her under her aunt's guardianship. Well, that was what we heard,' Melanie said and sat back haughtily.

'My mother does not like society. How would you know, Melanie Bains!' Daisy yelled as if the young woman could hear her. Phoebe rubbed her temple and momentarily closed her eyes.

'Are you implying, Miss Bains, that one of the ladies who felt jilted might have had grounds to harm Miss Dorchester?' Gilbert asked, returning to Melanie's earlier statement. 'If so, can you suggest who that might be? Some names, perhaps?'

'I could not, but her disrespect for the girls and Mr Foster would be grounds for confrontation.'

'But not murder, surely,' Hilda Dickinson said quietly beside her friend.

'The cut of her dresses was too low and may have attracted unwanted attention,' Melanie Bains continued.

Harland said in a hushed tone. 'Gilbert, could you see if Mr Eldon Foster has arrived yet? I wish to speak with him.'

Gilbert rose, went to the door, and was quickly advised in the negative by Mr Astin. He returned, took his seat and relayed the news to his superior.

Harland cleared his throat to break up the discussion between the debutantes. 'Ladies, I'm grateful for your contribution, but aside from Miss Dorchester's character, is there anyone you saw around Miss Dorchester that should not have been there, anyone suspicious, any activity that you thought was untoward or do you have any idea who might have wished to fatally harm Miss Dorchester?' Harland asked, focusing on Hilda, who seemed more objective and adopting a tone that implied he would soon send them on their way.

'Yes,' Miss Hilda Dickinson said.

The gentlemen looked more alert.

'Who might that be, Miss Dickinson?' Harland asked.

'Anyone who loved or respected Mr Eldon Foster. Sirs, I was present several times when Miss Dorchester ridiculed him for his kindness, sent him on his way after he had fetched a drink for her, or ran an errand, like he was dismissed. He was embarrassed but did not make a scene. If he were my friend, brother, or son, I would want him freed from a future with her.'

*'How dare she!'* Daisy screamed next to Phoebe. *'Her with the horsey laugh. Eldon loves me and would do anything for me. Tell them that, Phoebe.'*

'Noted, thank you, Miss Dickinson. Do you believe Mr Eldon capable of harming her?'

Both ladies gasped.

'Oh no, definitely not,' Melanie Bains spoke first.

'I believe he is a gentleman and a gentle soul,' Hilda Dickinson added.

Harland nodded and thanked them for their time. The ladies rose and departed the room as Gilbert held the door open for them.

Phoebe was distressed that the testimonies had been so nasty. Add to this, the room seemed small and hot, and Daisy crowded her. Suddenly, the deceased young woman gasped.

*'A scent. I remember a scent!'* Daisy proclaimed, and Phoebe jerked to look at her and then back to the table again. She could not give away that she was talking to the spirit world.

*'It was a scent... I smelt it before I was struck, I remember! And I can smell it lingering now in the air in this room.'* She sniffed loudly several times, identifying two of the ingredients. *'Phoebe, tell them, tell them now. My murderer was here or was wearing the same fragrance. Tell them!'*

Randolph Astin's priority had always been his family, and he did not like seeing Phoebe looking so anxious.

The front door opened, and a young man, tall, well-groomed and looking somewhat uncomfortable in the surroundings, entered. He was not handsome compared to the Astin brothers but looked pleasant and distinguished.

'Good day, Sir, I am Eldon Foster, here to pay my respects to Miss Dorchester,' he said, removing his hat.

'My condolences, Mr Foster,' Randolph said. 'Miss Dorchester's viewing room is to your right, and if you have no objections, Detectives Stone and Payne would like a quick word with those in attendance when you are ready in the room to the left.'

'I have previously spoken to them. So, they still believe a crime is afoot?' he asked, surprised.

'I could not say, Mr Eldon, but they specifically asked for you. I believe Miss Dorchester's guardian aunt may be seeking reassurances that there is nothing untoward about her ward's death.'

Eldon's lips tightened, but he restrained himself, adding, 'No doubt Mrs Stewart believes it to be otherwise.' He gathered himself and gave Randolph a small nod of thanks, moving toward the mourning room where Mrs Stewart held court despite Ambrose playing official host.

Randolph greeted two ladies as they exited the mourning room and directed them in to see the detectives; there was far too much activity underway for a business of a melancholy nature. As the door opened, Randolph noticed Phoebe sitting opposite the detectives, looking strained; her eyes met his momentarily before the door closed again.

'Will you take a cup of tea, Mr Astin, while you man the desk?' Mrs Dobbs asked, appearing from having refreshed the small spread she had prepared for mourners and still looking quite refreshed despite the foot traffic. Mrs Dobbs liked to be challenged and always rose to the occasion.

'Thank you, but I think I shall wait until the session ends and we have some peace,' he said as if sharing a confidence. 'Mrs Dobbs, would you kindly mind the desk for a moment while I fetch Julius from the back?' Randolph asked.

'Of course, Mr Astin. Mourners to the left, interviews to the right,' she said, having overhead Randolph's last instructions.

He smiled at her. 'Exactly so, thank you. You are grace under fire.'

She laughed. 'Go on with you. I would be useless to the business if I folded should we get busy.'

'I fear our Phoebe, however, is struggling,' he said in a low voice. 'I will fetch Julius to check on her. He is a friend of the detectives and will not be as officious as me.'

'Oh dear. Yes, that is a good idea,' Mrs Dobbs said, frowning. 'That debutante is quite a handful, I believe, and Phoebe is undoubtedly being pulled in all directions.'

He nodded, hurried down the hallway, and, opening the back door, saw Julius brushing down his favourite horse. He called out to his grandson.

'What is it?' Julius stopped, handing the brush to Claude, the stable manager, and hurried to his grandfather's side.

'I am concerned for Phoebe,' Randolph filled him in, and Julius gave a brief nod, passing him and entering the building, his grandfather close behind.

Julius saw his grandfather's concerns were warranted as he quietly knocked on the meeting room door and entered. He could see Daisy standing too close to Phoebe and talking. Phoebe was quietly advising Detective Payne of Daisy's comments while

Harland was speaking with the two debutants who had previously been in the mourning room.

Julius moved to Phoebe, and she touched his arm. He needed no further information.

'I apologise for interrupting, Detectives, ladies,' Julius addressed the gathering, but I must remove my sister; she is not well.' He took Phoebe under the elbow and raised her to a standing position. She did not protest but leant on him further.

Harland rose to his feet immediately. 'Forgive me, Miss Astin, I did not realise. That was insensitive of me.'

'I am sorry to have been asking so many questions,' Gilbert said, standing now and most concerned.

'No, not at all,' she assured them. 'You both have so much on your mind; I am only a little weary. Please do not let me interrupt you.'

Harland exhaled, most worried.

'Do not concern yourself, Harland,' Julius assured his friend, 'it has just been a long day for Phoebe with the viewing and other requirements. Please continue with your interviews; there is no hurry to conclude.'

Julius led Phoebe outside the room, and closing the door, she faltered as if she had been holding herself together for just that time. He placed his arm around her, insisting she leant on him, and supporting his sister, Julius walked her to the stairs, Randolph following close by.

'I have this, Grandpa,' Julius assured him, carefully helping Phoebe down the stairs to her workroom.

'I will send down a cup of tea,' Randolph said, returning to relieve Mrs Dobbs, who would busy herself with making fortifying refreshments for Phoebe.

'You are not to do that to yourself again,' Julius scolded her as he carried her down the stairs. 'You have no obligation to help them, and the spirits demand too much of your generous nature.'

He placed her on the sofa, and she leaned back with a sigh. Julius grabbed the knitted blanket nearby and draped it over her.

'Truly, I am all right; do not fuss over me. It was just too many of the living and too much of the dead.' She sighed as Daisy appeared.

'Not now, Daisy, please,' Phoebe said and closed her eyes.

'But we have no time to spare,' she wailed.

'Go,' Julius roared at the young woman's spirit, and she hurriedly disappeared.

'You saw her?'

'I spoke in the direction you were looking,' Julius said. In his usual style, Julius did not admit to seeing the spirits, nor did he deny it.

'Thank you, Julius.' Phoebe said. 'I am quite exhausted.'

'You should have sent for me; you are never alone,' he assured her and rose to meet Mrs Dobbs, taking the tea tray for two from her. She had put some extra slices on the tray as well.

'For fortitude,' she said with a wink, and Julius smiled and thanked her, returning to pour them both a cup of tea. Once served, he sat perched at the end of the couch near Phoebe's feet.

'Do you believe me now that I like working in solitude?' she asked her brother, and he gave her a wry look.

'I always believed you, but I like to encourage you to seek the sun and light sometimes. Plus, I would like to see you find someone and enjoy all you deserve in life.'

He felt Phoebe studying him.

'You told Mr Martin?'

'Yes.'

'Thank you. I sensed he was different towards me. I am sorry that I have pained him.'

Julius nodded. He did not mention his friend was devastated; that was not Phoebe's cross to bear.

'It is so complicated... love,' Phoebe said after a while. The colour was returning to her cheeks as they both sat comfortably in silence, regaining their strength away from the milling crowds. Despite the seven-year gap between them, they were the closest of siblings and similar in nature. Julius was most protective of his sister. Unlike Ambrose, neither of them sought company to buoy them.

*'I did not encourage her, and the feelings were not reciprocated.'*

Phoebe jumped at the voice behind Julius, and they both turned; Julius prepared to roar at another spirit. But he stopped in his tracks.

'Father Horan! Damien...' he said, shocked to see the ghost of the young priest that had officiated many a funeral with the Astin men. His body was not on the premises, but that never stopped persistent spirits from visiting. There was no denying to Phoebe now that he saw this spirit.

'Julius, I assure you I was true to my faith. I did not love that woman, and not doing so was the death of me.'

# Chapter 19

P HOEBE WAS TORN BETWEEN studying the deceased
Father Damien Horan in front of her pleading for
understanding, or confronting her brother, Julius, who was
speaking with the priest. Had Julius been able to see the spirits
all along? She had always suspected, and Uncle Reggie had
insisted he could, but now there was no refuting it.

Father Horan begged their attention. 'The young lady
upstairs to be buried today came to mass with her aunt and
afterwards asked if I would help her prepare for marriage in the
Catholic faith,' he explained. 'She was most devoted and came
several times on her own to speak with me about matters of
faith. But it did not take me long to realise her devotion was
not to her faith but to winning my affections.' He shook his
head.

'Forgive me, Father, but you are young and handsome. I suspect many parishioners hoped to win your heart,' Phoebe said respectfully.

'I have been the subject of some attention, Miss Astin,' he said humbly. 'But I am a Catholic priest and not permitted to take a wife, nor do I seek to do so. I am committed to my parish work and to spreading the Lord's good word.'

'Damien, forgive me for playing devil's advocate, especially with a man of the cloth,' Julius said, using the priest's Christian name as they had agreed to, having met many times on the job, 'but you kept the verse and lock of hair on your person, yet you say she meant nothing to you?'

'I was given the lock the day I departed the world, Julius. When I least expected it, Miss Dorchester threw her arms around my neck and pressed herself to me, confessing her love. I struggled to pull her off.'

'There was bruising around your neck,' Julius said, remembering Tavish's findings in the coroner's report.

'I was embarrassed and mortified someone might see us. She pledged her devotion but had no understanding of my faith. She spoke of having a large inheritance and assured me that I could leave the church and do as I wished as her husband. I intended to discard the lock of hair on my return to the presbytery and accepted it only to hurry her along. It is not my first gift from a young lady.'

'Will you tell us how you met your death?' Phoebe asked.

'I wish I could. I have walked those cliffs and stairs daily and am quite sure-footed, but someone appeared behind me; I felt their presence. Before I could turn to see them, I had been pushed and was tumbling, such a frightening sensation.' He inhaled sharply, his hand going to his heart, as he relived his untimely death again.

'Can you tell us anything that might help the detectives?' Phoebe asked.

'Like if there is a god?' the young priest teased, keeping the sense of humour that had befriended him to Julius and Ambrose, who were of similar age.

Julius laughed. 'We didn't dare ask.'

'Keep the faith,' Father Horan said with a smile. He sobered. 'No, Miss Astin, unfortunately, I recall nothing in regard to my assailant. But the detectives believe I was murdered?'

'At this stage, yes, and they are keen to seek justice for you,' Phoebe said.

Father Horan exhaled with relief. 'I wish I could think of something that might assist, but I did not come here to seek justice. I could not rest for fear it was thought I betrayed my holy vows. I did not. However, you will find some love verses in my Bible, tucked amongst the pages and lines underlined of great significance to me.' He looked abashed. 'They are not for a woman; they are to nature, to the beauty of this world where I tried to ground myself when people were so unchristian.'

'We understand, Damien. We see a range of temperaments in our line of work, too, but often, it is too late for redemption. The detectives know of Phoebe's skill,' Julius said, 'we will ensure they know that you were not in a relationship with anyone but your faith.'

'I thank you, both. If only I could also tell Father Morris.'

'If he knows you, he will never believe otherwise,' Phoebe said, comforting him. 'But we will ensure Detective Stone mentions to Father Morris that Daisy's love was unrequited.'

'My blessing to you both until we meet again, hopefully not for many years yet,' he said with a small smile, and Father Damien Horan bowed as he faded.

Ambrose greeted one of the few men to attend Miss Dorchester's viewing other than Mr Theodore Wright, who came and left just as quickly, and private investigator Bennet Martin, who stood nearby, observing as expected by his client. The viewing session was soon to come to an end; in total, a dozen mourners had attended, and the small room would have sufficed, Ambrose mused. He studied the late arrival – a man of his age who looked as if he wished he were in numerous other places and not a funeral home. But he could safely conclude that if this was the potential husband he had heard about and the reaction of Mrs Audrey Stewart confirmed it, the guest did not appear too heartbroken.

Eldon Foster stopped to say a few words to two departing ladies – Miss Melanie Bains and Miss Hilda Dickinson. He acknowledged them as they left the room to give him his privacy, and Miss Melanie Bains touched his arm in a showing of sympathy on her way out.

Eldon greeted Ambrose and joined Mrs Stewart while Daisy's wailing friends gathered themselves, and Kate moved away from the coffin toward Ambrose, offering her condolences to the pair.

'I said a quick prayer for her obnoxious soul,' Kate whispered, and Ambrose restrained a laugh.

'Do be kind. I am meant to be sombre, and you are making that quite difficult,' he said in jest.

Kate tried not to smile. 'I have printed our photograph, and may I say, I look particularly lovely. You look quite good yourself.'

Ambrose chuckled and disguised it as a cough, offering a nod of apology to Mrs Stewart. 'Are you returning to your office?'

'Done with me?' Kate asked with a raised eyebrow.

'On the contrary.' He leaned in closer to whisper, 'If you can wait a few moments for this charade to finish, I shall walk you back.'

'An offer I cannot refuse,' Kate said, trying not to look too happy in the room with a deceased body on display. 'I shall visit the ladies in the mourning wear store next door to tell them of the pending photograph.'

'I shall collect you from there,' Ambrose agreed. He watched Kate leave, and seeing his grandfather outside the door indicating the time, Ambrose stepped forward and announced, 'Ladies and gentlemen, the viewing will complete in five minutes. Please say your farewells, and you are most welcome to attend Miss Dorchester's burial this afternoon. Please consult Mrs Stewart for details.'

He stepped back again and watched the man beside Mrs Stewart move towards the body.

'Oh, Eldon, your heart must be broken,' Mrs Stewart said in a mournful voice accompanied by a shake of her head. Daisy's friends at the coffin moved aside as if sensing his approach and his superior grief to their own. They stepped back, watching Mr Eldon Foster lean down and kiss Miss Dorchester's forehead, causing the ladies in attendance to clutch their handkerchiefs. Several sobbed pitifully.

He then reached for his own handkerchief and hurriedly departed. Bennet Martin waited a moment and followed. Ambrose moved to the doorway and heard Eldon saying, 'Please make my excuses to the detectives. I am too overwrought to speak.'

'Of course,' Randolph said as the young man exited without looking back, Bennet a beat behind him. The two men were followed by the ladies who exited their interview around the same time, and one of them called after Eldon, hurrying out the door to follow.

'Grandpa, I wish to walk Kate back to her studio. Could you finish—'

'Of course,' Randolph said to his youngest grandson, 'off you go.'

Ambrose thanked him and hurried out to meet the woman who had caught his fancy, catching out of the corner of his eye the tall woman, Melanie, catching up with Mr Eldon Foster and her friend, trailing not far behind.

As he moved further away, Eldon Foster pocketed his handkerchief and exhaled. He stood straighter, his shoulders back. He was a different man now; everything had changed. Eldon had loved Daisy Dorchester once, when they were children. They had regularly promised to marry each other when brought together as their parents socialised. They had always been encouraged in their affections, and both families would benefit.

As he grew older, Eldon realised Daisy Dorchester was quite a catch, and he was the envy of his young friends. But it did not take long for Daisy to learn that as well. Character and integrity counted for very little – she taunted him with men who were more handsome and richer until, eventually, Daisy wore him down.

One evening, after dancing with a lovely lady at the request of a friend to save a wallflower, Eldon realised how easy conversation should flow, how nice it was to be considered handsome and obliging. Eldon Foster realised he did not like Daisy Dorchester, not one bit. But Eldon had a healthy respect for his mother and a fear of his father, thus he had no intention of dishonouring his obligation, and there was no doubt he would financially benefit from the marriage.

But today was a new day. He had his freedom. Freedom to love whom he wanted, to pursue respect and happiness. Eldon Foster was a new man; it was the happiest day of his life.

Bennet Martin stayed close to Eldon Foster but not close enough to draw attention. He was a better artist than a private detective, but the skills of observation that served his art so well proved very useful in his investigative work. He could confidently conclude that Eldon Foster was not heartbroken; quite the contrary. As for himself, he was relieved that Phoebe was working in a different room to himself today and that his exposure to her had been minimal. Still, it was as if he could feel her on the other side of the wall, and Bennet was pleased to leave and put *The Economic Undertaker* behind him. A great contrast to the many times he had previously tried to find reasons to visit.

He saw the well-groomed but plain-looking man stop when he heard his name called and effect a change to appear a defeated man as the two ladies approached. He recognised the ladies from the mourning room. A tall woman and a smaller, pretty woman who would not be noticed if Daisy Dorchester was in the room.

Studying the small group, Bennet could not see how such an unassuming man could live up to Daisy Dorchester and her demands from what he had heard of the young lady. He observed the ladies who hurried to speak with him. Were they sincere in their support or conscious that a new suitor was on the market once the mourning period was observed? The tallest, whom he had learnt was Miss Melanie Bains, was most insistent on holding court, but Eldon Foster seemed more attentive to her friend, the petite and pretty Miss Hilda Dickinson. Bennet watched as Mr Foster handed them into a cab and walked away.

Bennet determined he would attend the funeral this afternoon, study the guests in attendance, and then head to the site where Daisy met her death. He hoped his disinterest in the case wasn't as evident to his client, Mrs Stewart, as it felt to himself.

# Chapter 20

LILLY DREW A BREATH. 'And to conclude, Mr Cowan, there is very much a story to be investigated here – a beautiful but snippety debutante, murdered, the death of a Catholic priest who was providing pastoral care to her, the bashing of a friend of Miss Dorchester who was also to be the best man of her soon-to-be fiancé and a group of potential suspects including jealous girls some of whom Miss Dorchester slighted.'

'We have full access to the detective again, Mr Cowan, and the deceased's guardian aunt is very keen to press her case that her niece was murdered,' Fergus said, having had a full brief from Lilly and needing to appear as if he was very much part of this investigation, as they did their story pitch in the editor's smoky room. 'They are lining up to talk.'

Mr Cowan looked from one to the other and back to Lilly, pulling the cigar from his mouth and tapping on the paperwork before him.

'I just read your piece on the girl for the memorial column. If she was as obnoxious as you say, you did a good job hiding it.'

'It wasn't easy, Sir, trust me,' Lilly said. 'But I did my best to make it sound like she had talent and a shiny future ahead.'

He scoffed. 'You did all right.' Alex Cowan sat back and thought about their story pitch for a few moments before shooting questions at them.

'Why was she so unlikable?'

'Spoilt, Mr Cowan. Daisy Dorchester was told she was beautiful and deserving, and she believed it. I understand she usually got what she desired,' Lilly said.

'I believe she was considered the debutant who would be the belle of the ball,' Fergus added, 'and the photographer, Miss Kirby, said Miss Dorchester was very vocal in her criticism of other debutants even in their presence.'

'Are there any close friends who will disagree and provide some colour to your story?'

'Yes, a couple of weepers at the funeral who were in Daisy's tight circle of friends,' Lilly said.

'The potential husband, is he heartbroken?'

'No.'

'Good. Is he a suspect?'

'Yes. Detective Harland Stone has a few, and he is one of them,' Fergus answered.

Mr Cowan grunted. 'The priest, were they intimate?'

'Not to our knowledge, but Miss Dorchester told her friends she had a secret love.'

For a few seconds, Mr Cowan thought on that before firing back, 'What's the death scene like?'

'Steep, nasty, dangerous,' Lilly said, providing as many evocative words as possible.

He sat forward and slammed his hand on the desk like a judge's gravel. 'Do it! I want drama – the murder of a young beauty, jealousy, heartbreak... and direct quotes from the detectives. So, the photographer can provide the girl's portrait?'

'Yes, it is a beautiful one,' Lilly said.

'Excellent, get that too. Get quotes from her relatives the coroner, and talk about the death scene. Go, go, go!'

Lilly and Fergus jumped to their feet, trying not to grin. 'Thank you, Mr Cowan, you won't be sorry,' Lilly said.

'A story a day, and I'd better not be,' he called after them.

They exited the editor's office, pleased to be back in the fresh air and hurried back to their desks, grinning from ear to ear. For a moment, they sat and took a breath before they began the job of dividing their workload. Their colleagues could sense their excitement.

'Another scoop then, Lewis and Griffiths?' one of the older reporters asked with a grin. 'Good on you both.'

'Hopefully so, Ted, thank you,' Fergus said. 'The dead debutante.'

'Ah, yes, I thought that was an accident?'

'Apparently not,' Lilly answered, crossing her fingers for good luck, making the senior journalist laugh and shake his head at her.

'You'll need to keep your strength up. Allow me to take you to dinner, Lilly,' Lawrence Hulmes issued his regular invitation, and the men in the newsroom all chuckled at his persistence.

'As handsome as you may be and in much demand with the ladies, Lawrence, I'm not that hungry, thank you.'

The group laughed, and Lawrence took their ribbing in good humour.

'The day will come, Lilly Lewis, the day will come,' Lawrence waggled a finger at her.

'If you are so keen to eat together, Lawrence, you could always bring in some of your baking to share,' she teased, earning another round of laughs, and Lawrence held his hands up in surrender.

Lilly turned her attention to Fergus. 'I want to solve this, not just report it.'

'Then let's get to work,' he agreed. 'There's a murderer on the loose.'

Julius sat back beside Phoebe on the couch in her workroom.

'Have you always seen them?' Phoebe asked in a quiet voice, and Julius nodded.

'I was sorry when you declared you could,' Julius told his sister. 'It is sometimes confronting.' He studied his petite and fair sister and worried for her as he had always done since their parents departed the earth.

'But why did you not say? Are you afraid you will be ridiculed or considered a lunatic?'

Julius's jaw tightened as he thought of what to say. 'No,' he eventually spoke. 'Not that, and I have never thought of you that way. In truth, I don't want to live amongst the dead. It is enough that I see to their burial. It wearies me.'

'It doesn't usually weary me, but Daisy has been too much. Generally, I like that I can help, and aside from Daisy, most of my visitors are very respectful.'

Julius could feel Phoebe's hurt as she studied him. 'You could have trusted me.'

He nodded. 'I could have. But I hoped it would leave me if I ignored it often enough. It has not.'

'Uncle Reggie?'

'I see him regularly.' He turned to face her. 'Will you keep my secret?'

'Of course. It is not mine to tell,' she said, giving him a sympathetic look. 'I will tell the detectives what Father Damian Horan had to say.'

'Thank you.' Julius reached for his sister's hand, and she placed it in his. 'I am sorry, Phoebe. I know the burden for you might have been easier to share if you thought you were not alone.'

She smiled. 'It is not so dramatic; I felt special for being chosen.'

'And you still are,' he said, returning her smile. He looked to the top of the stairs and back to Phoebe. 'I believe it will be quieter upstairs now; the viewing session is over, and we will bury the debutante this afternoon. Let's hope that will be the end of it.'

As he spoke, the pair heard footsteps approaching the stairs, and Julius turned, exclaiming in surprise as a young man ran down the stairs.

'Tom!' He rose. 'Are you all right, is Violet?' In his moment of concern, he did not have time to feel the pain Violet's name caused him, but it soon rushed over him.

'We are both fine, Mr Astin... Julius, thank you. Hello Miss Astin,' the young man said, and Phoebe greeted him with a smile.

'You look well, Tom.'

'I am, thank you, Miss Astin,' Tom said, minding his manners as taught.

Tom turned to the man his sister loved. He had been invited to call Julius by his Christian name but was uncomfortable doing so. 'I was hoping we could speak, Julius, if you could spare the time for me?'

'Of course. Is everything satisfactory at your work?'

'Yes, I am on my lunch break. But I have something I need to discuss with you.'

'I shall give you some privacy,' Phoebe said, rising and preparing to leave her room.

'No, Miss, please don't depart. Maybe we could talk in the stable?' he suggested to Julius.

'Why don't I get the horse and cart and drive you back to work, and we can talk on the way?' Julius offered.

'That would be great,' Tom said, brightening now that he would not be late returning.

They bid Phoebe goodbye, and Julius glanced back at her. The smile she gave was either in the hope that Tom bought a message of goodwill from his sister or that she was now accepting of Julius's decision to keep his ghosts hidden and had forgiven him. Either way, Julius felt an enormous sense of relief not to hide his other side around one family member.

# Chapter 21

Ambrose placed himself street side, on Miss Kate Kirby's left, to protect her from the horses and carriages passing by.

'They are so fast sometimes,' she said as one whipped up a small dust storm in passing.

'We never have that problem with the hearse,' Ambrose joked. 'Lord knows I've tried to get the speed up, but Julius is a stickler for being dignified.'

Kate laughed. 'From what Phoebe tells me, you might be a little keener to hurry Miss Dorchester to the cemetery.'

Ambrose agreed. 'We were expecting large numbers this morning at her viewing; perhaps more will attend the funeral. Are you sure you do not wish to come?' he asked in jest.

'I have two bookings this afternoon, as luck would have it, but I'd find an excuse if I had none,' Kate said honestly and laughed at his shocked expression. 'I have a booking for a gentleman seeking a business portrait and a lovely photograph to take of newlyweds.'

'Who is this gentleman, and should I be concerned?' Ambrose teased, and Kate flushed with pleasure, her breathing quite shallow with the excitement of being escorted by the man she had thought non-stop about since she took their portrait.

'I imagine you should be,' she smiled up at him. 'I look particularly fetching with the cloth of the camera over my head and even more so when I appear from under with my hair a mess and blinking to adjust to the light. Who could resist?'

'Who indeed?' he asked, and on reaching her workplace, Ambrose reached for Kate's hand and placed a gentle kiss upon it. 'Good day, Kate.'

'Good day, Ambrose.'

And with a smile, she watched as he turned and made haste to do his afternoon shift. She watched, even though she knew that was very forward, and Kate was rewarded. Ambrose looked back as he reached the corner and gave her a smile and wave before disappearing around it.

The painful conversation with Violet was never far from his mind, but Julius was curious to know what brought Tom calling. He started the trap, giving the horse a gentle nudge, and once out onto the street heading to Tom's workplace, he glanced at the young man who had filled out and grown taller since the first time Julius set eyes on him at his grandmother's funeral.

'What is wrong, Tom, that brings you across town during the day?'

'It is Violet. She is upset that she offended you and does not want you to give up on her. She wants you to ask her out and to be interested in her again. I guess that's the best way to put it. Uncle persuaded her she was wrong to seek your affection as if she would be improper to do so. But now she believes he was wrong in asking that of her. I told her she was daft.' Tom looked over at Julius. 'Does that make sense? I said I would speak on her behalf, but I had intended to say it better than that.'

Julius smiled at him, a strange sensation of relief but hesitation fighting within him.

'I've always liked to be direct.'

'Me too,' Tom agreed. 'She loves you, I'm sure of it, and will you talk with her and invite her out? Please, Julius?'

Julius's breath hitched slightly at Tom's declaration of his sister's feelings. He rubbed his jaw with his free hand, holding the reins in the other.

'Ah, Tom...'

'You still like her, don't you?' Tom cut him off, but the matter was too raw and painful to engage a quick response from Julius, despite what Tom wanted.

Julius gave a brief nod to confirm his feelings, and when he finally responded to Tom's query, it was not what the young man wanted to hear.

'Your sister has my heart completely.' He saw the young man smile and relax, and Julius hurriedly added, 'But I have made my intentions clear to Violet several times now, and she made her position clear to me. Should she wish to pursue a relationship, she must come to me.'

Tom rolled his eyes. 'I knew you would say that. You are both the same: stubborn and used to taking charge.'

Julius gave a small smile, and Tom shrugged.

'Well, you said it was all right to be direct,' he added with a grin. 'Right then, I shall tell her that you love her and want to spend the rest of your life with her, but she must seek you out.'

Julius grimaced. 'Perhaps a little restraint is warranted.'

'If I leave it to the pair of you, she'll be an old maid living in our old neighbourhood, and you'll marry someone you don't love half as much. Oh, did I tell you we're moving back to our old neighbourhood?'

'No!' Julius glanced at Tom before returning his attention to the road. 'Why?'

'We like it there, and a smaller house near our old one has become available. It's cheaper, and we only need two rooms.' Tom spoke to Julius as if they were already brothers, not boss and worker.

'And Violet wants to move back?'

'She's as keen as me. We're not happy in the house Uncle insisted we take. In fact, we're not happy with most of Uncle's decisions,' Tom said again for emphasis. 'We're moving this Saturday.'

'Do you need help to relocate?' Julius asked, concerned, knowing they were alone in the world.

'I wish I had thought of that,' Tom said frowning, 'I could have brought you together that way.'

Julius chuckled.

'But I earn a good wage now, as you know, so I hired a horse and cart, and some of my friends from the neighbourhood are helping.'

Julius gave him a look of frustration. 'Save your hard-earned money. I will supply the horse and cart, and if you should need labour, let me know.'

'Thank you, Julius, that is really good of you,' Tom smiled and nodded, satisfied. 'If the cart could arrive after ten on Saturday, we'll be packed and ready.'

Julius glanced at him, a suspicious look on his face. 'You look like the cat that swallowed the cream. Are you sure you have hired this other cart?'

'Of course, but it is a friend who has given me a good price. I am happy to take up your offer, thank you. We will be there if you want to check on us.'

Julius nudged him as they stopped outside Tom's workplace, and the young man laughed.

'It was worth a try,' Tom said, jumping from the trap.

"Hmm, I still wish Violet to declare her emotions directly to me,' Julius said with an affectionate look at Tom.

Tom sighed dramatically. 'I shall organise it, and she shall. Thanks for the ride and helping us.'

'I'll come in and see Lucian,' Julius said, alighting and feeling like the world was a place of great promise yet again and his heart a little lighter. The two men entered the carpentry business looking like family.

# Chapter 22

A NEW DAY BROUGHT the promise of new things, and Gilbert Payne entered the Roma Street Police Station with renewed vigour to help his superior solve the case. He had experienced a disturbed night – thoughts of Miss Emily Yalden of the *Miss Emily Yalden School of Deportment* stayed foremost in his mind. A practical fellow by nature, Gilbert was as intrigued with the sensation as he was with the lady.

*Was this what it felt like to fall in love,* he mused. *It is odd and not conducive to getting work done, but feeling aglow is lovely. I can imagine the verses of poetry that have come from such feelings. But how does one function in the world when one's head is in the clouds? The feeling must pass, surely.*

Despite his state of surprise and mild euphoria, Gilbert had gone through his notes for the case, as was his normal practice each evening, and had reached some conclusions. But as he entered his shared office, Gilbert momentarily forgot the case. On the table were a dozen beautiful cream roses in their early stage of bloom. It was an unaccustomed sight in a police department, and could it be that Detective Stone was prepared to lose his heart too, although Gilbert could not proclaim that confidently yet of himself.

'Good morning, Gilbert,' Harland said.

'Sir. They are beautiful,' he said, staring at the bouquet.

'They are for Miss Astin. I was most frustrated yesterday during the interviews, and it was remiss of me to be so unaware of Miss Astin's comfort. Poor form.' He shook his head.

'It is a very thoughtful gesture, Sir. And cream is a perfect choice.'

'Yes.' Harland said and then frowned. He looked to his protégé to explain. 'Is it? Why? Should I not have got cream roses?'

'Sir, they are lovely. Cream roses mean someone – that is, the recipient – is on your mind, and you think them charming.'

'Is that true?' Harland exclaimed with surprise. 'Why do I not know this? Is it common knowledge?'

Gilbert shook his head. 'I don't believe so, Sir. Maybe amongst the ladies, I could not say. My mother is a keen rose grower and believes the colours are most significant.'

'Well, a colour that said thank you and my apologies would have been preferable,' he muttered. 'It is done now.' Harland moved along. 'I want to visit the scene of the crimes this morning,

Gilbert, and walk the route where the three incidents took place to find spots where witnesses may have had the opportunity to see something untoward. So, I shall drop the flowers into Miss Astin and meet you at the cliffs. Have you something to attend to prior?'

'Indeed, Sir. We received a message from Father Morris that he has found Father Horan's bible and some personal items if we wish to review them. I shall collect them from him and meet you nearby.'

'Excellent,' Harland said and frowned as he collected the roses. 'One hour, I shall see you then.'

'Yes, Sir,' Gilbert said, watching his superior departing with the flowers and a look of concern on his face.

Harland bore the comments from colleagues as he walked the hallway carrying the large bouquet and the ladies' smiles as he exited the building and waited for a hansom cab to take him to *The Economic Undertaker's* office. He was relieved the ride was quick so he could not berate himself further for his poor form.

He had thought about it all evening. Why had he not seen how overwhelmed and pale she was? Miss Astin was not the type of woman who enjoyed gossip or fuss, and heavens knows what that debutante was saying in her ear all afternoon. His behaviour was inexcusable, and Julius had shown him up, coming to relieve his sister. Harland could claim he did not have sisters and, as an only child, spent most of his growing years amongst other males at boarding school. But that would be making excuses for his being off balance.

If he wanted to be seen as her protector, a man who would care for and honour Miss Astin, then he had proven to be lacking. He had failed the first test he had faced and was ungentlemanly, demonstrating his work came first. Harland realised his large hands were grasping the bouquet too tightly as a thorn dug into him, drawing blood.

'No less than I deserve,' he muttered, sucking the blood away.

Phoebe ran a hand over her clean table and checked her makeup products were in order. She smiled, happy to see it all as she liked it and happy to have her room back to herself. Daisy Dorchester was laid to rest yesterday afternoon at a small ceremony – according to her brothers – and for a brief time, Phoebe's workroom was empty of visitors. That was not to say Daisy might not return, but it was often the case that the spirits did not unless they were strong or had unfulfilled business, like Mrs Tochborn, who discovered her missing child was on the other side, and Uncle Reggie, whose unfinished business remained a mystery.

Daisy had said all she could say about her death, and there was nothing further to add. However, Phoebe did wish to speak to the detectives about Daisy's perfume recollection and to tell them of Father Damien Horan's visit. It would also give her a chance to apologise for being unable to assist them yesterday afternoon.

Unlike her friend, reporter Lilly Lewis, Phoebe did not feel the need to compete in a man's world or avoid being vulnerable. She worked her trade and felt respected; her family had always protected her. Julius, especially, was most protective and in truth, she was a little surprised he did not have more to say about her future relationships. Perhaps she had not given him any reason to be concerned. Her mind moved naturally to Bennet Martin and Harland Stone. Such different men – Bennet was clearly uncomfortable with her spirit visitations, and she imagined he would want to protect and pamper her; Phoebe would feel stifled with that type of relationship. But Harland Stone was intriguing. He seemed to respect her work, showed no fear or disdain for it, and even found her of value. She liked his strength and yet gentle manner and could not help but wonder what it would be like to be kissed by him.

She heard a light knock on the door at the top of the stairs, and legs appeared. When the subject came a few steps further down her stairs, Phoebe realised it was the man himself, Detective Harland Stone. He stopped midway, and Phoebe's heart raced. She dared hope he might think of her, but knew the competition for his attention was most likely more interesting, more social, and more beautiful... and not working in a morgue.

'Miss Astin, may I enter?'

'Of course, Detective, I was just thinking about you.' She flushed and hurriedly added as he proceeded down the stairs, 'I have some new information which I hope will make up for my poor performance yesterday.'

Surprised, Harland stopped and then hurriedly reached the bottom of the staircase, where he presented a large bouquet of cream roses to Phoebe.

'On the contrary, Miss Astin. My actions were unforgivable. I was completely focused on my work at the expense of all else, of you, and I humbly beg your forgiveness. Please accept these flowers with my apologies.'

His sincerity captured Phoebe, and she wondered if he had prepared those lines... so many, so considered, his deep brown eyes fixed upon her, his countenance sober. She smiled as she reached for them and, holding them close, inhaled their scent.

'They are beautiful and unnecessary, but I will happily accept them, thank you,' she said with a smile. 'They will brighten my room.'

'It is a decidedly well-organised room, and feminine if I may say, given its purpose,' he said, admiring Phoebe's small touches of fabric and trinkets that made the room appear warm. 'I like an orderly environment.'

'As do I,' Phoebe agreed as she reached for a large crystal vase on a shelf of her bookcase.

They heard Mrs Dobbs on the staircase advising she was on her way – as if offering a warning should they be talking about something confidential or, worse, engaged in something untoward. She appeared halfway with a tea tray, and Harland took to the stairs to assist the kindly lady.

'I heard the Detective was in, and I know you are always in a rush, but there must be time to have a quick cup of tea and a slice of my fruit cake,' she said, handing Harland the tray.

'Mrs Dobbs, thank you! I would make time. Crime can wait,' he said, making her laugh. Harland relieved her of the tray and returned, whereby the young couple sat around Phoebe's table while she poured and encouraged the detective to help himself to a slice of cake.

'I must say before we move from the subject, I feel remiss at not noticing how you were suffering yesterday,' Harland said. Phoebe could feel his eyes searching her face, and she could read the anguish of his regret. 'I am often guilty of being too work-focused, but I hoped being a gentleman might have taken precedence—'

'Please, Detective Stone,' Phoebe cut him off, 'you are too hard on yourself. It was a very busy time, people were coming and going, there was a small window of time to study thoughts and reactions, and you could not have seen how persistent and dominant Daisy was at the time. I am sure if you could, you would have acted immediately.'

'That is very kind of you to say, Miss Astin, and some small consolation for the reproach I have felt.'

'Let us not speak of it again; your apology and the beautiful roses are more than enough if you felt any apology necessary,' Phoebe said graciously. She sipped her tea, and their eyes met momentarily, nothing was said, but the silence spoke volumes. Placing her cup in the saucer, Phoebe hurried to fill the silence. 'Now, regarding your investigation, Daisy said something very interesting yesterday afternoon, if I may tell you?'

'She is not here?'

'No, thank goodness. No one is here presently, well no one dead, if you know my meaning,' she said softly and with a smile, not wanting to invite the dearly departed to join them.

Phoebe wished Julius would arrive but was just as torn, hoping he would not. The large room seemed very small with just the two of them sitting opposite each other, breathing in the same air.

'Is it always tiring?' Harland asked with genuine curiosity.

'No, it is rarely tiring. I find the living much more exhausting.'

He laughed. 'I cannot disagree with that. Reading people all day is so wearing, especially when many choose to put on a mask once they know I am the law.'

'I can only imagine,' Phoebe said sympathetically. 'Most of my guests are respectful, and many are good company. But Daisy was in death as she was in life, I imagine. Too much.'

'I would hate that to be my legacy,' Harland said with a frown, taking another bite of his fruit cake and relishing it.

'If I may be so presumptuous, I don't think anyone would ever consider either of us the domineering presence in the room,' Phoebe said.

'Maybe not in a loud way that demands attention, but if I may say in a well-meaning fashion, I find your presence in a room very distracting.'

Phoebe flushed, her emotions racing. 'Thank you. I sometimes feel as if the world is moving on and I cannot catch up, but I am content going at my own pace. That must sound terribly old-fashioned and boring.'

'On the contrary, and I know how you feel. There are advances in policing every day. Why soon, I am sure the criminals will not get away with anything, and I will be obsolete!'

'What will you do for a job then?' Phoebe teased.

'Perhaps Julius will find a job for me.'

Phoebe laughed, and they were interrupted by a visitor hurrying down the stairs.

'I heard my name mentioned. What have I done now?' Julius said with a grin, and Phoebe was sure he had been sent to act as a chaperone. Her grandfather was quite old-fashioned in that way. Harland rose, and the men shook hands.

'I was hoping that should I find myself without a career, you might offer me a job.'

'You're certainly strong enough to carry a dead body or two. I am sure we'd find work for you,' Julius said in jest, slapping him on the back as they sat themselves at the table with Phoebe.

'Fear not, I am not out of work as yet, and I have come to apologise for being so inconsiderate yesterday, not to exhaust Miss Astin further,' Harland assured Julius.

'It was not you nor the investigation that was draining, Phoebe,' Julius assured Harland with a glance at his sister. 'That persistent woman.' Julius shook his head. 'Speaking of your case, has Phoebe told you what Father Damien Horan said on his visit?'

'The deceased priest? Has he visited? But you do not have his body, do you?'

'No, but that does not stop the odd spirit dropping in, and he did for a brief while,' Phoebe said.

'We had been discussing Miss Dorchester,' Harland told Julius, 'But now you have us back on track of the investigation, please tell.'

Phoebe rose to grab a spare cup and poured Julius a tea while telling Harland of Father Damien Horan's insistence that Miss Dorchester made advances, but they were not reciprocated. 'But I have more interesting news,' she concluded.

Harland touched the supplied napkin to his mouth and placed it on the plate, satisfied.

'An excellent morning then, thus far,' he joked. 'Gilbert will be disappointed I sent him elsewhere.'

'You are very kind to him,' Phoebe said, more relaxed in Harland's company with Julius on hand. 'I have heard not all superiors are to their underlings. Julius is quite tough on us.'

She laughed at her brother's incredulous expression.

'I am wounded,' Julius said in jest, his hand on his heart, 'and I shall dock your pay for that.'

'There you have it,' Phoebe said to Harland, who grinned at the pair of them.

'I am fortunate that Gilbert is a hard-working and conscientious young man. He is a fact collector and keen to learn.'

'I am fortunate that Phoebe is an artist and agreed to lend her skills to me,' Julius said with a smile at his sister, 'even if she is disrespectful of the boss sometimes.'

Phoebe laughed and nudged him, then returned her attention to Harland.

'I do not wish to hold you up, so allow me to tell you something I hope is of significance,' she said, becoming quite serious. Harland straightened, and she knew he would be keen for any insights that might close his current, loosely linked cases. 'Daisy remembered a scent she smelled moments before being struck. She had forgotten in all the drama, but during the interviews, Daisy caught a whiff of fragrance and proclaimed that it was familiar, that it was, in fact, a scent she inhaled just before her death.'

Harland's brow furrowed as he thought. 'So, Miss Dorchester is saying it might have been a woman who struck the fatal blow, and that woman was present in the interview room yesterday?'

'Well, no. I believe men or women could wear the fragrance or carry it on their handkerchiefs. But yes, she said that the scent was present yesterday, Detective, although it may be a popular fragrance,' Phoebe said apologetically. 'Daisy said the fragrance was lingering in the room, and when she told me, Miss Melanie Bains and Miss Hilda Dickinson were present.'

'But if it were a lingering scent, and her two friends had only just departed minutes earlier, it could be anyone,' Julius surmised.

'I did not discount the fairer sex as my murderer, but I confess I was focussed on a male killer; I shall have to widen my pool. Did she say what the fragrance was, Miss Astin?'

'Hopefully, not lavender, as I know ladies widely wear it, and we use it in abundance here to mask death odours,' Julius said candidly.

Harland groaned, 'Please, not that.'

'Fear not,' Phoebe assured him, 'it was not lavender. She believed it to be a modern fragrance, a mix of which Daisy claimed included bergamot and musk.'

Harland quickly grabbed his notebook and wrote down both.

They all turned to look at the stairs as Ambrose thundered down them.

'Oh, my apologies,' he said, seeing a meeting was in progress.

'Not at all,' Harland rose. 'I have taken up enough of everyone's time.'

'Then I shall take Julius, please,' Ambrose joked. 'It is not often I have to chase you up, brother. We have collections to make.'

'There is a first time for everything,' Julius said drily, rising to see Harland out and accompany Ambrose.

Harland shook the men's hands and turned to Phoebe. 'Miss Astin, your help has been invaluable yet again. Please leave this with me,' he said, 'I am on the hunt for a scent.'

# Chapter 23

DESPITE BEING EARLY SPRING and traditionally a warm time in Brisbane, it was a chilly breeze that whipped up from the cliff and had Gilbert Payne and Father Morris stepping back from the edge.

'Two deaths and an attack all within a short distance of each other, you say?' Father Morris asked.

Gilbert nodded. 'Most peculiar, and this morning we will retrace the path of the crimes. Who is to say what might come to mind. Ah, here is Detective Stone now.'

They turned to see Harland hurrying towards them and apologising for his delay. 'I was forced to stop and eat a superb slice of Mrs Dobbs' fruit cake,' he explained.

'It's important to keep the ladies happy,' Father Morris agreed with a laugh.

'Do not fear, Gilbert, I have procured you a slice,' he said, patting his pocket and earning a grin from the young detective.

'Most thoughtful, Sir.'

'But you have to earn it,' Harland said with a hint of mystery. 'I have some information I hope your fact-storing mind might sort out for me presently.'

Gilbert grinned. 'I shall take that assignment, Sir.'

Harland turned to the priest of St Patrick's Church. 'Father, I am glad you are here, I hoped to speak with you. Thank you for Father Horan's possessions,' he said, noticing the bundle under Gilbert's arm.

'You are welcome. So, you've decided to start coming to mass?' he teased.

'No. But your optimism is admirable,' Harland said with a smile, and Father Morris chuckled.

'I thought my prayers had been answered,' the priest said with a chuckle. 'What can I help you with and if I can, I shall happily.'

'Thank you. We are interested in several people, and I hoped you might shed some light on their character. I believe some are from your parish.'

The three men moved further away from the cliff, stopping in a small pavilion out of the wind while they spoke.

'Mr Eldon Foster, the deceased Miss Daisy Dorchester, and her debutante acquaintances.' Harland mentioned the two young ladies who claimed to be Daisy's friends and the other two ladies attending Daisy's viewing out of duty, Miss Melanie Bains and Miss Hilda Dickinson.

Father Morris nodded. 'I have come and gone from this parish over the years, but I can speak of several of the people you mentioned. However, I cannot provide any confidences spoken of in the confessional, of course.'

'Of course,' Gilbert said on behalf of both detectives.

'But observations would also be welcomed,' Harland said, hoping to take advantage of the man's perception.

Father Morris smiled at him. 'My observations would not compare to those of you two astute detectives. Mine tend to be about saving their souls.'

'I'll take them anyway, in confidence,' Harland said, assuring the priest of his discretion and inviting him to begin.

'Let's see,' Father Morris began. 'Eldon has been part of the parish since he was a child and was always a good lad. I think it is fair to say he has a healthy respect and fear of his father, and his mother is somewhat overbearing. I was not a supporter of his proposed union with Miss Dorchester. I believed them to be most unsuited and could not see it ending well. It did not.'

'Do you think him capable of harming anyone?' Harland asked.

'Namely Miss Dorchester herself? No. I know he would have met his duty, and they would have led separate lives, which is a great shame when a couple should be able to enjoy the pleasure of each other's company and the comfort and support provided by their matrimonial bond.'

Gilbert immediately thought of Miss Emily Yalden; he could imagine many enjoyable discussions and happy compliance in household matters. He glanced at his superior and wondered if Detective Stone thought the same of Miss Astin. He could not tell with the Detective's reserved look.

'Miss Dorchester, I barely knew,' Father Morris continued, running a hand through his thick mane of fair hair smattered with grey. 'She attended mass with her aunt, but her visitations coincided with Father Damien's time here, more so than mine. I confess I uncharitably found her affected with vanity.'

'As she was, sadly,' Harland agreed.

'We have heard the same said by many people,' Gilbert offered the priest to ease his conscience.

'I do not know of the two young ladies you say were close to her; I don't believe they are of this parish, nor was Miss Hilda Dickinson, but I do know her. Hilda is a gifted singer and has occasionally come to work with our choir. She has the voice of an angel.'

'But a horse-like laugh, according to an uncharitable comment from Miss Dorchester,' Gilbert said.

'I personally enjoy laughter of any manner but cannot recall being alarmed by Miss Dickinson's laugh,' Father Morris said. 'She is a quiet young lady, kind and patient, and believe me, some of the choir members would try the patience of Saint Christopher himself.'

The men smiled at his saintly reference.

Harland nodded. 'You do not believe Miss Dickinson could be driven to anger, to murder?'

'Goodness no,' Father Morris said alarmed and then laughed at the thought. 'Now, that would ruin my faith in humanity.'

'What about Miss Melanie Bains?' Harland asked, playing his last card and enquiring about the tallest and strongest of the women in the party.

'I know Melanie very well,' Father Morris said and smiled. 'Melanie has been a congregation member since she was young and was close to Eldon as children in our youth prayer group.'

'How close?' Harland asked and saw Father Morris's mind make the connection. The priest pursed his lips for a moment, thinking.

'It would be fair to say Melanie considers him a dear friend and is very protective of him, often defending him and always choosing to sit nearby him. Melanie brought Hilda along at the recent dance, and the young ladies spent some time in Eldon's company until Miss Dorchester arrived.'

'Do you think Eldon had feelings for Miss Bains?' Gilbert asked, understanding his superior's line of questioning, and wondering if perhaps Eldon Foster and Melanie Bains conspired to remove the obstacle to their love. But Father Morris diluted that theory.

'No. Eldon was never the first to seek out Melanie's company.'

They all turned at the sight of a man walking along the cliff.

'Ah, it is the private investigator, Bennet Martin,' Harland informed Father Morris. 'I thank you, Father, your insights have been extremely useful.'

'Well, I am pleased for that,' he said. 'Don't forget, there is always a glass of port and a sympathetic ear awaiting should either of you need it, and whether you like it or not, I shall keep you both in my prayers.'

'I would like that very much, thank you, Father,' Gilbert said.

'And it can't hurt where I'm concerned,' Harland said, giving the priest a quick grin.

Mid-morning, a little less than two hours since the Astin men had departed, the back door of *The Economic Undertaker* swung open, and Ambrose yelled from the door, 'Grandpa, there's been an accident.'

Randolph Astin moved with a speed that belied his age, his eyes falling on his eldest grandson being helped in by Ambrose and a stable hand.

'It is nothing,' Julius said calmly, watching as the panic unfolded around him.

Randolph called at the top of his lungs, 'Mrs Dobbs, Phoebe, we need help.'

Julius rolled his eyes. 'Do not trouble yourself, Grandpa; it is nothing, a flesh wound only.'

'It is not nothing,' Ambrose said, concern overriding his usual sunny countenance. 'We were attacked.'

'It was hardly an attack,' Julius said. 'We were collecting a body, and several angry family members were fighting with the hospital wardsmen over the release of the deceased.'

'That is appalling. You were stabbed? How did this come about? Could you not have left the body?' Randolph asked, taking over the stable lad's position as they helped Julius up the long hallway from the back of the building to the front rooms.

'Oh, my goodness,' Mrs Dobbs said, rushing in from the kitchen and seeing the blood seeping through Julius's white shirt. 'I shall get hot water and towels.'

'Julius!' Phoebe exclaimed, running into the hallway, her eyes wide with alarm. 'What happened?' She raced ahead of them into their meeting room and cleared the couch of cushions and effects for Julius to be lowered onto it.

'We were attacked,' Ambrose said.

'We were caught in a melee, a family feud. It is nothing, Phoebe, do not distress yourself,' Julius said, his words short and abrupt between sharp breaths. 'I need but a couple of sutures, and all will be well,' he assured her.

'We were loading the body when one of the men began to shove the hospital wardsmen. A boy swung with a knife, and Julius decided to stand in front of me and the wardsman,' Ambrose said.

'Ambrose, fetch the doctor,' Phoebe said, rising hurriedly. 'Grandpa, should we call for a constable or the detective as well?'

'I didn't stand in front of him, and do not call the doctor,' Julius continued, his voice the only calm one amongst the panic. 'Nor do we need the constabulary. It was an accident, a family distressed, and the lad swinging the knife was just protecting his father's body.'

'You are very caring to say so, Julius, but—' Randolph stopped mid-speech to grab at Julius's arm as he swayed. 'See, it is worse than you believe.'

Julius removed his hand from the wound as he was lowered onto the couch, and hands hurriedly removed his jacket despite his best efforts to ward them off.

'What became of the family?' Randolph asked, lifting Julius's shirt, his breath hitching. 'This is a wide wound, lad.'

'The boy was alarmed and ran off when he saw he had cut Julius. He left his mother and sister there, crying. There were two more men, I believe to be brothers of the deceased, and they were fighting with the widow. The wardsmen went inside, abandoning the body, and we exited the scene. Julius would not let me take him into the hospital,' Ambrose explained, 'he had the reins.'

'Stop fussing, Julius and sit still,' Phoebe ordered as she thanked Mrs Dobbs for the towels and hot water.

'Yes, sit still!' Ambrose added and saw the glare his brother gave him. 'I do not get to tell you what to do very often, brother, so I do not want to miss the opportunity,' he said in jest.

Before Julius realised what was happening, Phoebe applied some anaesthetic to his cut, startling him into profanity. Ambrose laughed, and Phoebe hid a smile.

Julius gathered himself and said through gritted teeth, 'Forgive me, Mrs Dobbs, Phoebe, I was caught by surprise.'

'Goodness, the last time I heard language like that was when my husband worked on the railway,' Mrs Dobbs said with a wink.

'There's a good fallback career for you, Julius,' Ambrose said. 'My brother, a navvy at heart.'

'Helpful as always, Ambrose,' his grandfather said, returning with the medical box and chided him with a grin. 'Could you fetch the doctor.' He held up his hands. 'Do not protest, Julius. I am sure Phoebe can stitch you, but I want to be sure your injury is not serious.'

'Will Julius be all right without me?' Ambrose asked, raising an eyebrow in his brother's direction.

'I will struggle on,' Julius assured him, and Ambrose departed down the hallway and out the back to take any available horse or cart. Voices were heard as the back door opened, and Mrs Nellie

Shaw from the dressmaking store next door hurried in, catching Mrs Dobbs in the hallway, their conversation easily overhead.

'Mrs Dobbs, we heard Ambrose say there had been an accident. Oh, dear me, is that blood?' Mrs Shaw said, spotting a bloodied item in Mrs Dobbs' hands.

'The boys met a disgruntled family when they attempted to collect a body from the hospital morgue. Julius was stabbed, but he is strong and claims it is only a flesh wound.'

'Can I go for a doctor?'

Julius groaned on hearing the comment, and Randolph hushed him.

'You are too kind, Mrs Shaw, but Ambrose has gone.'

He could not hear what else was said as Phoebe spoke, but footsteps indicated both ladies had moved away.

'I will leave the suturing to the doctor if he arrives soon enough,' Phoebe said, cleaning the wound.

'No, you do it, Phoebe, please. Get it done and over with,' Julius said, moving to a sitting position.

She nodded, rising. 'I have some silk thread; I shall be back.'

'Just rest and stay still, lad,' Randolph said calmly. 'We will get this sorted.'

Julius momentarily closed his eyes; he felt hot then clammy and did not want to admit to it or worry his family.

The door opened again, and footsteps hurried down the hall, too light to be that of Ambrose. Miss Violet Forrester rushed in, her face etched with fear.

Julius rushed to cover himself; he was not comfortable being vulnerable to anyone, let alone underdressed in the presence of ladies.

'Julius! Mr Astin,' she said, looking to Randolph and back to Julius. 'It is true then,' she said, dropping beside Julius and placing her hand on his forehead as if he were a child and she, his nurse. She had undoubtedly done the same for her brother, Tom, many times.

'You are a little feverish.'

He wanted to lean into her hand, but she was right, he felt unbalanced. He could feel her eyes searching his face, and her own was full of concern; Violet had lost so many, he could sense her fear.

'Ambrose has gone for the doctor and Phoebe for the thread to commence the sutures,' Randolph assured her. 'Miss Forrester, would you please stay with Julius while I fetch a constable? Pressure needs to be maintained on his wound, and the wad replaced if needed. Mrs Dobbs or Phoebe will be back momentarily.'

'Of course, Mr Astin,' Violet assured him, 'I shall not leave his side.'

Julius grimaced, preferring for the woman he loved not to see him this way. He had mastered the art of hiding his feelings, but the pain and his weakened state had made him more vulnerable.

And as Randolph departed and they found themselves alone, she added, 'I shall not leave your side ever again, if you will have me?'

# Chapter 24

THE DETECTIVES WALKED TO where Bennet Martin waited, not intruding on their meeting. Harland noted the private investigator seemed despondent, his usual surety replaced by rounded shoulders, a wistful look on his serious countenance. Harland wondered if Bennet wanted for anything despite his break away from his wealthy family to carve his own way in Australia. The man was not struggling when he kept a townhouse and two staff on hand. Good luck to him, Harland thought, never one to begrudge anyone their good fortune.

He considered Bennet's interest in Miss Phoebe Astin. The thought of another man stealing her heart did not sit well with him. But did Bennet truly understand and care for Miss Astin, or did her beauty captivate him? There was nothing amiss with that, Harland acknowledged, many relationships were based on less and

Miss Astin was beautiful. But she was also unique; those elements of her nature – her quietness, strength, spirit, and no dependence on society – made him believe they were kindred souls. She was also the most beautiful woman in his acquaintanceship, and he wanted to be the man privileged with caring for her.

'Good morning, Harland, Detective Payne, I've come to see the crime scene,' Bennet informed them.

'Good morning, Bennet, as have we, again. We are going to walk between the three incidents. Do you wish to accompany us?' Harland asked, and Bennet nodded.

'Thank you, I would appreciate that.'

The men descended the path and stairs to where Father Damien Horan's body was found.

'Do you have anything useful to share?' Gilbert asked, his eyes lit with hope.

Bennet gave a small shrug. 'I am sorry to say that I have barely started investigating. I am most unmotivated, I have to confess.'

'Then you are in the right place for a confession,' Gilbert said matter-of-factly as the church behind them bore down on them, and Bennet smiled at the young detective's humour.

'Are you not well? Has something happened?' Harland enquired, looking momentarily over his shoulder at the investigator and feeling obligated to ask.

'Thank you for your concern, but nothing that I won't recover from in time,' Bennet said and sighed most dramatically.

Harland did not push any further as his friendship with Bennet Martin was relatively new and only as a consequence of their connection to Julius. Harland did not believe Bennet would be a friend he would seek out without their common acquaintance.

'I would welcome anything you might share with me,' Bennet said, 'however, if you do catch the perpetrator, then my services are rendered null and void, so I am content not knowing.'

'You are indeed in the doldrums, Mr Martin, if you hope we solve the case before you are paid your compensation,' Gilbert observed as they moved down to the first landing of the cliffs.

'A matter of the heart,' the fair-haired man said in a low voice for Gilbert's ears only. 'I hear you are a poet; you will understand.'

Harland overheard and suspected he knew the cause of Bennet's doldrums, but Gilbert's reaction to being called a poet made the senior detective smile.

'I am an admirer of poetry but could not be described as a poet by any stretch of the imagination, Mr Martin, but thank you for the title and aspiration. I hope to rise to it one day.'

Nearing the base, Harland stopped, and the men drew around him. 'So, this is where Father Damien Horan was found. The coroner believes from the extent of his wounds that he did not slip on the stairs nearby but fell from the top.'

Gilbert frowned. 'Sir, it appears so. If he were to slip, there are plenty of handholds – trees, a railing – that he could have grabbed to have broken his fall. But if he fell or was pushed from the top, there is a reasonable freefall area.'

'Agreed, Gilbert,' Harland said, studying the area. 'It is also hard to fall from the top. It may look like a great height, but it is flat ground, and there is nothing to slip on.'

'Hello down there,' a female voice called, and all three men looked up to see reporter Miss Lilly Lewis at the top of the cliff stairs, looking refreshed in the cool morning air, her cheeks flushed, eyes bright and her enthusiasm obvious. 'May I join you?'

'We are on our way back up now, Miss Lewis,' Harland said, taking a few more moments to study the area before he began his ascent, Gilbert and Bennet in his trail.

'Well, what good timing,' she beamed on their arrival at the top and laughed at Harland's less-than-enthusiastic greeting. 'Come now, Detective, I have been playing by your rules; for all you know, I might have information.'

'Good morning, Miss Lewis, and do you? Have information, that is?' Harland smiled at her.

'No, I don't believe so,' she admitted. 'I was speaking with Father Morris about Father Horan, and he mentioned you were here. How opportune.'

'Indeed,' Harland said drily.

'You can help us re-enact our scene of the crime,' Gilbert suggested and gave an apologetic look to his superior when Harland looked less than pleased.

'Oh, that sounds fascinating, I would love to do so.' Lilly gave a small shiver in her functional long navy skirt and white blouse.

'Allow me,' Bennet said, removing his jacket and draping it over her shoulders.

'How kind and chivalrous, Mr Martin,' Lilly said. 'There is quite a cool breeze here.'

'You can repay that kindness by pretending to push Bennet off the cliff,' Harland suggested, 'in our reenactment, of course.'

'I am always happy to give a hansom gentleman a good nudge in the right direction,' Lilly teased, and Bennet grinned.

'I will do my best to fall at your feet, Miss Lewis,' Bennet teased, and Harland observed the smiles they exchanged; they were flirting, and he was right. Bennet was a man of some vanity and would feel better for having it stroked; the fair-haired English man with the silver spoon in his mouth looked brighter for it. Harland conceded that could be a very good thing.

'So, I am to be Father Horan, and a good push is required to topple me over the edge?' Bennet looked at the drop below.

'Yes. And an unsuspecting push might give the offender the upper hand, especially if it were from the weaker sex,' Harland said.

Gilbert looked to his superior. 'You know something, Sir, hence the questions about the relationship between Mr Foster and Miss Bains.'

'A theory, perhaps, but I am not discounting anyone at this stage,' Harland nodded. 'Let us say that Bennet, as Father Damien

Horan, has just accepted a lock of hair from Miss Daisy Dorchester and sent her on her way. Will you be so kind as to stand here, Bennet?'

Moving hurriedly into place, Bennet stood on the edge of the precipice, and Harland continued.

'If my hunch is correct, Miss Dorchester departed after being slighted, and Father Horan may have stayed here to pray or reflect, turning to face the view.'

'I will lift up mine eyes unto the hills, from whence cometh my help,' Gilbert said, and Harland raised an eyebrow in his direction.

'From the Bible, King James Version, Sir.'

'Interesting,' Harland said, never sure when Gilbert's facts might be useful. 'As for suspects...' he saw Miss Lewis keenly prepare to write down names and issued his usual warning that she was not to print them without his knowledge.

'Cross my heart, Detective,' she said.

Harland continued. 'Let's imagine a number of scenarios. First, Eldon Foster, a jealous husband-to-be, may have witnessed the scene and confronted Father Horan. He claims to have been nowhere near St Patrick's, which is questionable. Second, Miss Melanie Bains saw Father accept the lock of hair and was angry at the disrespect shown by Miss Dorchester to her good friend Eldon Foster, and appalled at the weakness of Father Horan. Thus, she confronted the priest. Or finally, Theodore Wright, keen to defend his friend's honour, saw the interaction between Miss Dorchester and Father Horan and acted to defend his friend.'

'Whoever the viewing party was, their motive might be jealousy or disgust,' Gilbert said, summarising the passions of the crime. 'A man of the cloth and the woman who is supposedly betrothed to Mr Eldon Foster involved in a liaison.'

'Would they be outraged enough to kill?' Bennet mused. 'Although people have killed for less.'

'Indeed,' Harland agreed.

'I believe Melanie Bains is in love with Mr Foster,' Lilly said, 'that is what Father Morris implied.'

'I agree, Miss Lewis,' Harland said, 'which makes her a vengeful suspect.'

'So, the culprit acts out of passion,' Bennet joins in. 'I noted at the viewing that Miss Bains was tall, but I doubt she would have the strength to fight and push the priest off the edge. The two gentlemen would have no issue doing so.'

'And may have fought with Father Damien Horan before he fell, hence the marks around his neck,' Gilbert said, referring to the post-mortem.

'Very possible,' Harland said. 'But if it was Miss Bains, she must have used the element of surprise as, despite her height, she would be no match for Father Horan's strength. Let us say that she viewed all this from afar and, in anger and disgust, approached him from behind and pushed Father Horan before he realised what was happening,' Harland said. 'Miss Lewis, can you approach Bennet as quietly and quickly as possible? Bennet, could you remain facing the view and tell me when you are aware of Miss Lewis's approach.'

Bennet nodded. 'The grassy mound and noise of the wind will certainly go a long way to masking the sound of an approaching person.'

Positions were taken, and Lilly had her hands on Bennet's back before he realised her presence, swinging around and slightly losing his balance.

'Ah, there you have it. That is how it may have played out if our murderer was a woman,' Harland said. 'So that might have been one way Father Horan met his death, or perhaps they were talking as friends, and he was relaxed, unsuspecting when the culprit was quick to anger and push him.'

'But that still leaves us with three likely suspects at this stage,' Gilbert said. 'Let us continue along the path. If our culprit saw Miss Dorchester and Father Horan, they might have wished to meter the same punishment on Miss Dorchester and gone in search of her.'

'Agreed, Gilbert,' Harland said.

Miss Lewis shrugged off the jacket as they walked to the next crime scene.

'Thank you, kind Sir,' she said, returning it to Bennet and refusing his arm. 'I am warmer now away from the cliffs and shall manage quite well.' She strode on, catching up with Harland, who thought she might have succumbed to Bennet's charms, but instead, she fired questions at him.

'Detective, so you are convinced there is a link between the priest's murder and Miss Dorchester's demise?'

'Yes.'

'Can I report that?'

Harland thought for a moment. 'Yes, I cannot see any harm in doing so. The clergy are aware we believe his death to be suspicious.'

'Do you think they were involved?'

'No, I believe Father Damien Horan was a man true to his faith.'

'Was Miss Dorchester trying to corrupt him?'

'I cannot speak for her mindset.'

'Her aunt told me that Miss Dorchester hoped to get married here in St Patrick's and was soon to be engaged to the gentleman you mentioned before, a Mr...,' she looked at her notes, 'Eldon Foster, one of your suspects.'

'That is also my understanding.'

'Here is another theory: could she have killed Father Horan when he refuted her advances and then took her own life out of despair?'

'It is possible, but—' Harland hesitated, not wishing to admit he had discounted that theory because of Miss Astin's discussion with the deceased.

Gilbert spoke up, 'Her manner of death was consistent with an attack, and there are easier ways to take one's own life. She could have thrown herself from the cliff after doing the same to Father Horan.'

'I agree, Gilbert,' Harland said and added for Lilly Lewis's benefit. 'From all my interviews, I believe the young lady's vanity would have precluded her from feeling that her life was of no consequence if slighted.'

'Yes, I could not agree more,' Lilly said and stepped back, realising the detective had stopped at a small inlet designed to encourage viewers to stop and admire the view. Gilbert joined him, and Bennet Martin studied the area.

'Is this relevant?' Bennet asked.

'This is where Mr Theodore Wright was found, alive, but assaulted. Why and by whom?' Harland asked. 'He claims to have not seen who struck him, but it was a reasonable blow that felled him.'

'Sir, there are loose rocks around the edges of this inlet. They are decorative, I believe, but they could easily be picked up and used as a weapon,' Gilbert said, and both men dropped to their knees and lifted each rock.

'This one has a dark stain, Sir; it might be blood,' Gilbert said, showing his superior.

'Excellent work, Gilbert.' Harland pulled out a handkerchief and wrapped it around the rock, handing it back to Gilbert.

After checking the remaining rocks, they rose, brushed off and continued to the final location.

'Who is this, Mr Wright? I know so little of him other than what you have mentioned?' Lilly asked, and Gilbert explained the relationship between Mr Wright and Mr Eldon.

Bennet thought out loud as they walked to the next crime scene – the cemetery on the edge of the church grounds and the death place of Miss Daisy Dorchester.

'They are both crimes that could have been committed by a man or a strong, determined woman,' he mused. 'A push down the cliff, a strike with a rock... or committed by two people. Lovers? Perhaps the theory of Eldon Foster and Miss Melanie Bains clearing the path to their future together is not so unlikely? Although I did follow him after Miss Dorchester's viewing and saw Miss Bains hurrying to catch up to him. There was no obvious ardour. In fact, he put Miss Bains and her friend in a hansom cab fairly quickly.'

'Father Morris believes they have a friendship, but the devotion is one way,' Gilbert said, 'Sir, your thoughts?'

'My thoughts exactly, Gilbert,' Harland agreed. He sighed and continued leading the party to the next location.

They left the gardens surrounding St Patrick's church and entered the small nearby cemetery, making their way to the grave where Daisy Dorchester was found dead under the watchful eye of a large angel statue. The inscription on the grave reads: "The truth will set you free."

'The verse is actually " You will know the truth, and the truth will set you free", Sir,' Gilbert said. 'It is from the Bible... so perhaps we are meant to know the truth of her deception. If the culprit is God-fearing, they will know the verse.'

'Eldon Foster and Miss Melanie Bains are certainly that after years of church attendance,' Harland said, studying the grave. 'Again, we have a victim struck from behind, but the blow was fatal this time.'

'Is the location significant?' Lilly asked, brushing away dirt and vines to read the name on the headstone. 'It is the grave of a lady named Constance Kemp, a young woman aged twenty.'

'We can only surmise,' Harland said. 'Perhaps this grave and the deceased within it is significant or just a grave of convenience for the attack.'

'I shall find out, Sir,' Gilbert said, writing down the name and dates from the tombstone. 'Father Morris may remember the lady and can tell us more.'

Harland nodded as he thought. 'We have one more clue.' All eyes turned to Harland as he addressed his fellow detective. 'Hence, the challenge for you that requires some understanding of facts and fragrances.'

'Ah, the puzzle that I must solve to earn my slice of fruit cake,' Gilbert said with a grin. 'I will do my best, Sir.'

'A scent or fragrance featuring bergamot and musk. Do you know of one?'

'That is a modern fragrance, Sir,' Gilbert said.

Harland raised an eyebrow, surprised as he exclaimed, 'That is what Miss Astin said.'

'You have seen her?' Bennet asked, too quickly as to betray his emotions.

'Today, with Julius. Miss Astin had some information to share.' Harland moved on quickly, 'What do you know of it then, Gilbert?'

'I read that modern fragrances blend several essences, Sir, but unfortunately for our investigation, gentlemen and ladies both wear bergamot and musk. The men's fragrance pairs bergamot with musk or cedar for a crisp scent, and the ladies' fragrance also uses musk but may use other scents.'

'That is very true, Detective Payne,' Bennet spoke up. 'I wear Bergamot with musk.'

'Then we should inhale you, Mr Martin,' Lilly suggested, 'so we recognise the scent.'

'Unfortunately, it does not help narrow down our suspects. In fact, all three could be wearing the fragrance Miss Dorchester identified to Miss Astin, not to mention the young ladies who claimed to be her friend.' Harland fished in his pocket and handed over a package of cake. 'You have earned it.'

Gilbert smiled. 'Thank you, Sir. Do not despair, at least we do have suspects.'

'True,' Harland said. 'Miss Lewis, will you do something for me?'

'Of course, Detective.'

'Will you ask for witnesses who may have seen Miss Dorchester, Father Horan or Mr Wright on that fateful day to present themselves to the station.'

'You may be inundated,' Bennet warned.

'We can only hope,' Harland said as Gilbert pocketed his slice of cake and agreed that would not be such a bad situation to find themselves in.

# Chapter 25

J ULIUS CAUGHT A GLIMPSE of Mrs Dobbs at the door, but she disappeared just as quickly, leaving the two young people alone for a moment.

'Miss Forrester,' Julius began filling the silence in the room. He grimaced with pain as he moved slightly to speak with her.

'Do not move, Mr Astin... Julius,' she said, dabbing his forehead with a wet cloth.

'I assure you, I am quite well, Violet. Do not be concerned,' he said softly, although he was not convinced of that himself but did his best to persuade her.

'On the contrary, you are pale, and I suspect you have lost quite a bit of blood on the bumpy ride back here. It would have been best if you had allowed your brother to assist you into the hospital,' she scolded.

He gave a small smile, accepting her reprimand, but had to close his eyes again as a feeling of faintness overtook him.

*Good God*, he thought to himself, *first stabbed, now the woman I love sees me being pathetic. Could this day get any worse? Still, it is better me than Ambrose, and I am alive.*

'Julius!'

'What?' his eyes sprung open, alarmed as Phoebe stood over him, Violet on her knees beside him, and his grandfather pacing in the hallway.

'Oh, sorry, I thought you were unconscious, I have been trying to wake you. This may hurt.'

'Then you should not have woken me,' he said testily.

'You might have struck me if you awoke at the feeling of a needle piercing you,' Phoebe said.

'Very true, it is best you did, Phoebe,' Julius conceded. 'Violet, please do not stay to see this. I may use profanity.'

Violet smiled. 'I am not so delicate, Julius,' she said, which engaged a smile from Phoebe as she studied them both. 'I shall assist Phoebe if she will let me?'

'I welcome that,' Phoebe said. 'We will clean the wound again.' She offered the pad and alcohol to Violet. 'Brace yourself, brother.'

Julius held his breath, closed his eyes and let Phoebe push him back onto the cushions as she commenced her work.

'I fear he is pale and may have lost a lot of blood,' Violet whispered.

'As do I,' Phoebe said. 'The doctor will be here shortly, I hope. Julius is so stubborn he will not admit to feeling weakened.'

'I can hear you,' he muttered through gritted teeth, keeping his eyes closed and not wanting to see the pitying look on Violet's face or his sister performing her stitching.

'He may need a saline solution,' Violet said. 'My father had one after a bad accident at work when he bled profusely.'

'Did it help?' Phoebe asked.

'Well, it did not hinder him; he may have become more serious, less sweet of nature,' Violet said in jest.

'It would be impossible for Julius to become more serious,' Phoebe said, 'so it may have the opposite effect.'

'Still here and in possession of all my faculties, serious or not,' he added again for their benefit, making both girls chuckle.

'That is lovely work, Phoebe,' Violet said. 'Better than some of our stitching,' she teased.

'Perhaps we can exhibit my brother and his scar for business purposes,' Phoebe suggested.

Julius's lips twitched in a smile. 'You are both merciless.'

'There, I have finished,' Phoebe declared.

'Thank you, both,' Julius said, sighing, and opened his eyes to examine the work.

'Goodness, you are pale; it is quite disarming,' Violet said again, touching his face and causing him to shiver. He had ached for this woman, wanted her with a passion he had never felt before, and now that she had said she was his, he could do nothing about it for the moment.

'There are no other cuts, are there Julius?' Phoebe asked, breaking into his thoughts, running her hands over his shoulders and neck and looking at his arms.

'Phoebe, cease, there are no other cuts. It was a lad wielding a knife in a moment of panic. A flesh wound; it was unfortunate I was in the way. Stop,' he ordered between clenched teeth. She stopped, but not without giving him a frown.

'Here is the doctor,' Violet announced, pleased on seeing Ambrose through the window with a man carrying a doctor's bag in close pursuit. 'I shall leave you.'

Julius caught her hand and held it for a few moments before releasing it and giving in to the doctor, who dismissed all from the room except Ambrose, who insisted on staying.

Phoebe returned quite distressed to her room down the stairs; Violet accompanied her, as did Randolph.

'What if it is more serious than Julius is telling us,' Phoebe said, 'you know he cannot take sympathy and what if he has lost too much blood.'

Violet's hand was on her heart, her breathing hitched.

'He is in good hands and was very alert,' Randolph assured them. 'I have seen these injuries before, in my younger years, and I think with good care, we have no cause for concern.'

Violet exhaled, releasing the breath she was holding. 'That is comforting, Mr Astin. I best return to my ladies next door. Will you keep me informed?'

'Of course,' Phoebe said and gave a small start. 'Daisy is back.'

'The grave.'

'I beg your pardon, Daisy? What was that?' Phoebe asked.

'The grave,' she said again and disappeared.

'She is gone and said but two words – "the grave". What could that mean? Her grave, the grave where she struck her head and died?' Phoebe gave a small shrug. 'It is not my concern now until the doctor declares Julius shall be all right.'

The bell went upstairs, and Randolph glanced up the stairs. 'I shall see to that.'

'I shall accompany you and return to my work,' Violet said and giving Phoebe a quick hug, the small group disbanded.

The two ladies – Miss Mary Pollard and Mrs Nellie Shaw – were relieved to see Violet as she entered the *In Mourning – Attire for the Family* dressmaking business. They stopped their work, peppering her with questions.

'Oh, Miss, is Mr Astin hurt? So many people are coming and going next door,' Mary said with a good view of the entrance door of *The Economic Undertaker* from her desk.

'How is our beloved manager, Violet dear? Please tell me he is not harmed?'

Violet nodded, taking in their questions, and slipped into her chair.

'He claims it is a minor flesh wound inflicted by a lad trying to stop his uncles from taking the boy's father's body away. I understand the mother and boy wanted him buried in the cemetery, and the uncles wanted him returned to the family land.'

'How terrible, the poor wife and son,' Mrs Shaw said, 'and at such a distressing time. But is it only a small cut?'

'It is wide but hopefully not deep. Phoebe says Julius would not admit to being in pain or feeling weak. He looked very pale and was a little feverish. Thank goodness the doctor is there.'

'Did he have sutures, Miss?' Mary asked.

'Yes, Phoebe did them with silk, which she told me is being used widely these days. She did a very good job.'

Nellie sighed with relief. 'Goodness, what a state of affair. Were you able to assist, dear?' she asked as subtly as possible.

Violet gave a small smile. 'He allowed me to do so, Nellie. I am much relieved.'

Nellie nodded and gave her a knowing smile. 'I did not doubt it for a moment. Now, do you have a good vegetable broth recipe? I believe it can work wonders for healing.'

# Chapter 26

LILLY LEWIS THANKED THE detectives at the conclusion of their morning investigation as Bennet Martin hailed a hansom. Addressing Lilly, he asked, 'May I offer you a lift back to your newspaper premises? It is not far off route for me.'

'Yes, you may,' she said, her face lighting up. 'That would be appreciated as the afternoon is bearing upon us, and I have much to write for a pressing deadline.'

The detectives departed on foot as a hansom pulled up, and Lilly accepted Bennet's hand and settled into the cab. Lilly straightened her skirt and patted down her brunette hair after the windy morning by the cliff.

'Your job must be very exciting at times,' Bennet said, sitting opposite and studying her with the eye of an artist as their ride got on its way. Lilly believed him to be sincere in his comment.

'It all depends on having the right story to report, and at the moment, Fergus and I are in the editor's favour. I imagine it is the same with you, Mr Martin, that the quality of your job depends on your client. But I guess you can be selective about which cases you take, whereas I must fight for each story.'

'I take my hat off to you then, Miss Lewis. Given the calibre of your stories to date, you have fought well, they were very impressive indeed,' he said, flattering her again. He mused on his own predicament. 'Yes, I can pick and choose to some degree, but I do have staff to support, so I must bear that in mind.'

'Oh,' she said, surprised, 'forgive me. I thought you were... well, entitled.'

He laughed, and she smiled, enchanted by how handsome he looked, as most women would be. He was a very appealing man, his appearance enhanced by his British accent and expensive tailoring.

'I am entitled, I suppose, but I am cut off. Well, not entirely. My mother fears I will starve to death, so she sends financial support unbeknown to my father, and while he threatens to disinherit me completely, he will not do so.' Bennet gave a confident smile. 'It is a ruse to get me to return home and take up work with the London police.'

'And why does that not appeal to you? You clearly have some talent in the area of investigation.'

'Thank you. But fundamentally, I am an artist at heart, and that is the occupation I seek. Besides, I like living here, I have no intentions of returning.'

'I see.' Lilly said and winced as a carriage passed by too close for her liking and, teasing him, asked, 'Won't your father be angry should you choose an Australian bride and never return to the motherland?'

'No doubt.'

'Very wilful, Mr Martin. I do admire that.'

'Well, that is heartening. Perhaps I am not an entitled bore after all?' he said with a raised eyebrow and expectation of her refute.

'Hmm.' Cocking her head to the side, she considered him. Bennet presented as pressed and polished, not a hair out of place, with refinement and an air of arrogance oozing from every pore. He was like no one she knew – her brothers were rather rough and tumble – only one was undertaking formal studies, and the rest had taken a trade like her father. While the Lewis family lived comfortably, they were middle class at best. The man she most admired, Julius, was more handsome, in her opinion and not arrogant but rather aloof. Knowing Phoebe was not interested in pursuing a romance with the man before her now, Lilly wondered what kind of woman drew his attention. She was, after all, quite different from Phoebe, physically and by nature.

Bennet laughed at her expression. 'Are you trying to get the measure of me, Miss Lewis?'

'I am hardly in a position to judge you, Mr Martin, nor do you care what I think, I imagine.'

'Oh, on the contrary,' he said, smiling most charmingly.

'I am sure that smile works on many ladies, Mr Martin, but I am spicier than most,' she rebuked him, which he seemed to enjoy. 'You are very different from most men I know and work with, including my five brothers.'

'Five brothers!' he exclaimed. 'Good gracious. Will they all wish to approve of any brave man who comes to call?'

'Without a doubt, especially as I am the family's only girl. Does the thought strike fear into your heart?' Lilly asked with a laugh.

'No, caution more so than fear,' he chuckled. 'I imagine your parents are keen for you to make a good match.'

'My father despairs that I won't since I am running around reporting on murders,' she said and sighed. 'Perhaps that is off-putting for a gentleman.'

'I can't imagine why. If a man is threatened by an intelligent lady who seeks stimulation of her mind, the fault is his.'

Lilly huffed. 'Really, Mr Martin, you surprise me again. I thought you would surely favour a dainty little lady who would run your household and dote on you.'

'I would certainly like my future wife to dote on me,' he said and smiled at her, 'but I've been known to paint for days on end, and the idea of having a wife with her own passion that is not reliant on me to be her source of company around the clock has much appeal. You, too, Miss Lewis, are quite different from the ladies of my acquaintance, with the exception of Miss Astin, of course.'

'How so?'

'They simper and preen and put forward their best side as they have been encouraged to do,' he said, appraising her.

'And you do not do the same, puffing out your chest, standing tall and looking your best?'

'Oh touché, Miss Lewis,' he said and laughed at himself as he glanced at his attire – his most expensive waistcoat. 'I feel you do not care to impress me, and yet you cannot help but do so.'

'Too kind, thank you, Mr Martin,' she said, pleased with his analysis of her character.

A momentary silence fell on them as they reflected on all that had been said, and Lilly watched the world go by. She looked to Bennet Martin and decided to ask a most impertinent question.

'I know of your affection for my dear friend, Phoebe. May I ask, do you see in her a future wife?'

His face reflected his surprise.

'Forgive me, you need not answer, of course. I am a reporter and think nothing of asking questions that may or may not be intrusive.'

He cleared his throat and looked at the passing vehicles while speaking. 'It is a moot point, as Miss Astin has advised me indirectly, that she does not reciprocate my feelings.'

'Ah, I am sorry then. What is it you saw in my dear friend? Of course, I know all her best attributes, but I often wonder what draws a gentleman to any woman.'

'She is beautiful, feminine, and, like me, artistic. But...' he sighed, 'Miss Astin is probably not suited to my lifestyle nor me to hers. I find all that spirit chatting quite fearful. Does that unman me?'

'Not at all. I believe everyone has something they fear. My father is a large man and cannot stand spiders, and we get our fair share at home.'

'I believe the climate encourages them. And you, Miss Lewis, will you share what you fear in the spirit of exchange?'

Lilly grimaced. 'I suppose it is only fair. I am frightened of... birds. There I have said it.'

'Birds!' Bennet exclaimed. 'Extraordinary. Why?'

'Oh, I love their songs and pretty features; even the dark crows and the handsome magpies are beautiful, but those nasty claws and sharp beaks frighten me. If they all stay at a distance, we will get on just fine.'

Bennet could not hide his grin. He leapt from the hansom as it pulled up at Lilly's place of business, offering his hand for her dismount.

'It has been a pleasure,' he said.

'It has been enlightening,' Lilly added and made him chuckle.

Racing inside, the delightful short trip with Bennet Martin fell from her consciousness for the immediate time, but little did she know it did not fall from his as he ventured home to capture her image on his canvas.

Lilly was pleased to find Fergus busily writing as she arrived. 'I have plenty – I have just accompanied the detectives on a walk of the site of the crimes,' she informed him.

'Excellent, I spoke with the mother.'

'Daisy Dorchester's mother? Oh, that is good,' Lilly smiled, and the pair got to work to meet the end-of-day deadline and get their copy in to make the morning edition as the afternoon paper was already on its way to the press.

Lilly did not look up again until the late afternoon shadows appeared, and Fergus stretched beside her.

'I believe we are done,' he said.

'I agree. We will only keep changing it if we continue to fuss. I am pleased with it.'

'As am I. Let us hope Mr Cowan is as well,' Fergus said, rising, and the young reporters hurried their copy into the editor.

Now, for the next angle, Lilly mused.

The Astin family business closed early, and the family was home by sundown to make Julius comfortable and wait for the doctor's second visit.

'It is not necessary,' he grumbled, walking up the stairs of his grandparents' home unaided. 'I can return to my own home for the evening.'

'Absolutely not,' Randolph said, 'I am putting my foot down about this, Julius.'

'You have been ordered, brother, so be quiet and do as you are told,' Ambrose said, not leaving his brother's side.

Julius stopped on the verandah, his hand gripping the rail while a wave of nauseousness passed over him. He waved off Ambrose's assistance, but his grandmother, Maria Astin, rushed out the front door, ordering him as she did two decades again when he was but eight. 'Into bed immediately, Julius, you are whiter than the sheets. Randolph, Ambrose, help him.'

'I am quite alright, Grandma, I assure you.'

'We'll see what the doctor says about that,' Randolph said, steering Julius through the door, down the hallway and into the bedroom where Phoebe had been freshening the room in preparation. Julius sat heavily on the bed, allowing his brother and grandfather to remove his outer garments and shoes.

'Modern nursing studies say that sleep is needed so your body can fight an illness or infection, Julius,' his grandmother continued. 'I have been reading widely during my volunteer work at the hospital. If you wish to get back on your feet, then you will be off them tonight.'

'So there, brother,' Ambrose said and gave a small shrug at the look of annoyance from Julius.

'We shall make some broth,' Phoebe said, looking in on him and hurrying after her grandmother into the kitchen.

'This is all unnecessary,' Julius bemoaned but laid back and sighed as his head hit the pillow. Within moments, he was asleep.

# Chapter 27

T HE PAST WAS BURIED deep within Julius Astin, but in his weakened state, it intruded on the present. For a moment, as he lay on the bed of his youth in the small downstairs bedroom, he became once more the eldest boy who must help his grandparents following his parents' tragic death. He felt responsible for himself and his siblings and the strain they put on his mourning grandparents. In the coming days, months, and years, they would have little of a material nature but abundant affection, love, and security – enough to cocoon them for the altered lives ahead of them. The room held all the memories of the latter years of his childhood; he grew up too quickly. Phoebe and Ambrose's bedrooms were upstairs, his grandparents in front of his own in the middle of the house. Small, comfortable, their home.

The night seemed endless; surely it was over, but it was still dark outside.

'Lie still, Julius darling, it is time to sleep,' his grandmother said, pushing him gently back onto the pillow after insisting he sip at some broth.

'Is he all right?' Ambrose's voice, the same question over and over. 'How is his temperature? He is shivering with cold... he is too hot...'

'We cannot lose him.' Phoebe's voice hitched.

'We will not lose him. The doctor says he is in no danger,' Randolph assured his grandchildren, 'but he needs to rest. Tomorrow, he will be on his way to being his usual self if not able to lift anything for a little while.'

Julius agreed but did not have the energy to say so or reassure them, as he had long since made it his business to provide for their needs. But tonight, he was weary and weak and happy to lay down and close his eyes while others fussed around him, something he normally abhorred. The doctor came to his bedside, accompanied by Randolph, and declared Julius was improved but would need to sleep to recover from blood loss and his body's shock reaction. It would not have been so severe had he gone into the nearby hospital, the doctor had added, and he heard his grandfather's sigh of frustration.

'He is not one to accept help.'

'Then tonight he must; it is a sizeable wound,' the doctor had said and administered a tincture which had made Julius weary but pleasantly pain-free.

Several times early in the evening, he woke and felt the relief of a cold washer on his face, his grandmother administering it. He heard Violet's gentle and concerned voice and desperately wanted her by his side, but his grandmother would not allow such impropriety. He woke momentarily to find Bennet nearby, worry etched on his face. Ambrose was there and gone and back again. Phoebe had entered to change Julius's dressing and check his stitches, which the doctor had admired.

'Thank you, Phoebe,' he thought he said but only heard her humming in reply.

Uncle Reggie sat nearby for a while.

'You have not come to escort me?' Julius asked, and Reggie laughed.

'Not yet, not for a long time.'

'But you will come?'

'You will be well met and most welcomed when that day arrives. Do not rush here, though, nephew. To quote Ecclesiastes, which is most fitting to you now, "Enjoy life with the woman whom you love all the days of your fleeting life which He has given to you under the sun". That's an order,' Reggie added and laughed.

'Ah,' Julius smiled as his grandmother entered the room, and he saw the reason for Uncle Reggie's presence.

'She is still so beautiful,' Reggie said softly.

'Do not torture yourself so, Uncle Reggie,' Julius said, forgetting he straddled the world between the living and the dead and unconsciously spoke to the deceased with his grandmother present.

'Hush now,' his grandmother said, not understanding his mutterings, but his grandfather, Randolph, had entered in time to hear his words.

'Is it time to get up?' Julius asked.

'It is barely midnight, darling; go back to sleep,' she had said, brushing the dark hair from his forehead and cooling him again with a cloth.

'I shall sit with him for a while,' Randolph said, kissing Maria as she passed.

'Go to bed, Grandpa,' Julius heard himself saying as if he was outside his body observing all that was going on. 'I am perfectly fine, just fatigued from the tincture.'

'It is all right, lad, I shall go when I am weary. Allow us to care for you, for a change.'

Hours passed, and still, it was not light. Julius slept fitfully.

'When is the morning coming?'

'Soon,' someone answered, but he did not know who spoke.

More hours passed, or so it seemed. It was the longest night in history. Perhaps the day would never come.

'Is it still dark?'

'It is the night, and everyone is resting. Rest now, my lad.'

The memory returned, and he was not strong enough to close it down; in moments, Julius was drawn in. It was as real as if it were anew. It played out in his mind like an old film track that never fades... his parents crossing the wide road, their arms linked, laughing at something his father said. It was their anniversary. A horse and cart were coming around the corner fast, too fast.

'Dad, Dad, stop!' Julius yelled the warning as he did that day, watching them and waving from the verandah of the house.

'Julius, wake up,' he heard Ambrose's voice and the slight shaking of his shoulder, but he had to stop his father from crossing.

'Stop, stop!'

The memory unfurled. The realisation that his parents were unable to go back or forward, his father shielding his mother, the impact, the sound of the thud, the yelling, the scream, his father falling, his mother being thrown. Then his father was dying before him, begging him to see to his mother.

'I cannot help her, Dad.'

'Julius, lad, wake up,' his grandfather insisted, but his father's hand gripped his arm.

'I can't help her, Dad. Mum is gone. Her head is not right, her neck...'

Julius sat up gasping and saw Ambrose hurriedly departing the room.

'It is alright, lad. That time is gone now and has been grieved. Return to the living,' his grandfather said, his eyes awash with tears, 'return to the living.'

# Chapter 28

*M*ORNING EDITION

MURDER OF DEBUTANTE AND PRIEST LINKED
ASSAULTED MAN ALSO CONNECTED
DETECTIVES SEEKING WITNESSES

*The Courier* presents an exclusive report by Lilly Lewis and Fergus
Griffiths.

Two recent deaths and the assault of a man near St Patrick's
Cathedral, New Farm, have come to the attention of detectives
from Roma Street Police Station, and *The Courier* can report that
the detectives on the case believe them to be linked.

The death last Sunday evening of the debutante, Miss Daisy
Dorchester, aged 18 years, who was thought to have slipped and

struck her head on a graveyard headstone, is now being treated as murder. In a sensational twist, the death of Father Damien Horan, aged 28 years, found the morning after at the base of the cliff, has been declared intentional, and an assault in the same vicinity on Mr Theodore Wright, aged 22, of South Brisbane, has also been linked.

Detectives Harland Stone and Gilbert Payne – two of the city's finest – wished to assure the public that there was no concern for alarm as they did not consider the killings to be random but believed Miss Dorchester to be the link between all three cases that took place within walking distance of each other. The culprit is still at large.

'All parties were connected through mutual acquaintances,' Detective Stone said, 'and the three victims were carrying a verse upon them by Robert Browning.'

The poem's lines were in Miss Dorchester's possession, in Father Horan's pocket, and scribbled on a scrap of paper in the possession of Mr Theodore Wright, who is believed to have engraved the lines on a ring; the ring has not been found. The random fact, which might have been easily overlooked as victims' possessions are returned to family and often not scrutinised or compared, was discovered due to impressive detective work, allowing for the link to be confirmed between the three cases.

Interviews with family and friends of Miss Dorchester painted a wider picture of the young lady about to embark on the next stage of her life. After making her debut, she was expected to announce her engagement to Mr Eldon Foster and had been visiting Father Damien Horan to discuss her pending nuptials. It is believed that Miss Dorchester may have formed an attachment to the Catholic priest that was not reciprocated and had gifted him a lock of hair and the verse *"Grow old along with me, the best is yet to be"*. Miss Dorchester's aunt/guardian, Mrs Audrey Stewart, strenuously denies this claim. Mrs Stewart has been vocal in her belief that her niece was murdered and has hired renowned private detective, Mr Bennet Martin, to investigate.

Father Morris of St Patrick's parish said it was not uncommon for Father Damien Horan to receive notes and gifts of affection from young ladies as he was a most charismatic young man. Still, he insisted that the priest was devoted to his faith and may have pocketed the gift to avoid embarrassing the young lady. However, his verbal rejection may have offended Miss Dorchester or been misconstrued by a parishioner, resulting in the death of both parties.

Mr Theodore Wright was attacked near where Miss Dorchester had met with Father Horan. He told *The Courier* that he had been collecting the engraved engagement ring from the jeweller on behalf of his best friend, Mr Eldon Foster, soon to be betrothed to Miss Dorchester. Mr Wright said he spoke briefly with Miss Dorchester that day before they continued, going their separate ways.

Friends of Miss Dorchester spoke of her boasting of a secret love, but she would not reveal whom that might be. Your reporters also uncovered that Mr Eldon Foster did not wish to wed the young lady, but having promised to do so in their youth and as it was the desire of both families, he was honourable in his intent to offer for her.

We can also reveal from an exclusive interview with Miss Dorchester's mother, Mrs Faith Dorchester, that her daughter was ambitious to make a good match. Mrs Dorchester admitted to being estranged from her daughter – a daughter whom her mother idolised until three years ago. The source of the estrangement was the pending marriage of Miss Dorchester to Mr Foster, which Mrs Dorchester did not believe should take place as no real affection existed between the pair.

Mrs Dorchester – a gentle soul – described her daughter, Daisy, as talented and beautiful. While she spoke of her daughter commendably, Mrs Dorchester admitted to being intimated by Miss Dorchester and allowing her sister-in-law, who supported the pending nuptials, to stand as guardian to Miss Dorchester.

The investigation into the two deaths and assault continues. Detective Stone requests anyone who might have seen the three victims on Sunday or been in the vicinity and recall anything of interest to attend Roma Street Police Station at their earliest convenience.

The residents of the Astin household had a restless night, and an emotional current ran through the family as they arrived for work at *The Economic Undertaker* to begin their day. Julius was not with them. Having spent the night in fitful sleep, he fell into a deep sleep and did not stir as the household aroused.

Randolph took his usual post behind the desk at the front of the reception area, Phoebe departed to her room to prepare for an incoming body, Mrs Dobbs fussed with tea and baking, expecting their first clients after nine o'clock, and Ambrose hovered to receive today's collections before briefing the senior stable hand, Will, who was sent home to suit up and undertake the collections with Ambrose in Julius's absence.

The mood was sombre, like a wheel was missing from the cart, and the office limped along.

'It is peculiar, isn't it?' Ambrose mused, getting his grandfather's attention. 'Julius is so often serious, some might unkindly say moody, and we are all more so now in his absence.'

'It does feel very empty here without him,' Randolph agreed. 'But he will be back tomorrow, I have no doubt.' He handed his grandson a list of today's collections. 'It might not hurt to let Will know he may be stepping up for a while. Julius should not be lifting anything heavy for a matter of weeks.'

Ambrose sighed. 'I will miss his witty banter on our trips.'

Randolph chuckled. 'It will make you appreciate your brother more, I am sure.'

Ambrose accepted the list but hesitated, not leaving his grandfather's side.

'What is it, lad?' Randolph studied the young man who reminded him of his brother, Reggie, in nature.

Ambrose frowned and, swallowing, looked toward the window as he spoke. 'Last night, what Julius saw...'

His grandfather did not fill the silence. Ambrose continued. 'He was with our father when he died. He saw Mum with...' he indicated his neck but could not say the words. 'He saw that.'

'I have always known,' Randolph said with regret.

'He has kept that inside him,' Ambrose said, facing his grandfather. 'I never knew. I never thought about it, not once.'

'Julius has always wanted to shield you and Phoebe. He loves you both with a fierce protectiveness.'

'But I have been no comfort to him, quite the contrary, and he has carried that vision every day, every night.'

Randolph placed his hand on Ambrose's shoulder. 'You were but a boy. Your grandmother and I did our best to help Julius, and we were lucky that his sense of responsibility overtook his rebellion. In that regard, you and Phoebe may have saved him by providing a distraction from his rage and a purpose in helping to keep the family together. As for your nature – your teasing of your brother – I believe that keeps his nature lighter. Do not change; he needs you to be just you.'

Ambrose thought on his grandfather's words for a moment. Then, he nodded but could not speak, and waving the list, quickly headed down the hallway to fetch Will and begin his work day.

# Chapter 29

D ETECTIVE GILBERT PAYNE WAS quite at home in a church, although not so much the Catholic type. Nevertheless, he believed God was present and would recognise him there. Clean and pressed, as he was most days, but a little more so today if possible, knowing he was visiting the house of God, he pondered if Miss Emily Yalden was a church-going lady and was pleased to have another reason to think about her.

'Bless my soul, you have come to convert,' Father Morris said, walking down the aisle of St Patrick's towards the young detective. He clapped his hands together and raised them to heaven, but sported a grin that said he was teasing Detective Payne.

Gilbert grinned. 'Good morning, Rev... uh, Father. Not today, but it is always comforting to be in the house of God.'

'It is, I agree, which is good given the hours I spend in His house. How may I be of assistance to you, Detective Payne,' Father Morris said as they walked towards the entrance.

'I am here about a grave, Father Morris. The grave on which Miss Daisy Dorchester struck her head and died. Detective Stone and I would like to determine if it is significant to the case.'

Father Morris looked surprised. 'Oh, that is an interesting thought. Do you have the name of the interred?'

'I do,' Gilbert said, consulting his notes again.

'Should we walk there? It is but a short distance.'

'Yes, please,' he said, exiting the church with Father Morris. 'It is the grave of a lady named Constance Kemp, of twenty years of age. The headstone reads, "The truth will set you free." Do you know it, Father?'

Father Morris said the name again. 'I know the interred, and I know the verse. I have buried many a parishioner in my time at this presbytery, including Miss Kemp.'

'She was a miss. So, did you know her well?' Gilbert prodded, impatient.

'Oh yes, Detective. That I did, I knew Miss Kemp very well.'

They arrived within minutes and stood in front of the grave, which was dark grey from the weather and neglected, a vine entwined around the angel's feet. The area where Daisy struck her head was clear of vine.

'Miss Kemp's death was unfortunate,' Father Morris said. 'She was a victim of her own vanity.'

Violet gathered herself, took a deep breath and knocked on the front door of the Astin family home. It was late morning, and she did not want to intrude at lunchtime, but it was the best time to be away from the business as trade lessened during this hour. Her choice of dress that morning had been most deliberate – it was the one most flattering in colour and fit, the blue bringing out the blue of her eyes, but her exhaustion could not be hidden.

'Miss Forrester, well, this is a lovely surprise,' Mrs Astin said, opening the door widely and ushering Violet in.

'Please forgive the intrusion, Mrs Astin, but I just dropped in to ask after Julius and to leave a small gift.'

'How considerate,' Maria Astin said with a smile that said she knew her grandson would be very welcoming of the visit. 'Julius will be delighted to see you.' She offered Violet a seat at the table and put the kettle on. 'I shall fetch him, but you will have a cup of tea?'

'That would be lovely, thank you. Then Julius is awake and moving freely?'

'He slept most of the morning as he was awake most of the night. But I heard him moving around moments ago. He is much recovered.'

Violet's hand went to her heart. 'Well, that is a relief.'

The door to the living room opened, and Julius appeared with his shirt unbuttoned as if he had shrugged it on, sleeves rolled up, and unshaven. His eyes widened in surprise as he realised how he looked in front of the woman who occupied his thoughts every waking hour and whom he attempted to look his best for any day he might see her. Julius stepped back and realised he could not disappear into the room; he had been seen.

'Violet!'

'Miss Astin has come to ask after you,' his grandmother said, placing three cups and saucers on the table. 'I was just coming to fetch you.'

Violet rose to her feet. She had never seen Julius in such a state of undress but could see through the fabric of his shirt that his physique was well developed – no doubt from the constant lifting that both he and Ambrose performed in their duties.

'I am sorry to come unexpected,' she offered.

'Not at all,' he said, doing up his shirt buttons and rolling down his sleeves. 'Forgive my appearance; I thought you were Phoebe, returned.' He rubbed a hand over his jaw.

'You have been ill,' she said, her eyes searching his face with concern.

'Had I known you were visiting... my apologies.'

Violet could not but help study him, a glint of amusement in her eyes to see the usually very-put-together Julius Astin ruffled. It was intriguing to see him unguarded as he would be in the fold of his family.

'Mrs Astin tells me you feel much stronger this morning,'

'I do, thank you.'

Violet returned to her seat as Mrs Astin placed the pot of tea and plate of biscuits on the table and turned her attention to Julius.

'Take a seat, and you will eat some toast,' his grandmother said, bossing him into a chair. 'Julius, Ambrose and Phoebe remain my children in this house; I like to pull rank when I can,' she said in jest, making Violet laugh.

'And heaven forbid we disobey,' Julius added drily, accepting the tea with thanks.

Violet pushed the gift towards Julius. 'I made you a new shirt since your other one was torn.'

His eyes lit up, and he accepted the shirt, opening it and holding it before him. 'It is perfect, thank you, and looks to be a good fit.'

'I had your other shirt that was removed after the accident; Mrs Dobbs reluctantly gave it to me, and I have to say,' she said sheepishly, 'Tom was most fascinated with the cut in the shirt and the blood. He believed you to be very lucky the wound was not a little higher near your heart. I could not sleep at the thought of it.'

'Heaven forbid,' Mrs Astin said, sitting with the young couple and pouring herself tea, now they were both served.

'The cut is quite shallow, fear not, Grandma. The young man was slashing wildly, not plunging. He was panicking.' Julius continued to admire the shirt. 'You must have worked all night on making this.'

'I could not sleep. I was quite anxious. Fortunately, my grandmother had some fabric stashed away for an order she never finished.'

'I am sorry for that, but it has served me well, thank you. It will be my favourite shirt, I assure you.'

The pair exchanged a smile while Mrs Astin pretended to fuss buttering toast. Violet liked his unkempt appearance, stubble-roughened jaw, and mussed hair. She broke their gaze and said, 'Mrs Dobbs dropped in with a treat for us and said that everyone missed you terribly this morning and were quite glum, especially Ambrose, who vowed to Mrs Dobbs never to vex you again.'

Julius laughed, delighting his grandmother, who rarely saw her eldest grandson appearing happy. Violet noticed that Mrs Astin, in turn, smiled at her as if she had performed a miracle.

'I give that one day,' Julius said.

'Goodness, that long? How optimistic you are,' Violet teased. She sipped her tea and added, 'I must return to the office. The owner-manager is a terrible taskmaster.'

'I have heard that too,' Mrs Astin said, enjoying their teasing of Julius.

'Since you were working all night on such a beautiful garment, I am sure he has no grounds for censure.' Julius played along. 'I shall see you out and find a hansom.'

'There is no need. I am happy to walk; it is not that far,' Violet said, rising.

'No, it is too warm,' Julius said, walking to the door with her.

It was a wonderful feeling to have someone thinking of her comfort. Violet had never experienced that.

'Thank you for the tea and hospitality, Mrs Astin. Good day.'

'You are welcome any time, my dear.'

Violet hoped that soon that would be true, and she would be an Astin herself.

Having had a quick visit from Violet to assure her that Julius seemed much better and was preparing to return to his own home for the evening, Phoebe felt much lighter of heart and could turn her mind to other matters. Namely, the odd appearance of Miss Daisy Dorchester and her utterance of the words "the grave". In truth, she was weary of the debutante and grateful she had gone to her final resting place, but perhaps it was a clue and significant. Phoebe thought it might be worth passing on to

Detective Harland Stone but curbed her desire to see him with the thought that he was no doubt very busy and did not need to be hindered by her messages from the dearly departed.

Phoebe moved to the body that Ambrose and Will had brought in just an hour earlier and removed the cloth from the deceased's face. She stepped back, surprised, a hand going to her mouth as she emitted a small gasp.

'Well, hello, Miss Phoebe Astin. I wondered when you would get to me,' a friendly voice said nearby, and she looked around to see a fellow student from her mortician course standing nearby. He was, as she remembered him when they studied together several years ago – slim, splendidly dressed and a self-confessed dandy.

She squealed with delight, which was very unlike Phoebe, but her pleasure was evident. 'Hyde! Is it really you, Hyde Barker?' she asked, clapping her hands together, and then Phoebe paused. 'Oh dear, you are dead.'

'Sad but true, my dear. Can you believe it?'

'No, no, I cannot, Hyde. My goodness, this is terrible. How, may I ask?'

He sighed and moved over to his body. 'Pneumonia. I put up quite a fight, I assure you. I do look quite peaceful in death. Handsome even.'

'It becomes you,' Phoebe agreed, moving closer. 'But I am sorry to have your lovely warm presence gone from amongst the living.'

'Thank you, dear Phoebe. Now, I must say, I am very pleased to be here in your care; I did mention you quite a bit to my family. Someone must have remembered, which is surprising because Lord knows they are a flighty lot.' He rolled his eyes. 'I shall miss them, however.'

'You are having a viewing, so I will get to meet them.' She brightened, 'You can assist me with your appearance.'

'Oh, I know exactly what tint to use, but I don't want to step on your toes.'

Phoebe smiled. 'You won't. It can be your last and best work upon this earth.'

Hyde gave her a warm smile and clasped his hands before him. 'Thank you, dear Phoebe, for my swansong.'

'While you have left this life too soon, Hyde, I am so pleased to see you again, so honoured to be able to prepare you. You were always the one to put a smile on everyone's face during our studies.'

'We were a good group, were we not?'

'Some, as I recall,' Phoebe said, recalling her days in study. 'But you were the most accepting of a lady mortician in the class.'

Hyde waved his hand. 'Those men that were not pleased to have you amongst their ranks were jealous of your talents.'

Phoebe laughed and touched Hyde's face as he lay on the table. 'Let us begin.'

Hyde stopped, gasped and stepped back.

'What is it?' Phoebe asked, alarmed, and glanced around, expecting someone to have entered. She was usually most vigilant about not talking should the living be present unless it was family who knew of her visions.

Hyde put his hands to his temple. 'I am getting a message for you, goodness.'

'How odd. Most spirits appear directly.'

'A young lady by the name of Miss Daisy Dorchester. Do you know of her?'

Phoebe involuntarily grimaced and scolded herself. 'Yes, a client, but she was recently laid to rest. Gone too soon from this life.' She tried to say something kind, but it was challenging where Daisy was concerned.

'She is struggling to come back... perhaps she did not go above,' he said and gasped at the thought. 'Oh, good Lord, I hope I do.'

'You are a good and kind soul; you will be amongst the angels,' Phoebe assured him without a doubt.

'I would like wings. I digress.' He frowned. 'She is quite persistent, isn't she?'

Phoebe nodded. 'Yes, a fair assessment. I imagine her presence will be stronger at the cemetery now, where she died and was buried.'

'I am coming, Miss Pushy,' he said, looking skyward, but Phoebe could not see or hear the voice coming through to Hyde. 'Daisy... I shall call you Daisy or nothing at all.'

Phoebe tried to hide her smile but knew Daisy had met her match. Hyde would not put up with a young miss bossing him around.

'I shall tell her. Enough now, we are busy.' With that, he dismissed her, and Hyde returned his attention to Phoebe. 'Daisy said to please relay to you not to go to the grave.'

'Ah, the grave message again. Did she say which one? Her new resting place perhaps, or the one where her mortal remains were found?'

'She did not say, so perhaps, do not go near either. That would fix that,' he said firmly, with a hint of disinterest in anything Miss Daisy Dorchester said.

'Most odd,' Phoebe said. 'I had no intention of doing so.'

'Good. Back to you and me.'

Phoebe gave him a warm smile. 'Let us spend the afternoon preparing your body for the viewing. I have some lovely new tints, so do consider those, even if you have a favourite.'

'Ooh, well, I best have a look then.'

'You will look, as you always did,' she assured him, 'nothing but your best.'

# Chapter 30

F ATHER MORRIS WAS MOST regretful as he recalled his parishioner, Miss Constance Kemp. Her headstone had long since fallen into neglect.

'Her mother died not long after Constance's death, her father took to drinking, and her only sibling, a brother, left the country. I do not know what became of him. Constance would be my age if she were alive today,' Father Morris observed. Perhaps a mother, a grandmother, who is to say.'

'What had befallen her?' Gilbert asked of the young woman cut down in her prime.

'Ah, that was a tragedy no one could imagine. You must understand that Constance was a lovely young lady from a very good family, and she committed to a young man from the parish, Richard Canning, also from good people. I believed them to be in love, and certainly Richard was smitten.' Father Morris added, 'Constance was a great beauty.'

'I see,' Gilbert said, realising where the comparison to Miss Daisy Dorchester began.

Father Morris continued. 'A travelling salesman visited the Kempt household selling products to enhance a lady's beauty. He took quite a shine to Constance – whether to increase his sales or because he fell for her, but I later heard he visited on several occasions and took some liberties. Compared to Richard, a hardworking farm lad, he was quite a sophisticated and charming man.'

'The salesman's charm and gift of the gab?' Gilbert asked.

'Exactly so, Detective. I believe he promised her the world, and they were a strikingly handsome couple. Richard was usually so mild-mannered, but he went berserk. He took an axe from his farm and presented at her home.'

'Good Lord,' Gilbert said aghast.

Father Morris gave a brief nod and continued. 'Constance tried to block the door of the room in which she had hidden, but she was no match for Richard, especially in his stage of rage. He forced it open and murdered her, striking her down the forehead. Her life, her beauty, gone forever.'

'Like Miss Daisy Dorchester,' Gilbert said, staring at the grave before him. 'Beautiful, spoken for, and had her head turned by a man more handsome and, in this case, unattainable. What became of Richard, her intended? Did he flee?'

'Quite the opposite. After taking Constance's life, he sat upon the fence, waiting, and soon enough, Constance's father appeared, tormented, and accused him of murdering his daughter. Richard replied that he did and, jumping down off the fence, told Mr Kemp that his daughter deceived him and he would now hang for her death.'

'What a waste of two young lives.'

'Tragic,' Father Morris agreed. 'Richard tried to shoot himself but did not succeed in making it a fatal shot and thus was hanged. You can imagine how distraught the families were and the community... they were both so loved.'

'Did you tend to Richard in prison?'

'Often. He was completely unmanned and frequently cried like a child. He lost his future – his wife-to-be and the family he had hoped to raise with her. Richard had much sympathy and support, and some tried to prove his actions were due to an illness of the brain. But it was not so. After his execution, Richard's brain was studied, and there was no evidence of disease.'

'It was just the frenzy of a man betrayed and broken,' Gilbert said. 'Beauty is a dangerous thing.'

'And yet, in nature, there is so much to be found,' Father Morris said.

The words made Gilbert recall Father Horan's study and love of nature, and it made him wonder, 'Do you think that is why Father Horan turned to nature when faced with the challenge of beauty in the human form?'

'That is a very interesting observation, but I could not say. Everything changed so quickly. Richard was dead five months after Constance's death; now Miss Dorchester and Father Horan are gone in the blink of an eye. There is nothing beautiful about jealousy.'

Detective Harland Stone stood back, looked at his board and then moved a piece of paper from one side to the other. Satisfied, he started on the next pile of witnesses' accounts.

'Another dozen, Detective,' Sergeant Henderson said, entering Harland's office and handing him a wad of hand-written notes. 'Hopefully, we're through the last of them now.'

'Thank you, Sergeant, and to your constables. I know the invasion was an imposition.'

'It kept us busy for the morning, and it was a nice change from the usual lawbreakers,' the mature sergeant said with a smile and departed for the front desk with a wave of his hand.

Harland looked at the latest batch of notes. Since asking the public to share any sightings on the morning of Miss Daisy

Dorchester and Father Damien Horan's death and Theodore Wright's assault, the constabulary was inundated with witnesses and extra constables were assigned to get statements and contact details.

Harland mumbled as he categorised the statements. 'Three more debutante sightings... another of Father Horan, and another, two of Mr Wright... Miss Dorchester again....'

'Sir, that's promising!' Gilbert said, entering their shared office and removing his hat. He looked at the board, his eyes wide with enthusiasm.

'Indeed it is, Gilbert. The public has stepped up, and our victims were seen in multiple places. I am hopeful that we might be able to determine a clear suspect from the sightings.'

'Oh, that is good news, Sir. I feel that suspects only tell us half the story or untruths, thus delaying our investigation.'

'By the nature of our roles, people are defensive around us, but the truth always prevails. It is also difficult to be guided by the spirit world but unable to find what we need to support the assertions.' Harland marked another sighting on the board, forming a map from the cliffs where Father Horan fell to his death to where Theodore Wright was assaulted, culminating in where Daisy Dorchester met her death.

'Goodness, so many sightings,' Gilbert said, looking at the discarded pile of notes already marked on the board.

'Yes, we are fortunate that the crimes were after mass on Sunday, near a popular walk and a cemetery. It must have been challenging for the culprit to get away with their acts.'

'I found that once the church service ends, most people leave promptly, especially those with a young family. But a cemetery will always have a visitor or two present.'

'Speaking of which, how did you go with the grave connection?' Harand remembered where his protégé had been this morning.

'A most interesting connection, and Father Morris well remembered the grave owner, Miss Constance Kemp.'

'Tell me while I finish marking these sightings.'

Gilbert recounted the sad tale of Miss Constance Kemp and the uncanny resemblance to the debutante's nature. When he finished, Harland gave a firm nod.

'As I suspected. I believe that is the final piece of our puzzle. A clear message from the culprit, would you not say so?'

'I would, Sir,' Gilbert agreed, 'very clever.'

'Then consider this, Gilbert, as I believe we have our murderer.' Harland turned to the board, and Gilbert came and stood beside him. 'We have several sightings of Father Damien Horan after church and later, near the cliffs. A couple confirmed they saw him talking with a young lady who matched Miss Dorchester's description. No one saw him falling to his death.'

'That is unfortunate but not unexpected.'

'True,' Harland agreed. 'We have sightings of Mr Theodore Wright near the church and a sighting of Miss Dorchester in the cemetery.'

'Hmm,' Gilbert mused. 'And any of her friends... Miss Bains, Miss Dickinson, or Mr Eldon Foster himself?'

'Only of the ladies after mass.'

'Could it have been... that is to say, could there be more than one killer?'

'There could, but I don't believe so.' Harland moved closer to the board. 'Look at this, Gilbert. There is but one person seen at every location and one only.'

Gilbert saw the name and groaned.

'The timing of the sightings is most significant. They were in the right place at the times we believed our victims to be harmed. Shall we pay a visit?'

'I cannot believe it,' Gilbert said, staring at the board.

'Come then,' Harland hurried him along. 'The murderer thinks they have got away with it. '

# Chapter 31

I T WAS NEARING TWO o'clock when the door to *The Economic Undertaker* office opened, and Randolph adopted his best sincere expression only to frown moments later.

'You are meant to be resting, lad,' he said with a shake of his head and a sigh of frustration.

'I find I cannot,' Julius said, entering and closing the door behind him. 'It is difficult to do. I think I take after my grandfather.'

Randolph chuckled. 'The cheek. Your colour looks much better.'

'I feel better.'

'Oh, you are here and looking much better than you did this time yesterday,' Mrs Dobbs said, entering the room and clasping her hands together.

'I am sorry to cause you concern, Mrs Dobbs, and for the profanity,' Julius said and grimaced.

'Oh, do not give it a second thought. Having you back safe and well is reward enough. Tea then. And should you get the chance, do drop in next door, Mr Astin. The ladies were so worried about you. I believe you received the shirt Miss Forrester spent the night making?' She did not wait for a response. 'Young Miss Pollard went to mass for you last night to offer prayers for your recovery, and Mrs Shaw cooked and brought in her special broth for you today.'

'You are held in high regard, my boy,' Randolph said proudly, and Julius flushed with embarrassment.

'I will, Mrs Dobbs, thank you. That is very kind of everyone. Forgive me, but I must sit,' he said, excusing himself for sitting while Mrs Dobbs stood; he lowered himself into a seat in the reception area, and his grandfather joined him.

'I am a little weary,' he conceded.

'And will be for a short while. There will be no going on collections for you for some time. It may be your business, but I am putting my foot down about that.'

'Thank goodness,' Mrs Dobbs said. 'I shall make us all a cup of tea.'

'Speaking of collections, I've been thinking about the future of the business for a while, Grandpa, but this stabbing incident has convinced me it is time for a few modifications.'

'Oh. I did not know you were wanting a change, Julius. Are you thinking of selling?' Randolph was not one for surprises and had no inkling of his grandson's discontent.

'No, definitely not, nothing like that,' Julius assured him. 'But my bookkeeper and I have been working on a restructure, as such. Cousin Lucian inspired it, and I'm conscious that our stable hands may want some new challenges. I wanted to talk with you first.'

'Do tell then,' Randolph encouraged him, feeling apprehensive. Julius was the most consistent of his three grandchildren and not given to impulsiveness, so Randolph knew whatever his eldest grandson suggested was most likely final.

'It will take a little more finessing as I heard you speaking with Grandma while I was drifting in and out of sleep.'

Randolph frowned, trying to recall what Julius might have heard. His grandson continued, clearing his throat as if introducing an awkward topic.

'I suspect I also said somethings that caused distress.'

'You were feverish and at the mercy of the tincture; you said nothing that caused offence, only concern for your welfare.' Randolph did not mention he heard Julius speaking with Reggie or that he now had an inkling as to why Reggie remained between both worlds, his soul not at rest. But he would not raise that until Julius was stronger. He added for Julius's comfort, 'It was to be expected that you might feel displaced with the fever and tincture.'

Julius gave a small nod but did not want to speak of it and hurried on. 'I think we are all ready for a change. So, Grandma would like you to have a couple of days to attend her, and I know you wish to do so.'

'I did not like to let you down.'

'Grandpa, you never could. Did you wish to retire? We will work around it, and you have earned it.'

'No, definitely not,' Randolph assured him. 'I cannot bear to be idle, and I enjoy this work. But in fairness to your grandmother, I should give her a couple of days of my time. She is undoubtedly happy to have me out of the house on the other days.'

Julius smiled. 'Excellent, that is a relief; we would miss you. I would miss you.'

Randolph smiled sincerely. 'Thank you, my boy.' Neither man was adept at expressing their emotions. 'So, who shall replace me then for two days at the desk?'

Ambrose burst through the front door as Mrs Dobbs entered with the tea tray for the two men.

'Who is leaving? Did you say you were leaving, Grandpa? Why? Tell me it is not so? I knew this day would come,' Ambrose moaned. Coming fully into the room, he saw his brother and added, 'You are meant to be resting, but you do look much better.'

'I am not leaving,' Randolph assured him.

'I feel better. Sorry if I caused you to spend the night awake.'

'You caused me a great deal more aggravation than that,' Ambrose said, scolding his brother. 'I should have taken you into the hospital. Lord knows why I did as you asked.'

'Because I had the reins.'

'Yes, that was probably why,' Ambrose conceded, and he happily accepted the offering of tea and a biscuit when Mrs Dobbs appeared with an extra cup. He sat, joining the men, and dipped his biscuit into his tea. 'I thought you were gone to us, and I would have to decide which burial package to give you – our top, middle, or the paupers' package.'

'I seem to recall,' Mrs Dobbs began as she finished serving the tea, 'that you vowed never to vex your brother ever again.'

'Oh, that's right, I did,' Ambrose said and enjoyed the amused looks of his brother and grandfather. 'But Grandpa convinced me otherwise.'

'I did?' Randolph spluttered.

'Yes. You said Julius needed me to be my lighthearted, loveable self if I am to keep him from being morose.'

'Hmm,' Randolph mused. 'A very literal interpretation of my words, but not untrue.'

Julius scoffed. 'Well, you are here now, so you may as well stay and hear my suggestions for the business going forward. You are welcome to stay too, Mrs Dobbs.'

'Thank you, Mr Astin, but I shall tidy the kitchen and do my grocery list for tomorrow's clients.' She departed with their thanks ringing in her ears.

'You will not be much good doing collections with me for a while since you can't stretch,' Ambrose said.

'Precisely. Do continue now that Ambrose has stopped interrupting us,' Randolph teased his youngest grandson.

'Well, some months back, Lucian told me he wanted to do less management at the carpentry businessmen and be more hands-on. He is missing the tools and the satisfaction of creating. Grandpa needs two days a week to himself,' he told Ambrose, 'And my bookkeeper wants me to dedicate at least one day a week to the books, supplies and advertising.'

'A change is timely then,' Randolph said as Julius paused to drink his tea.

'It is, but I also want to remain active in the business.'

'Of course you do; you would miss me terribly,' Ambrose said, and Julius continued ignoring him.

'I believe we all need to take a step up or sideways a couple of days a week,' Julius said. 'I will take your role two days a week, Grandpa, at the desk—'

'You will be inundated with young ladies! That will never work,' Ambrose interrupted him.

'Not if I am a married man,' Julius said.

'That would be wonderful,' Randolph smiled at his grandson.

'They would all want to see me then,' Ambrose agreed with a smile as Julius shook his head and smiled at his little brother.

'As I was saying, I will take the desk two days a week, and when I'm not seeing clients in-house, I will manage the bookwork, looking at what each business needs. The other days, I will continue to work with Ambrose, attending funerals. Grandpa will be our office manager on the days he is in. Ambrose, you will step into my role on those two days I am absent and take the manager title and the pay raise that goes with it.'

'Excellent,' Ambrose said, his eyes widening. 'That would be great, brother, as I am considering my future and may look to buy a house.'

'Are you? At last. Have you met someone?' Julius asked, his voice laced with suspicion.

'Do I need to in order to act more mature?'

'Yes, I suspect so.'

'Fine then,' Ambrose gave him a wry look. 'I may wish to court Miss Kate Kirby.'

'Oh, such a lovely young lady,' Randolph said delightedly.

'Phoebe's friend, the photographer? She is lovely,' Julius agreed.

'As am I,' Ambrose said.

'Does she know of your feelings?' Julius asked.

'She knows, and I believe she reciprocates.'

Julius smiled. 'That is why you wanted to set up our office photographs.'

'No, but it led to where we are now, so I guess I have you to thank for that, brother.'

'Wonderful,' Julius said, still smiling, as was Randolph.

Ambrose looked from one to the other. 'Enough about me then, as interesting as I am, carry on with your business plan, Julius, I am all ears.'

Julius moved forward slightly and winced. 'I keep forgetting it is there,' he said by way of explanation as he gingerly touched his side. 'Ambrose, please know that my bookkeeper has funds for you and Phoebe to contribute to a house purchase when ready. Perhaps make an appointment with him.'

Ambrose put his cup down. 'No, Julius, you are generous enough and do not need to provide anything more than the good salary you pay. Those funds, however much they amount to, should stay in the business.'

'They were not expected,' Julius said and attempted to explain. 'Any time we received a tip or bonus, which we have received quite a few from estates over the years, I put them aside for your homes. So, we were not expecting those funds, nor were they counted on to keep the businesses afloat.'

'But—'

'You are a generous and good man, Julius and have always looked after your family,' Randolph said. 'Ambrose, you have worked hard, and your brother has planned for you and your sister. Allow him to do so.'

'If you are sure I am not taking from your pocket,' Ambrose said and grinned. 'It is very exciting.'

Julius agreed. 'It is amazing to have the keys to your own home. It will make you feel grown up,' he teased before continuing. 'But back to my work plan. To assist you, Ambrose, we shall promote our stable manager, Will, on the two days I will be office-bound. His wife has just had a child; I imagine he could use some extra funds. You can break him in for a few days while I am out of action. Claude will be promoted into Will's role two days a week, and we will hire a new junior stable hand to fill Claude's role for those two days. The newly hired hand can help out in general across all the businesses as needed on the remaining days. He could be a good runner for you, Grandpa, get the mail, and so forth. What do you think?'

'I think that is an excellent plan, lad, and timely. I am sure a new challenge will suit everyone and keep us all on our toes. Would you not say so, Ambrose?'

'Absolutely. What of Phoebe?'

'I have not spoken to her yet, but she should take on an apprentice. Thus, if she should find herself overworked or with a husband and child in the near future, she can trust her predecessor, as can we knowing that Phoebe trained them.'

'She is not one for company,' Randolph said. 'You might find yourself hiring someone with qualifications if and when the day comes that Phoebe needs to step down.'

'I thought as much, too, but I shall give her the option,' Julius said as the door swung open, and they all hurriedly rose to their feet, Julius stumbling up a little slower than his grandfather and brother.

Ambrose moved swiftly in front of his brother as a woman entered with a young boy behind her – the boy who had stabbed Julius.

# Chapter 32

ST PATRICK'S CHURCH WAS the third place that the detectives tried in their search for their main suspect, Miss Melanie Bains. On calling at her home, they were advised by Mrs Bains that her daughter was a good girl, and Harland assured her that her daughter was assisting with enquiries only. At this stage, there was no point alarming the poor woman nor warning Miss Bains should she arrive home after their departure. They were directed to call at Miss Kate Kirby's photographic studio, where Melanie was heading to collect her portrait and then to the church to arrange flowers as she did every Tuesday for the mid-week masses.

'I am sorry you have gone out of your way, Detectives, but she has come and gone,' Miss Kirby said as another young lady arrived to collect her portrait at the allotted collection time. 'You have only missed her by fifteen minutes or so. I believe she was heading to the church.'

'St Patrick's by any chance?' Harland asked.

'She did not say, unfortunately.'

They bid Miss Kirby farewell, and before departing, Gilbert asked as casually as he could manage with a heart inflamed with romantic potential, 'Miss Kirby, may I enquire after your friend's well-being, Miss Yalden?'

'Emily? Why she is well, Detective, thank you for your concern. That is, as well as one can be as a single lady managing a business and a household.'

'Of course, very admirable. You are all so talented. Good day, Miss Kirby.'

Harland glanced back to see what was delaying his detective and noted Miss Kirby seemed to study Gilbert with much interest, which made him flush slightly to Harland's amusement. When they were far enough away not to be overheard, Harland said, 'I believe Miss Kirby might hold a candle for you.'

'I don't believe so, Sir. I am hoping it is more than that. Her friend, Miss Emily Yalden and I have recently struck up a friendship, and perhaps she has confided something to Miss Kirby, and her opinion of me is favourable.'

'Ah,' Harland said, 'The lady who runs the deportment school?'

'I own no claim to her, Sir, but I think she is wonderful.'

'Good for you, Gilbert. What would the people of the earth be without woman? Mark Twain asked the question, I am but paraphrasing.'

Gilbert grinned. 'Very good, Sir, and I believe Mr Twain's answer was "scarce".'

Both men laughed, enjoying the temporary release before the gruesome task of interviewing and arresting a lady was to be undertaken. They arrived at the church and entered, their eyes adjusting to the dark interior.

'She is here, Sir,' Gilbert said on spotting her at the altar, arranging flowers.

Harland drew a deep breath.

'I shall go tell Father Morris of our intentions should he care to join us or offer Miss Bains support... even if she is proven to be guilty and was not as compassionate to her victims,' Gilbert said.

'Excellent idea, thank you, Gilbert.' Harland walked up the aisle. 'Miss Bains, good afternoon. A word if I may.'

'Detective Stone. Has something happened? Is mother—'

'I assure you, everyone is fine. Please do come and take a seat.'

Melanie Bains put down the flowers she was arranging and stepped down from the altar. To conceive she could commit such a crime seemed unimaginable to Harland as she walked towards him in a modest dress of light lavender, her hair restrained neatly at the nape of her neck, and carrying several flowers as if that might enhance her appeal to the single detective. He frowned at the act and turned to see Father Morris entering with Gilbert.

'Goodness, what is going on? Good afternoon to you, Miss Bains, Detective Stone.'

'Father, thank you for your time. We have an unpleasant line of questioning for Miss Bains and thought it best you were in attendance.'

'What on earth do you mean?' Melanie asked, pausing in the aisle.

'Please, Miss Bains, sit. We can talk here or down at our station.'

She dropped onto the seat, her mouth dropping open at the same time. Gilbert stood nearby as Father Morris sat beside her.

Harland began. 'Miss Bains, we have conducted a thorough investigation and received many eye-witness accounts from the public. I think it is time you told us the truth... that you saw all the victims on the day of their death and were, in fact, their murderer.'

She gasped, her hand going to her heart, and Melanie snapped to look at Father Morris, who looked equally shocked.

'I swear to you, Father, on the bible and all I hold dear, that I did not harm anyone. I could not. It is a mortal sin. I would never commit such an act and risk the fires of hell, nor harm any of God's children, even if I did not agree with their actions or morals.'

'And there we have it,' Harland said, not taking his eyes from her, studying her reactions and denials. 'Do you think you are a moral crusader acting on behalf of the Lord and administering punishment?'

She shook her head again, quite bewildered, which Harland found to be sincere and thus frustrating. Perhaps she was not their culprit after all.

'I do not, I could not cast the first stone, I am not without sin, although I try, I do try to be a good person.'

Father Morris nodded and gave her a small smile of comfort.

'Then, since I have you placed at every crime scene and with every victim, it is best you tell me everything, Miss Bains, and do not omit any details as that will only convince me you are capable of lying and self-preservation.'

Harland had her where he wanted – alarmed, breathing fast and ready to confess. She gave a nod and began her tale.

At *The Economic Undertaker*, the woman came no further than the doorway, and the boy beside her reached for his cap and took it off, clutching it to his chest. Julius stepped to the side of Ambrose, and the woman gasped.

'Sir, you are alive, God be praised.' She reached for her handkerchief hidden in her sleeve and pressed it against her lips momentarily before rushing on. 'I have only my son left in the world now, but we are here to do the right thing, to beg your forgiveness and appeal for your mercy.' She was a small, thin woman who, while not yet thirty, looked older than her years, no doubt from her labours.

'Sir, I did not mean to harm you. I didn't mean to hurt anyone; I was just protecting Pa, and I had the knife, but I didn't—'

Julius held up his hands to stop their tirade of words. 'I do not doubt that,' he assured them both and asked the young man, 'What is your name?'

'Charlie Ewing, Sir, and this is my Ma.'

'Mrs Ewing. I am sorry for your loss. I believe we were to have the privilege of burying your husband?' Julius asked.

'Yes, Sir, you are too kind. He is still at the hospital morgue. His brothers tried to take him, but Charlie, well, he was standing up for his father. He is very sorry.'

'I am.'

'He is a good, hard-working boy,' she added as tears ran down her face and her son took her arm, a look of great regret upon his face.

'Madame, please do not distress yourself,' Randolph said, 'I insist you take a seat. Ambrose, a cup of tea for Mrs Ewing.'

'You are too kind, thank you, but we do not wish to impose. We, that is, Charlie, has come to face his punishment,' she said, accepting the seat and looking up at her son standing before her.

'How old are you, Charlie?' Julius asked, gingerly lowering himself beside Mrs Ewing.

'Fifteen, Sir. I am the breadwinner now, so if you wish to call the police, I will understand, but my mother—'

Mrs Ewing's bout of tears began again.

'Please calm yourself, Madame. I am alive and well, and there will be no police required or punishment metered,' Julius assured her. His words made her cry afresh, and she apologised as her body shook. Julius could only imagine the courage it took for her to bring her son here today.

'Mind you, Charlie, he was in a lot of pain and delirious all night,' Ambrose said, returning to the room and giving the young boy a lesson. 'Every action has a consequence; that's what Grandpa spent years telling me.'

'And I never knew I got through to you until now,' Randolph said and smiled, easing the tension a little.

Mrs Dobbs entered, bearing a cup of tea for the distressed mother. 'There's milk and sugar in there, my dear; it will do you good,' Mrs Dobbs said kindly and departed just as quickly.

'I am so grateful, Mr Astin,' Mrs Ewing said, looking at Julius while she steadied the cup in one hand and dabbed her eyes with the other. 'But we have no money to compensate you for your medical bills or loss of work income. We will pay you back if we can work out a plan. I assure you we have enough for my husband's funeral – Charlie sold my husband's tools.'

'And I can labour for you at no cost to make up for your losses,' Charlie said.

Julius gave a small groan at their desperation, which he knew only too well. He had planned to avenge his parents' death when he was a boy of Charlie's age, but fate had intervened to prevent him from acting. Who is to say what might have become of him? He assured them, 'Mrs Ewing, Charlie, it is not necessary. I know it was an accident.'

Charlie was nodding with great vigour.

'I saw your uncles wishing to take your father home to the farm and you and your mother wanting to keep him nearby in the local cemetery. It was just unfortunate you had such a good swing.'

Charlie smiled and looked sheepish. 'I am on the cricket team.'

'As I recall,' Ambrose added, 'Julius did lots of stupid things when he was your age.'

Julius gave his brother a wry look as Mrs Ewings gave a small laugh, making her look younger than her years.

'What are your plans, Mrs Ewing, may I ask?' Julius enquired.

She swallowed a sip of tea and answered, 'My husband's brothers have shown us great kindness and allowed us to return to their farm and offered Charlie work, but it is on the condition that we bury my husband there.'

'Ah, it has a condition. But you do not wish to go?' Randolph asked gently.

Mrs Ewing shook her head. 'I am grateful for their kindness, but my husband never wanted to stay on the land. We've always lived here, and the memory of my husband is everywhere. Charlie knows no other home.'

Charlie nodded. 'Mum and I don't want to leave our house. It's not much, but...' he shrugged.

'Do you have work lined up, young man?' Randolph asked.

'I will have, Sir, if I am not sent to prison,' he said with a glance at Julius. 'I am going to look for labouring work, and my mum does washing and ironing. We'll be alright.' He looked at his mother and assured her with a confidence that belied his future.

Julius exchanged a look with his grandfather, who gave a subtle nod.

'We best discuss your husband's funeral, Mrs Ewing, as the hospital will not hold his body for much longer,' Julius said. 'If you will excuse me for a moment, my grandfather can tell you of our plans.' He rose with a small wince and motioned for Ambrose to follow him as Randolph suggested the best package for them.

'What is wrong? Are you in pain?' Ambrose studied him as they moved into the room with the coffin range on display. 'You look a little pale.'

'No, I am well, thank you.'

'I can see you home.'

'I am fine, brother, and thank you for your gallant act earlier. I wish to consult with you – I am thinking we should offer Charlie the job of a junior stable hand. What do you think?'

Ambrose's eyes widened in shock. 'You want to consult with me? Why?'

'Because you are a manager now, you will be more involved with our workers, helping to oversee them and train them where required.'

'Oh, right. Thank you, Julius,' Ambrose said, surprised and then frowned. 'The boy stabs you, and you want to give him a job?'

'He seems a good lad; they are a family needing a break, and we need a stable hand.'

'You are a rescuer, Julius. You cannot help but take in the needy.' Ambrose sighed. 'But I agree, it would be wonderful for them, and Mrs Ewing could use some good news. It will also mean we have someone ready to step into the role now, everyone can step up as you are no use to me at the moment.'

'Forgive me,' Julius said in jest. 'It all works out perfectly.' He smiled at his brother and returned to reception as his grandfather pushed the cheapest package upon the Ewing family.

'Julius, you have a thought?' Randolph asked, reading his grandson perfectly.

'Yes. Charlie, are you any good with horses, preparing carriages, cleaning, delivering goods, collecting parcels, stocking inventory and re-stocking?'

Mrs Ewing's breath hitched as she looked from Julius to Charlie and back again.

'I can be good at all of those things. I love animals, and I am very orderly, aren't I, Mum?'

'He is a very neat and organised boy. He works hard and sees what needs to be done without being asked. My husband always said so when he took Charlie to work with him.'

'What work was that, Mrs Ewing?' Randolph asked.

'He was a jack of all trades. Did repairs and odd jobs. Charlie is handy, too.'

'That could work out very well then.' Julius said. 'We have a job going for a junior stable hand. Would you be interested?'

'It comes with a free funeral package,' Ambrose added and shrugged, seeing Julius's small smile.

'Oh, that is too generous, Sirs. We cannot possibly accept after the aggravation we have caused you,' Mrs Ewing said, not believing it to be true.

'You can and you must, Mrs Ewing,' Randolph said, insisting as if there was no way of denying the elderly family statesman his wishes. 'You have suffered quite enough, and now it is time to accept a little help when it comes your way.'

'It is more than we ever hoped for. I cannot believe it,' she said, looking at Charlie and dabbing the tears away again.

'I won't let you down, Sir,' Charlie promised Julius. 'I'll be the hardest working stable hand you've ever had.'

'Just stay away from the knives in the kitchen,' Ambrose teased.

'Yes, Sir, I promise.'

'Then, let us prepare your father's funeral and give him a respectful send-off,' Julius said, concluding their meeting. 'I will give you a letter of employment, Charlie, and we will expect you bright and early the day after you lay your father to rest to begin your new occupation.'

Mrs Ewing began crying again, and Charlie's grin went from ear to ear. 'I told you everything would be all right, Ma, didn't I? I told you.'

# Chapter 33

MELANIE BAINS LOOKED TO the altar, lifted her eyes to the stained-glass windows as if for inspiration, then turned to Detectives Harland Stone and Gilbert Payne and began her story.

'I stayed after mass to gather the song sheets as I normally do, and when I came out of the church, I saw Daisy Dorchester with her arms around Father Damien Horan's neck. You can imagine my shock and disgust. Father Horan, a man of God and Daisy Dorchester, who was promised to a good man.'

Harland was not going to interrupt her story, but Father Morris could not help but defend his colleague.

'He was faithful to the end and shunned Miss Dorchester politely. He kept her gifts so as not to cause offence but felt nothing for the young lady. That is your findings too, is it not, Detective?'

Harland nodded. 'That is correct, she was rejected.'

Melanie Bains gasped. 'Oh my, I have been so judgemental.' Her voice hitched. 'Father Horan told me so when I accosted him over the matter, but I would only believe my eyes.'

Father Morris made the sign of the cross upon himself and said, "Blessed are those who have not seen, and have believed". You remember that from your Bible, Melanie?'

'Yes, Father. John: 20:29. Perhaps you will hear my confession and forgive me, Father?'

'Please continue, Miss Bain,' Harland said, impatient with the preaching.

'Well, that was it, Detective. I told him I was shocked and disappointed and he had betrayed my faith in him. I told him to repent. I had intended to tell my mother, but I hoped he might redeem himself, so I decided not to tell her.'

'When you left him, he was still alive? You did not push or see him lose his footing on the cliff stairs?' Gilbert asked.

'Of course I did not push him. How could you think so?'

'Stranger things have happened, Miss Bains,' Harland responded. 'Where did you go after that?'

'I went to the cemetery to place flowers on my father's grave. I always bring extra so I can have some for him when I finish the church flowers.' Melanie took a deep breath. 'That is where I saw Daisy Dorchester; she was also tending her father's grave, which is not far from my father's. I was surprised, to be honest, I thought her too selfish for that.'

With that, she looked apologetically at Father Morris again. 'It is just that she was so nasty, Father.'

He nodded but did not interrupt.

'Your confessional will be time-consuming,' Gilbert muttered under his breath, and Harland did his best not to laugh.

'Did you speak with Miss Dorchester?' Harland continued.

'Yes. I only intended to say good day. She looked me up and down as if I was not fashionable enough for a visit to the cemetery. Honestly, that girl,' Melanie shook her head. 'But then we did exchange a few words that were not pleasant.'

Harland's eyes narrowed. 'So, you did not raise a hand to strike her.'

'Absolutely not, I did no such thing.' Melanie flushed and looked away quickly.

'Your body language tells me you did something, Miss Bains. Pray tell us what it was?' Gilbert asked. Harland gave him a nod of approval, knowing Gilbert had been reading scholarly articles on how the body betrayed guilt.

Melanie swallowed and, glancing at Father Morris, said, 'I told her that I had seen her with Father Horan, and she was no better than Constance Kemp.'

'I see. Did she know who Miss Kemp was?' Harland asked.

Melanie scoffed. 'Of course, we all know about her. She was from our parish, and even though she died long before Miss

Dorchester and I were born, she is used as a warning against straying and vanity.'

'Was Miss Dorchester angry when you compared her to Miss Kemp?'

'She did not care what I said or thought of her; Daisy Dorchester was like that. She told me that I was jealous because I could not get a man, and then she went and took some flowers from her father's grave and put them on Constance Kemp's grave.'

'That was kind,' Father Morris said.

'She was just making a point that she admired Miss Kemp, and my thoughts meant nothing to her,' Melanie sniffed. 'So, I left.'

Harland studied her momentarily to see if she would add further to her story, but she did not. 'And when did you see Mr Theodore Wright? Witnesses placed you together, but you did not tell us you had seen him.'

'No, I did not think it was relevant,' Melanie said. 'I saw him in the cemetery with Miss Dorchester.'

Both detectives froze.

'You saw Theodore Wright with Miss Dorchester in the cemetery? Are you sure of that, Miss Bains?' Gilbert asked.

'Absolutely.'

'Were they together?' Harland asked.

'Not then. I saw him after I left her. Mr Wright was walking through the cemetery, and I said good morning to him, and he looked uncomfortable, as if he did not want to be seen. I thought it odd at the time. He put his head down and hurried on. When I got to the cemetery gate, I looked back, and he was talking with Miss Dorchester. They were still at Constance's grave.'

Harland rose, and Gilbert, surprised, jumped to his feet beside him.

'Thank you, Miss Bains. Do you have anything else to tell us, no matter how trivial? You cannot know what holds weight and what does not in an investigation.'

She thought for a moment and added, 'No, Sir, after that, I returned home.'

'One last question, Miss Bains, what fragrance do you wear?' Harland asked.

Melanie looked up at him, a look of surprise relaxing her worried countenance. 'Jasmine, Sir. It is my favourite.'

'Indulge me, if you will? Do you have an acquaintance who wears a fragrance of bergamot and musk?'

'How peculiar, Detective Stone,' Father Morris said. 'Do you associate the scent with the killer?'

'Not necessarily, Father, it is just another line of enquiry,' Harland assured him, not wanting to have them pointing the finger at some unsuspecting person as they had just done with Miss Bains.

Melanie responded. 'Yes, Sir, I have several friends who wear that fragrance. I only remember it because it is an unusual pairing, according to my mother, and quite modern. She is very knowledgeable in fragrances and flowers.'

'Hence your good taste in flowers,' Gilbert said kindly, glancing at the altar arrangements and trying to make amends for their former accusations.

'Thank you, Detective Payne,' Melanie said and coloured lightly. She was a practical girl by nature and not given to swooning. 'My friend Mr Foster wears it, and so does his friend, Mr Wright. In fact, Mr Wright kindly gave me his handkerchief at Miss Dorchester's viewing, which was liberally sprinkled with the fragrance.'

The detectives exchanged looks, and the men departed with a hurried goodbye and thanks to Father Morris.

'Miss Bains may have been in our interview room with that handkerchief when Miss Daisy Dorchester placed the scent,' Gilbert said, excited.

'Yes, I may have got it wrong with Miss Bains, but Mr Wright being with the debutante in the cemetery and wearing that fragrance is very promising.'

'Sir, you did not get it wrong if I may be so bold. We had to pursue that line of enquiry, and the witnesses placed Miss Bains with all three people.'

'True, thank you, Gilbert. Did you believe Miss Bains?'

'I find myself doing so, Sir. She was most sincere and convincing.'

'I believe she is telling the truth,' Harland said, his stride relaying his impatience. 'Let us return to the office, revisit the witness sightings once more, and refine our strategy. Then, Theodore Wright, the best-man-to-be, will get a visit from us first thing in the morning.'

Julius was weary and needed a moment alone. His grandfather was right; bed rest at home was called for, but before then, he had to go next door and thank the ladies. His wound burned, and after such a restless night, Julius could have curled up in one of the display coffins and slept for hours. He left the reception area, bidding Mrs Ewing and Charlie goodbye for now, and in an attempt to avoid everyone and their concerned looks, took the stairs down to Phoebe's room.

She was with a man her age, the same man lying on the table that she was preparing. They were smiling, and then the spirit looked at him.

'Oh my, who is this most beautiful man?'

Phoebe turned and huffed at the sight of Julius. 'My brother, who is meant to be at home resting,' she told Hyde and then turned to Julius. 'I am glad you are here; I need to change your bandaging.'

'There is no need for you to bother with that, but thank you,' he said, coming around to her side.

'I promised the doctor I would, and you don't want to risk infection.'

'I shall leave you to attend to your brother; we are done here, Phoebe, and thank you. You have made me look better than I did in life. Although nowhere near as handsome as your brother. He is very striking, isn't it?'

Phoebe smiled. 'He is indeed. Julius, may I introduce Mr Hyde Barker.'

Hyde gasped. 'Oh my Lord, he can see and hear me. I am mortified.'

Julius smiled. 'It is not widely known, and I beg you to keep my secret. I am sorry for your passing, Mr Barker.'

'Thank you,' Hyde said, 'It was a disappointment, but my father always said life is short.'

'I can attest to that in this industry,' Julius agreed.

'Hyde and I studied together at the mortician school. He was most kind to me,' Phoebe said.

'Ah, yes, I remember your name now, Mr Barker. Phoebe spoke of you often.' He exhaled. 'I must sit, Phoebe.'

Her face furrowed with concern. 'Then do so,' she said, seeing him to the couch.

'I will give you privacy,' Hyde said with a small bow and departed.

'Take off your jacket, and I shall clean and rebandage the wound,' she ordered her brother and Julius, with a sigh, shrugged off his jacket, kicked off his shoes and lay on the couch. His body relaxed with relief as he lay down, exhausted.

'You should not have come in this afternoon.'

'So I have been told. We have made some changes; I want to talk with you about them... and you have the most comfortable couch in the office.'

Phoebe smiled. 'Who are you escaping from?'

'Everyone who is well-meaning but exhausting.'

'I understand. Tell me your plans later, or Ambrose or Grandpa can tell me. Quiet now, you are pale.'

As he closed his eyes, Julius saw Uncle Reggie appear, and before Phoebe had returned with her kit, Julius was asleep.

# Chapter 34

Miss Phoebe Astin left work early shortly after Ambrose accompanied Julius home. It has been a tiring day with the surprise visit from her dearly departed friend, Julius refusing to admit he needed to slow down and still looking quite ill, and the news of adjustments to the business. The changes made good sense, but Phoebe was not one for change. She liked her life's pace and routines; they provided comfort. As for the option of training an assistant, Phoebe would think about it but did not feel inclined to do so right now. Perhaps in years to come, if she were with child or could no longer keep up with the demand for her services. Phoebe made her way to Kate's home.

Miss Kate Kirby also left work early as she was hosting the *Vexed Vixens'* dinner. Her parents and sisters were at the theatre for the evening, and it was one of the rare times Kate had the run of the place to herself for several hours. Her mother had happily prepared a supper for the ladies. As they sat around the dining table usually occupied by the Kirby family, Kate called the *Vexed Vixens'* dinner to order and welcomed the ladies.

'Thank you, dear Kate, and for hosting us,' Lilly said on behalf of herself and fellow *Vexed Vixens* – Emily, Phoebe and Violet. 'Now, Phoebe, I must ask, how is your brother? I saw Detective Stone today for an update on the Miss Dorchester case – which, mind you, seems to be going around in circles – and he told me of the unfortunate stabbing incident.'

'I thought Julius was not reporting it to the police,' Violet said, surprised, pausing with the serving spoon in hand. She realised she had used his Christian name and flushed. No one else seemed surprised, so she continued serving to provide a distraction.

'You are right, Violet, he did not, but the hospital staff did.' Phoebe filled the ladies in on the incident. 'I believe he is much improved,' she concluded. 'Would you not say so, Violet?' she asked her friend, whom she hoped would soon be her sister-in-law.

Violet smiled. 'Indeed. Before departing for the day, he dropped in to thank me and the ladies at the dress store for our concern. Mary has been praying for him, and Nellie made him a vegetable broth,' Violet explained. 'He would improve faster if he had spent the day in bed, but I imagine there is no telling him that.'

Phoebe agreed. 'He was at work for a brief time but was quickly tired.'

Violet laughed, remembering something, and shared it with the girls. 'Mr Astin – Ambrose that is – was with him, and poor little Mary is completely tongue-tied around them both.'

At the mention of Ambrose's name, Kate's eyes widened. 'I cannot blame her. They are so handsome the pair of them, especially Ambrose. I have had the pleasure of his company a little of late. I hope you do not mind, Phoebe?'

'Of course not,' Phoebe declared, smiling. 'You are two of my favourite people.'

Kate beamed.

'Men are terrible patients,' Lilly said and then shrugged. 'My five brothers will get a sniffle and think they are dying, but they will break an arm and say it is nothing. Strange creatures.'

'I am sure they say the same of us,' Emily said and then laughed. 'I recall my father's bemusement when I screamed and ran away from a spider, but the next night, on hearing a noise, went downstairs with the poker ready to confront a stranger.'

The ladies all laughed at the ridiculousness of the situation.

'If I might start with my vexation?' Phoebe asked and continued without waiting for an answer, 'Julius has invited me to take on an apprentice. The very thought vexes me.'

'Oh, I would love an apprentice,' Kate said, 'it would ease my load at the photographic studio. They could take the bookings, collect supplies and clean up. I must think about it,' she mused.

'It would be time-consuming to teach someone, not to mention that it would mean you have constant company,' Violet sympathised with Phoebe. 'I am fortunate that my two ladies are both good at what they do and came qualified. Speaking of jobs, I understand Julius has employed the boy who injured him. He is a generous soul. Tom, my brother, and I can attest to that.'

Phoebe smiled at the surprised looks around her. 'Julius has great compassion for those dealt the fickle hand of misfortune.'

'He has experienced it first hand,' Emily said with sympathy. 'That can change a person for life.'

There was a short silence as they considered this and life's fortunes and misfortunes.

'Oh, I am supposed to keep the gathering on track; I forgot my role as hostess,' Kate said, moving onto a lighter subject. 'Like Lilly, I, too, saw the detectives today. They dropped by my studio seeking Melanie Bains, but she had just left after collecting her photograph.'

'They think she was capable of murder,' Lilly whispered as if there was a chance someone might overhear. 'Oh, Kate, I am sorry. Was that your gossip?'

'Luckily no, or you would have been in trouble for stealing my thunder,' Kate nudged her with a smile, and Lilly exhaled, relieved. 'It is much more exciting than that. Detective Gilbert Payne asked after your health, Emily.'

All eyes turned to Emily, the eldest of the group at twenty-eight and so well presented and sensible, as one would expect from the proprietor of the *Emily Yalden School of Deportment*. Phoebe expected Emily to offer a flippant remark, shutting down his interest, but her reaction was quite the opposite. She smiled, her eyes lit up, and Emily declared, 'Did he? How very kind.'

'And you alone,' Kate continued. 'He did not care for my health, or Phoebe's, Violet's or Lilly's at all,' Kate teased. 'Just your health, Emily dear.'

Emily flushed, her olive skin a pretty hue, and she did not reply, unaccustomed to being teased in matters of love, despite tutoring her students in conversational starters and retorts.

'He is such a kind and lovely gentleman,' Phoebe said, coming to her rescue. 'It would be an honour to win his affection, and you are so worthy, Emily.'

'Thank you, dear Phoebe, and I do admire him,' Emily said with a grateful smile. 'We recently talked briefly and found we have similar outlooks.'

'And he is in a very solid occupation,' Lilly observed.

'I ensured he knew you were single, Emily, fear not,' Kate said.

Emily groaned. 'Oh dear. Not wishing to cause offence, but Kate, you are not known for discretion.'

The ladies tried to hide their smiles, and Kate gave them all a playful, stern look.

'I saw that look, Vixens, and I assure you all, I was the soul of discretion.' She turned to Emily. 'I just said that you worked so hard, as we single girls must do when managing our businesses.'

'Oh, well, that is good, thank you, Kate.' Emily exhaled with relief and brightened again at the thought of the lovely detective thinking of her.

'Mr Eldon Foster also came into the studio today,' Kate said, giving a small shake of her head. 'He wanted to order a photograph of Miss Daisy Dorchester. Poor man, I believe he is quite upset. I suspect he had imagined their life together and is at a loss.'

'Really?' Phoebe asked surprised.

'Yes. Her aunt took the print she was entitled to, but Mr Foster wanted something to remember Daisy by, or so he said.'

'He is a suspect too but is not the main suspect,' Lilly said. 'Oh, that is between us and to go no further, of course.'

The *Vexed Vixens* agreed with solemn promises.

'Sadly, Daisy did not return his affections,' Phoebe said. 'She told me their proposed union was an obligation from a childhood friendship and to better both families. I believe she hoped he would release her from it.' She lowered her voice. 'I met him briefly, but they seemed most unsuited.'

'He is very plain, and she is vain. If he had considerable money, perhaps he might be more handsome,' Lilly said.

'Lilly, you are outrageous,' Emily said with a shake of her head but a small smile.

'Sadly, it is true for a woman with Daisy's confidence,' Phoebe said. 'She was excited by the attention her beauty attracted and wanted to make the best match. I guess we cannot fault that.'

'Except she was stringing along poor Mr Foster, who was most charming when he called to order the photograph today,' Kate said. 'I felt very sad and sorry for him.'

'Has she stopped visiting you, Phoebe?' Violet asked.

'Yes, thank goodness. She was most exhausting. Which was the vexation I intended to offer tonight – when spirits do not move on and are exceedingly bossy.'

'Well, I don't think anyone can match that,' Kate said with a laugh, 'but we'll try.' And the ladies each took a turn stating what vexed them since the last meet.

As Phoebe listened and contributed, she could not help but think of Daisy. Phoebe's instincts warned her she had not seen the last of her yet.

# Chapter 35

WEDNESDAY MORNING WAS GREY, wet, miserable, and most unusual for a spring morning in Brisbane. It did little to improve Detective Harland Stone's mood as he had spent the night tossing and turning, going over the case in his head until he gave up in frustration and sought out a very early morning boxing session to release some tension. Now, showered, suited and at work, everything seemed a little clearer.

'I was wrong about Miss Melanie Bains, so I want to be confident of a case against Mr Theodore Wright before I accost him,' he said, annoyed at the assumptions he drew. He rubbed a thumb over his bottom lip and stared at the board covered in names and sightings.

'As was I, Sir. I thought a lot about this case last night,' Detective Gilbert Payne said, flipping through his notes.

I, too, spent many hours pondering it.'

'Good morning, detectives,' Lilly Lewis said, breezing into the office with a bright yellow dress on to compensate for the lack of sunshine in the day. Unlike the detectives, Lilly looked energised, with her blue eyes sparkling and her complexion fresh.

'Miss Lewis,' Harland said wearily.

'Good morning,' Gilbert said with a small smile and nod.

'Goodness, you are both so glum this morning; it cannot be just because of the weather. I have brought Mr Martin with me,' she said, and he arrived at the door on cue.

'I was paying the hansom driver,' he explained, shoving a large umbrella into the detectives' bin, removing his hat and running a hand through his blonde hair. 'Good morning to you both. I hope you do not mind the intrusion, but I discovered something of interest since catching you at the boxing rink this morning, Harland. As Miss Lewis dropped by my office with her hypothesis, we thought we would put on a united front.'

'Ah, so you are collaborating now?' Harland asked with interest.

'I would not say that,' Lilly said, 'but I had an arty question and thought Mr Martin the more artistic amongst us to answer it.'

'That's the truth,' Gilbert agreed. 'Shall we sit?'

The small group seated themselves while Harland remained standing near the board.

'Let us begin then,' Harland said.

'I shall scribe if needed, Sir,' Gilbert said and rose quickly, moving to the board.

'I confess I have not thrown myself into this case with much gusto, but I have got back on my feet after a setback,' Bennet said with a glance to Lilly as if she assisted in his recovery from Miss Phoebe Astin's rejection.

'Another resurrection of sorts,' Gilbert said, eliciting a chuckle from all.

'Precisely, Detective Payne,' Bennet said in good humour. 'As a consequence, I have made up for lost time, hopefully, and spoken with every living person I could find connected to the deceased,' he exaggerated in good humour. 'Thus, I believe we all know that Miss Dorchester was in love with another – Father Damien Horan?'

'Yes, we are across that,' Harland answered.

'Did you know that if Mr Eldon Foster did not wed Miss Dorchester, he would not be gifted the house promised by his father on their betrothal?'

'Yes, we have that,' Gilbert said. 'It was in Mr Foster's best interests to wed, but we understand that his father has gifted it to him in sympathy.'

'I see. You are a tough group to impress.' Bennet looked to his notes. 'You know that Miss Dorchester was not widely liked because of her caustic tongue, not that you would tell that from the diplomatic obituary Miss Lewis wrote.'

Lilly smiled. 'It was most challenging.'

Bennet continued. 'And that Miss Melanie Bains is in love with Mr Eldon Foster and despised Miss Dorchester for the manner in which she treated him.'

'In love? I knew she held him in high regard,' Harland said.

'Jealousy is a very respectable motive for murder,' Lilly suggested.

Harland tapped the board where a note bearing Miss Bains's name was at the top of the suspect list. 'As of yesterday, we believed her to be our main suspect, especially as the crimes committed were manageable by a woman's hand. But now, I believe our killer is a male, and my partner concurs.' He nodded at Gilbert.

'I do, Sir. I am of the opinion we need to resurrect a suspect – with apologies to the church for that reference – a suspect who has not been honest with us.'

'Are they ever?' Lilly asked, dramatically rolling her eyes. 'May we ask to whom you are referring?'

'Mr Eldon Foster?' Bennet cut in.

'Maybe, but not our first choice,' Harland said with hesitation in his voice. He saw Miss Lewis and Bennet exchange a smile. 'What is it you know?'

'We believe he may be the culprit; we both have something to add to your list, Detective Stone,' Lilly said. 'Last evening, my friend Miss Kate Kirby advised that Mr Foster came by requesting a print of Miss Dorchester's photograph.'

'He is dialling up the sympathy and ensuring he looks appropriately bereaved,' Bennet said.

'Perhaps he is feeling melancholy, given they were once childhood friends,' Gilbert suggested.

'I have something even more interesting,' Bennet said with a grin at Lilly as if challenging her.

'We shall see about that,' Lilly retorted.

'My client, Mrs Audrey Stewart – Miss Dorchester's aunt and guardian – advised me yesterday that Mr Foster had approached her solicitor to ask for a portion of Miss Dorchester's dowry as he had been assured of it and given his intention to honour their agreement, he believed he earned it as any widower would.'

'Goodness, that is outrageous,' Gilbert exclaimed.

'And definitely more interesting than my information,' Lilly conceded, 'thus far.'

Bennet raised an eyebrow and gave her a small smile.

'Most unorthodox and very interesting, thank you, Bennet. Mr Eldon Foster is setting himself up very nicely for a comfortable life with a wife of his choosing,' Harland said with eyes narrowed and focused on the board.

'But witnesses do not place Mr Foster at the scene, and he has an alibi. Focus instead on Mr Theodore Wright,' Harland suggested.

'The question is, why was Mr Wright in the cemetery?' Gilbert asked.

'Why indeed.' Harland paced. 'Did he see Miss Dorchester throw her arms around Father Horan and blame the priest for encouraging her advances? He may have been defending his best friend's honour and confronted the priest or defending his own. He has told us of his declaration of love to Miss Dorchester.'

'So, if he saw Miss Dorchester give the priest a lock of her hair, might he have confronted Father Horan, given him a good shove that led to the priest toppling backwards?' Lilly mused.

'Did he then hurry to catch up with Miss Dorchester and find her in the cemetery talking with Miss Bains and get into a disagreement with her?' Bennet added.

'Yes,' Gilbert continued. 'If he declared his love to Miss Dorchester and she rejected him, was the humiliation sufficient to act irrationally?'

'Passionately, fuelled with anger,' Lilly said in a hushed voice as she thought about the hypothesis.

'Look at the sightings of him,' Harland pointed to the board. 'He may have collected the ring and followed her, knowing Miss Dorchester was seeing Father Horan for counsel. Where is the ring? Why was it not found upon his person?'

Bennet shook his head. 'But he was a victim and struck on the head. What of Mr Eldon Foster? What if he had decided to join Miss Dorchester for counsel, saw her embrace the priest, and then saw his best friend declare himself? He has a better motive for harming all three. You believe him capable of it, don't you?'

'Physically, yes,' Harland hesitated.

'But morally, no,' Gilbert concluded, and Harland agreed. 'From speaking with Mr Foster, I felt he had a quiet desperation to be wanted by Miss Dorchester, that he hoped the wedding might make her settle into life with him as his wife.'

'Interesting,' Lilly said, 'as I believed the same when I spoke with him. He displayed an off-hand bravado as if her insults were expected, that it was the Daisy Dorchester he had always known. He might have even despised her sometimes, but he did not want the humiliation of being cast aside by her, and she had not done that despite loving another.'

'Very true, Miss Lewis, an interesting perspective,' Harland said. 'Yesterday, Gilbert and I questioned Miss Melanie Bains in-depth, and she revealed something very interesting – that she saw Mr Theodore Wright in the cemetery. She is the only witness to do so. He did not mention that he was in St Patrick's Cemetery or saw Miss Dorchester there when we interviewed him.'

'Sir, there was something else I found last night while going through all my notes,' Gilbert said.

Go on,' Harland invited his protégé.

'It is an odd thought, but the wounds on Theodore Wright's scalp were on the front of his scalp, left-hand side. So, he must have seen his attacker unless he was pushed forward and struck something, but he claimed to be hit from behind but did not see his assailant.'

Bennet hurriedly rose to his feet. 'Might they have been in it together? Theodore Wright and Eldon Foster conspiring to get rid of Miss Dorchester and share her wealth?'

'It is as good a theory as any, except that Theodore Wright declared his love to Miss Dorchester and betrayed his best friend. I saw them in the hospital ward when the truth came out, and I don't believe their reactions to each to be rehearsed.'

'Then tell us your theory about Mr Theodore Wright, Detective?' Lilly asked. 'You have your suspicions.'

'I do, and Gilbert has just confirmed they might be valid.' He turned to the group. 'I know Theodore Wright was passionately in love with Miss Dorchester, and she did not rebuke his attentions, thus leaving him to believe she might feel the same. In that depth of passion, he was prepared to forsake his friendship and ask for her hand, except Mr Wright saw Miss Dorchester giving Father Horan the lock of hair and confronted him when she left.'

'He pushed the priest to his death, then headed to the cemetery where he found Miss Dorchester, professed his love and was rejected,' Gilbert said.

'Yes. The humiliation and devastation made him snap,' Lilly said, 'and he killed her then and there in a fit of jealousy. But what of his wounds?'

Harland smiled. 'I believe they are self-inflicted.'

He thought momentarily, revisiting Gilbert's odd observations as he had found himself doing in each of their cases, raking through them should there be a missed gem.

'What is it, Sir?' Gilbert asked, hoping to assist as Harland directed a quizzical look his way.

'The murderer has provided clues illustrating his state of mind. The inscription on the grave, Gilbert, spoke of truth?'

'Yes. It says, "You will know the truth, and the truth will set you free", Sir,' Gilbert said.

Bennet added enthusiastically, 'So the murderer chose the grave of Constance Kemp to show his disgust of Miss Dorchester's misplaced and false affection and to tell us that if we looked for the truth, we would know why she met her maker.'

'That would mean he planned the murder,' Harland mused. 'That could be possible if Miss Dorchester visited her father's grave every week at the same time.'

'But you don't think it was planned to such a degree, Sir?' Gilbert asked.

'Correct. I feel this is a random, jealous, vicious attack, and the murderer is not telling us that Miss Dorchester deserved it or justifying his actions; he was telling *her* why she deserved it,' Harland said. He drew in a deep breath. 'Gilbert, let us question Mr Wright again. We will head to his place of work now. Miss Lewis, prepare your copy but do not print it yet. Bennet, would you see if the hospital kept the clothing Mr Wright was in when he arrived unconscious?'

'I shall immediately.'

'And be cautious, everyone,' Harland said, 'he is not a big man or naturally violent, but a man cornered is capable of anything.'

# Chapter 36

JULIUS THOUGHT HE MIGHT feel somewhat bereft watching Ambrose head out with Will when the brothers had always managed the funerals together, but he did not – it was, after all, only going to be an absence of two days a week and until he recovered. He checked the boys over, declared they looked the part and promised Ambrose he would be all right.

'I know you will miss me and our time together today,' Ambrose teased.

'Yes, lucky Will,' Julius retorted, making Randolph and their newly promoted funeral assistant laugh.

'Right, lads, you have all you need,' Randolph said. Lowering his voice, he added, 'This is very important to Phoebe. I believe Mr Barker was very kind to her when they studied together.'

'One of the few men in her class who happily accepted a lady student,' Julius confirmed.

'It was a good showing at the viewing, so let us hope they come along and pay their respects at the funeral too,' Ambrose said. 'I hate small funerals.'

'That's thoughtful of you, Ambrose,' Will said, 'but maybe they have close friends rather than many friends.'

'It's only because he gets bored with no one to distract him,' Julius told Will the truth of it.

Ambrose scowled at his brother as Phoebe arrived at the top of the staircase, looking quite ethereal in a tasteful black mourning gown with her fair hair loose and feminine.

'We all here then, shall we go?' Ambrose asked.

'Do not over-exert yourself, Julius. Will you promise?' she asked of him.

'Perhaps go next door and check on your other business and Miss Forrester,' Ambrose teased as he walked down the hallway.

'I will keep an eye on him,' Randolph assured them, issuing umbrellas and hurrying them along. 'Let's not keep the dead waiting.'

The door closed behind them, and Julius exhaled with relief.

'I do need you to go next door, lad,' Randolph said and smiled at Julius's expression. 'I assure you it is not a ruse, although I am happy for it. I could go, but I have two customers arriving shortly.'

'That's fortunate,' Julius said with a raised eyebrow and a small smile. 'What is it you need from next door?'

'I need Miss Forrester to confirm orders were filled for a package we did – funeral and mourning clothes for a family of four. I know the funeral was delivered, but if Miss Forrester can confirm the order was collected and they did not ask for anything more, I can finalise the bill.'

'I shall do so now.'

'Then my accounts will be ready for you to take to your bookkeeper. You also need to approve Miss Kirby's photographic plan and suggested date, plus the advertisements for this week's *Courier* needs to be checked, and you are meeting with Lucian mid-morning to co-sign a delivery of timber. After that, I have scheduled you to rest on the couch for the afternoon.' Randolph handed Julius the paperwork.

'Thank you, Grandpa. I don't know how I will fill your shoes two days a week.'

'Fear not, if chaos ensues, I will clean it up the next day,' he said with a wink at his grandson.

Julius chuckled and took the paperwork. To his grandfather's amusement, Julius straightened his tie and checked his appearance before heading out the front door to the mourning wear shop.

Miss Mary Pollard gasped as she saw the tall, handsome figure of Mr Julius Astin heading their way.

'Mr Astin is coming, and he is not walking as confidently as he once did.' She straightened and returned to work, not seeing Violet and Nellie exchanging smiles.

Julius knocked lightly on the door and opened it cautiously. 'May I enter?'

'Of course, Mr Astin,' Nellie responded as she was in his line of sight. 'How are you feeling?'

'Much better, thank you, no doubt because of your broth, Mrs Shaw, Miss Pollard's prayers and Miss Forrester's new shirt that buoyed me no end.'

The ladies laughed at his charm.

'If that were truly the case, Mr Astin, we would be in great demand at hospitals all over the country,' Violet told him. She reverted to addressing him formally in front of her staff. 'Would you like a cup of tea?'

'No, thank you. Mrs Dobbs keeps us well supplied with refreshments. I fear I will expand considerably while out of action.'

'Perish the thought,' Violet teased.

'I have some paperwork that needs your attention when convenient, Miss Forrester.'

'Shall I take a look now? The meeting room?'

'That would be appreciated,' Julius thanked her and followed Violet into the room where the ladies normally enjoyed their breaks, keeping the door ajar. The back door was also opened that led to the yards and stables. He waited for Violet to sit before lowering himself into a chair.

Then, to Julius's surprise and dismay, the spirit of Miss Daisy Dorchester appeared nearby him.

He gasped.

'What is it? Are you in pain?' Violet touched his arm.

'I am not, thank you,' he said, trying not to look at the spirit, but Daisy lingered.

*The grave, Phoebe is in danger.'*

Julius rushed to his feet, tripping as he righted himself, tearing at the stitches, the blood appearing on his shirt. He rarely saw spirits outside the confines of Phoebe's office, nor did he encourage it, but here was Daisy, looking pale and ghastly and uttering a warning.

'Julius!' Violet hastened to her feet to grab his arm, believing him to be falling.

*'The grave,'* the spirit said again. The apparition disappeared.

'Violet, please get Claude,' Julius said as he covered the bloody patch with his hand and hastened as best he could.

'Let me help you.'

'No, please, call Claude.'

341

She nodded and rushed to the rear door. Julius stumbled behind her as Violet took the stairs down to the yard, catching the attention of Claude in the stables, who came running.

'What has happened, Miss? Oh, Julius, you are bleeding.'

'A horse, quickly Claude, quickly.'

Claude raced to the stable and hurriedly affixed their remaining horse to the trap.

'You cannot ride, Julius,' Violet said, taking his arm. 'Send Claude. Tell me, and I—'

'Phoebe is in danger. I cannot explain; I am sorry.'

He stumbled down the stairs, meeting Claude halfway with the trap.

'You cannot ride, Julius, get in.'

Julius hauled himself up beside Claude, leaving Violet gaping at him. They tore off at a dangerous pace for a crowded area and an injured man. It was fortunate it was a wet day and fewer people had braved the weather; it was fortunate Julius knew many shortcuts to all the cemeteries – tricks of the trade.

'It is a befitting day for a funeral,' Phoebe said, accepting Will's hand as she stepped down from the hearse and touched the coffin of her friend. A good-sized group had gathered, and many had followed the hearse in from the cemetery gates.

'This is the third burial we have had at St Patrick's these last few weeks,' Ambrose said. 'If I were a parishioner, I would be getting worried.'

Will chuckled subtly. 'Should we mention the packages we have available?'

'A fine idea,' Ambrose said in jest. 'Julius will promote you again if you keep thinking like that.'

'My friend is not a practising Catholic, but his father and ancestors are buried here. It is a coming home if you will,' Phoebe said, ignoring their banter.

'I hope we are all buried together,' Ambrose said sobering before adding, 'I am sure you and Julius will want to spend eternity with me.'

'It is such a long time,' Phoebe said and sighed but gave Ambrose a small grin when he turned to scold her. 'I hope to lay near Mum and Dad. You can join me there if you like.'

They stopped talking as the family gathered, and Ambrose and Will undertook the formalities. The prayers were said, the blessing offered, and eventually, the coffin was lowered into the ground. Phoebe dabbed her eyes with a small lace handkerchief; Hyde Barker had been taken too soon for such a good soul.

As the crowds dispersed and only the working parties remained – the funeral directors, Father Morris, and the gravediggers ready to fill in the plot – Phoebe looked about her.

'Where was Daisy buried?' she asked Ambrose.

'Over there near that large angel statue with the clipped wing.'

Phoebe spotted it. 'I shall pay my respects while you finish up. I shan't be long.' Taking her umbrella, she trod on the small path to avoid the puddles and went further into the cemetery to visit Daisy and her grave.

Amidst the drama of the loss of her friend and the injury to Julius, Phoebe completely forgot the warning that Daisy had tried so hard to get to her and headed towards the grave.

# Chapter 37

DETECTIVES STONE AND PAYNE arrived at Theodore Wright's place of business – a narrow building a little like Mr Wright himself – unassuming and somewhat drab.

'He is not in today,' a gentleman with a pencil behind his ear told the detectives. 'He returned to work a few days after his assault but has been struck down by headaches. Perhaps try him at home.'

They requested the address, thanked the gentleman, and returned to the hansom cab, which Harland had requested wait for them.

'At least he lives nearby,' Gilbert said, glancing at the address. They arrived within minutes only to receive a similar reception from the landlady.

'He went for a walk to clear his head, the poor dear,' she said with a sympathetic expression on her weathered face. 'Not only is he nursing a wound, but he has lost a dear friend.'

'You know Mr Eldon Foster then, Madame?' Harland asked. 'I understand they had a falling out.'

'I do, but I was not referring to him. I meant the young lady who was murdered. Mr Wright told me she was his sweetheart, and he intended to propose.' She lowered her voice and leaned in closer to them. 'I confess I thought him most ambitious, but who am I to say.'

'Thank you, Ma'am. Which direction did he walk in?'

She pointed the way, and the detectives departed, returning to the dry interior of their hansom cab.

'Most frustrating,' Harland said.

'St Patrick's is in the direction indicated, Sir. Do you think he has gone to the church to pray or perhaps to visit Miss Dorchester's grave? He might have forgiven her and is feeling melancholy.'

'Let us try that. I would leave you here to wait for Mr Wright, but if I should encounter him, I may need backup.' Harland leant out and instructed the driver where to take them, and shaking off the rain drops, the two gentlemen astutely watched the path along the journey lest Mr Theodore Wright should be spotted.

'We are nearly there, and do not leap from the trap on arrival,' Claude warned Julius.

'Since when did you become so bossy? That promotion has barely kicked in, and you have taken charge,' Julius said, unhappy to have another person giving him orders, especially his staff.

'Mr Astin senior said if you were to try and get a horse or the cart or attempt to do anything silly, we were to curtail you for your own good. He was right.' Claude nodded towards the blood streak evident on Julius's white shirt.

'Hmph!' was the best that Julius could reply to his grandfather's directive, but he felt relief coursing through him as St Patrick's church came into sight.

'Go to the cemetery entrance, Claude; it is at the back of the church.'

'Right away,' Claude said, turning the trap as quickly as was safe. As they approached the corner, they saw the departing funeral group ambling out slowly – a possession of black umbrellas adding to the dreary day.

Julius swore under his breath. 'You will have to let me go by foot from here; we cannot rush through the grounds with the mourners present.'

'I'll take you to the other gate and get you as close as possible to the entrance. May I suggest you do up your jacket to hide the blood?'

Julius scrambled to do so and leapt from the trap as soon as Claude had pulled to a stop. He raced through the gates, his breath hitching with the sharp pain. He tapped his hat and bowed his head, acknowledging the small group of mourners departing from the gate he chose to enter. Then he saw Ambrose and Will across the cemetery grounds, but Phoebe was not in sight.

'Sir, is that not Mr Astin arriving?' Gilbert asked as the two men descended from the hansom and paid the driver. Julius Astin was entering the gate further afield from them.

'Yes, and Julius should not be moving that fast. I wonder what is happening?' Harland frowned, watching his friend, who did not move freely.

On seeing a small crowd of mourners seeking a cab, Harland released the driver from waiting. He hurriedly assisted an elderly lady into the hansom the men had abandoned, impatiently keeping his eyes on Julius's movements as best he could.

He accepted her thanks, and nudging Gilbert, they hurried to find out what was happening within the St Patrick's Cemetery grounds.

# Chapter 38

P HOEBE READ THE HEADSTONES as she made her way to Daisy's grave. She loved the messages from the heart – "much-loved wife", "never forgotten father", "heart and soul of the family" – and the names of those that had gone before telling a little of their origins – Scottish, Irish, German. She paused at the headstones that told of the means of death – young Samuel was taken too soon by pneumonia... Sarah, sadly missed, died in childbirth... a horse kicked Albert, causing his death... and goodness, Beatrice died in a ferry accident. Several graves did not speak of the manner of death but featured a prayer of hope and consolation.

She came to the angel statue, and there was the sizeable headstone of Miss Constance Kemp, whose headstone featured a verse about truth and another reading: "But the Lord said to

Samuel, 'People look at the outward appearance, but the Lord looks at the heart'." Phoebe wondered what fate had befallen poor Constance to spend eternity branded by vanity.

Nearby was Daisy's grave. The mound of dirt had not yet received its headstone – that would come sometime later – but it featured a small sign bearing Daisy's name and life and death dates as written by her brothers and supplied by *The Economic Undertaker*. The grave was covered in flowers now past their prime. Phoebe gasped with surprise as she rounded the large angel statue and lifted her umbrella slightly. A man in a dark, waterproof coat was on his hands and knees at the foot of Miss Constance Kemp's grave. He patted the ground with his hands as if looking for a lost possession.

He turned sharply and hurried to his feet.

'Who are you?'

Phoebe's eyes widened at the abruptness of his question.

'Good day, Sir. I am an acquaintance of Miss Daisy Dorchester. I have come to pay my respects.' She said and nodded in the direction of the fresh mound of earth. Phoebe did not inquire who he might be but expected an introduction as she studied his face.

She recognised him. He had briefly been at Daisy's viewing. But why was he fossicking at the foot of Miss Kemp's grave and right near Daisy's place of burial? She gathered herself as a thousand thoughts rushed through her head – Daisy warned her, and now she was at the grave, both graves!

Phoebe shivered. 'I am sorry if I am interrupting you,' she offered politely, expecting he would announce himself now and offer an apology of sorts for his abruptness, but that was not to be.

'Well, you are, so do what you must and hurry on.'

Phoebe stepped back as if she had been slapped. Such rudeness was uncalled for, and accepting that she did not seek the company of people very often, surely manners had not deteriorated to this degree from the gentlemen of the city.

'Can I help you look for something?'

'No, I've lost a valuable item, and I don't need you or anyone else trodding it into the ground.'

As the breeze picked up slightly, making her shiver again, Phoebe caught a whiff of his fragrance in the air – bergamot and musk.

'Your scent. It is bergamot and musk, is it not?'

Her question surprised him. 'What of it then?'

'It is most pleasant.'

He glared at Phoebe. 'I know you from somewhere.'

Realisation dawned on Phoebe. She remembered who the gentleman in front of her was... he had come to Daisy's viewing but was excused by Detective Stone from an interview. He wore a bandage then. Now, he wore none.

'Oh, you are...'

His eyes narrowed. 'Yes, who am I?'

Phoebe looked behind. Where was Ambrose? She could not see him, but the hearse was still in sight. A glance at the only weapon at hand – the umbrella – reminded her she was alone, vulnerable and out of sight. Phoebe hurriedly returned her attention to the gentleman before her, fear coursing through her.

*Daisy warned me not to go to the grave.*

*I had dismissed her counsel.*

*It was Hyde's funeral that drew me here.*

*Is this him? Is this the man who murdered Daisy? Mr Theodore Wright.*

*He is wearing the scent Daisy identified.*

*But he did not come into the interview room where she smelt it.*

*Did he have an accomplice?*

She glanced around nervously. 'I best get going then and leave you to your business.'

'What do you know of me?' he hissed.

'Nothing sinister, I assure you. If I recall correctly, you were attacked, yourself a victim,' she said, hurriedly trying to diffuse the situation.

'Yes, that is so. I was the victim of a brutal attack.'

That seemed to appease him, and Phoebe continued lacing her voice with sympathy. 'I believe I read of it, Sir. It must have been frightening.'

'Is that all you know of me?'

'I don't know why I would know you at all, Sir.' She glanced behind her again. 'I best return to my brother; he is waiting for me, and the rain is getting heavier; he will want to depart.'

Theodore Wright's jaw dropped open, and he swore in anger. Phoebe turned to see what had caught his attention.

'They are here, those detectives entering the grounds.'

Phoebe began to step away. 'Forgive me for interrupting you. I shall leave you to your toil.'

'Not so fast,' Theodore Wright said, his eyes narrowing. 'I saw you at Daisy's viewing. You were talking with the police, the tall one. What do they know of me?'

'Sir, I assure you, they would not share their thoughts or investigation with me.'

He suddenly leaned forward and grabbed her arm tightly, shaking her. Phoebe yelped in fright.

'You recognised me. What do they know? Tell me, or you will find yourself next to her,' he said with a sneer on his face and a nod to the mound of earth where Daisy rested for eternity.

'I know you are the friend of the bereaved, Mr Eldon.'

'Bereaved,' he scoffed. 'That's rich. He never loved her. Now, he's free from marrying her and still inherits his father's house. He would never have made her happy.'

Phoebe knew had she been Lilly or a stronger person, she would have asked more questions, perhaps eliciting a confession, but she wasn't, and she was frightened.

'Are they looking for me?' he asked, shaking Phoebe's arm and standing over her.

'Who, Sir?'

'The detectives, your *friends*,' he said the word with a hiss. 'They interviewed me at the hospital.' Theodore Wright stepped closer again, his stance threatening. 'You will not mention to anyone that you saw me here.'

*'Run, Phoebe, he is the one.'*

'Daisy!' Phoebe exclaimed in fright, relieved to see the debutante – her presence ever so faint – and forgetting for a moment that Daisy was in spirit form and could not assist her.

*'I told you not to come here, did I not?'*

'Daisy? Who are you talking to?' Theodore's eyes were wide with fright as he looked behind him and back to Phoebe.

*'Tell him I know it was him. Tell him, Phoebe!'* Daisy demanded.

Phoebe nodded, pulling away a little and feeling her shoes squelch into the mud. 'Daisy said to tell you she knows you took her life.'

He gasped in fright, releasing her arm and stumbling backward, looking around wildly.

*'Tell him I know his fragrance.'*

Against her better judgment, Phoebe passed on the message, hoping it might frighten Theodore Wright enough to turn and run.

'She knows your fragrance.'

'I didn't...' he started to protest. 'You're making this up. Who are you?'

*'Tell him he proposed to me on bended knee at Constance Kemp's grave.'*

Phoebe repeated her words, and Theodore gave a small cry of terror.

*'I know where the ring is that he dropped, the engagement ring. Tell him.'* Daisy faded and then returned as if the effort of saying too much drained her ghostly form.

'Where is she?' he demanded, frantically looking around. 'I didn't mean to harm her. It was an accident, a moment of passion. I loved her.'

'She knows where the engagement ring is. Daisy is standing right beside you now.'

He screamed in terror and thrashed out. 'No! Get her away from me.' Theodore Wright ran at Phoebe, his hands going to her throat to stop her from talking, and it was then he ran into a tall, enraged Astin and a punch that struck him to the ground.

Ambrose could not believe what he was seeing. From afar, he saw his brother, Julius, entering the cemetery at a pace that alarmed Ambrose. Moments later, Claude appeared, running behind Julius. Had he been tying up the horses? Then, Detectives

Harland Stone and Gilbert Payne hurried towards Ambrose and Will from the other entrance.

'What is happening?' Ambrose asked, panic rising.

'We are not sure,' Harland said, 'but we are seeking Theodore Wright to arrest him for murder; he may be here. Your brother has also arrived at a great pace.'

'Theodore Wright? Was he part of our funeral party?' Ambrose asked, confused.

'No. He was the assault victim, injured on the day Miss Dorchester and Father Horan were murdered. You would not know him if you saw him?'

'No!' Ambrose started running towards Daisy's grave, calling back, 'Phoebe went this way.' The detectives followed at a great pace. 'She is at Daisy's grave. If he is there, then...' he didn't finish; his heart was in his mouth.

Then he saw Phoebe holding her umbrella over her head, and nearby, a man in a dark coat was standing too close to her.

'That is him,' Gilbert said, picking up his pace as they all did.

Ambrose called her name as they slipped on the wet grass and mud, and the rain beat down. Then the main lunged at her, Phoebe screamed with fright, and Julius appeared, his fist impacting the man's face, knocking him clear away and to the ground.

Everyone seemed to arrive at once, yet Ambrose felt like he was seeing events unfold in slow motion as he scrambled for

Phoebe's umbrella, shaking it and holding it over his sister. Julius was shaking out his hand; Harland raced to Phoebe's side, shirking off his wet coat and wrapping it around her shivering form; Gilbert and Claude pulled Theodore Wright up from where he lay, his nose bloodied, his eyes wild and screaming for Daisy to stay away from him; and Will, arriving moments after the other men, removed his tie, offering it to Gilbert to secure the murderer's hands behind his back.

'Why are you here?' Ambrose asked his brother. 'How did you know Phoebe was in danger?'

Unlike his two siblings, Ambrose could not see Daisy or hear her exclaim with delight, *'Your most handsome brother, Julius, has come to save my honour, Phoebe. I told you I was murdered, see! Theodore just confessed.'*

'I just put two and two together,' Julius mumbled.

'You are not well, and you're bleeding again,' Ambrose said, his tone abrupt, which was most out of character but relayed his concern. 'Phoebe, are you harmed?'

'No. He just frightened me.' Addressing Detective Stone, Phoebe said, 'He was here looking for the engagement ring. I could smell his scent – bergamot and musk.'

'Daisy warned you not to come here,' Julius said in a low voice so only those who knew of Phoebe's unique skills could hear. He moved closer, and she wrapped her arms around him, seeking comfort.

'I never gave it a second thought when I came to Hyde's funeral,' Phoebe said, looking up at her eldest brother.

'Nor I when you said you were going,' Julius agreed regarding his sister with concern.

'You still have a good right hook. Perhaps you should spar with me again soon,' Harland said with a small smile to Julius to lighten the mood.

'I have just had practice,' Julius said in jest, 'and done my bit for the law. That should see me out for a while.' While Phoebe clung to him, Julius leaned against the angel statue for support, prompting Ambrose to take charge.

'You have done yourself a disservice and set back your recovery, brother. Will, bring the hearse. Julius, you will lay down and rest on the return.'

'I shall see to it,' Phoebe said, feeling stronger now and returning Harland's coat. 'Thank you, Detective Stone.'

Ambrose did not notice Phoebe and the detective's eyes locked, and for a brief moment, their hands touched in the exchange. Nor did he realise his sister was falling in love, and he could not see the spirit of Daisy nearby, looking pleased with herself. He stepped up and continued to issue orders. 'Claude, can you take the detectives and their prisoner back to the station in the trap?'

'That would be much appreciated,' Harland said, breaking eye contact with Phoebe.

As the hearse and trap arrived, the group disbanded with the sound of Theodore Wright's voice yelling, 'Forgive me, Daisy, please do not haunt me,' and the two Astin family members who could pay heed to the dead heard Daisy's voice faintly insisting, *'I told you I was murdered! See!'*

Ambrose assisted his brother into the hearse and then offered his hand to Phoebe to sit her nearby Julius, ignoring their conversation as Phoebe suggested, 'Perhaps Daisy was not so awful after all; she had my welfare at heart,' she whispered to Julius as she studied him with concern.

'Perhaps,' Julius agreed, and they shared a smile that said neither truly believed that.

# Chapter 39

M ORNING EDITION

SENSATIONAL CONFESSION TO MURDER
DEBUTANTE AND PRIEST KILLED BY JEALOUS
SUITOR
ASSAULT WOUND SELF-INFLICTED
DETECTIVES THANK PUBLIC
*The Courier* concludes its exclusive report
by Lilly Lewis and Fergus Griffiths.

A sensational confession to murder has been recorded, and
your reporters can reveal the motive is one of the oldest known
to man – jealousy.

The two recent deaths and the assault of a man near St Patrick's Church, New Farm, were first thought to be unconnected and accidental. But the bereaved families can take comfort in knowing that justice has not eluded the man who was found to have caused both deaths, and it is due to the superior investigation work of Detectives Harland Stone and Gilbert Payne from the Roma Street Police Headquarters.

The culprit, Mr Theodore Wright, a public accountant from South Brisbane, aged 22 years, had the great misfortune of falling in love with the debutante beauty Miss Daisy Dorchester, who was thought to have slipped and struck her head on a graveyard headstone, causing her death.

Mr Wright, a close friend of the deceased's beau, Mr Eldon Foster, was to be the best man at their wedding – a proposal was forthcoming. But Mr Wright lost his heart so passionately that he was prepared to sacrifice his long-term friendship to ask for Miss Dorchester's hand in marriage.

Having collected the engagement ring with a verse he selected and engraved within its gold band for his friend, Mr Wright decided to use it for his own means. He knew Miss Dorchester was attending mass at St. Patrick's and seeking marriage counsel after mass. However, he had not expected to see Miss Dorchester offering Father Damien Horan a lock of her hair and slinging her arms around the priest's neck.

Father Horan's compassionate rebuff left Miss Dorchester distressed, and she hurriedly departed to the cemetery in the grounds nearby to visit her father's grave. Mr Wright challenged the Catholic priest, demanding an explanation.

Detective Harland Stone has told *The Courier* that 'Mr Wright confessed, saying, "The priest had no right to be romancing any woman, let alone a woman seeking his blessing and guidance for her nuptials." He then pushed Father Horan, who was innocent of the accusation, sending him falling to his death down the cliff stairs.'

By his admission, Mr Wright hurried to catch up with Miss Dorchester, claiming Miss Dorchester had returned his affections and been attentive to him in the past. Finding her by her father's grave, he dropped to one knee and proposed. Miss Dorchester was said to have ridiculed him and threatened to tell the man she was promised to after her debut, his close friend, Mr Eldon Foster.

Humiliated and embarrassed, Mr Wright confessed to the detectives that he grabbed Miss Dorchester by the neck and dragged her to the grave of Miss Constance Kemp, shaking her and telling Miss Dorchester that she was as vain as the woman who possessed the headstone before them.

Mr Wright told the detectives that he left Miss Dorchester but returned moments later out of fear and anger of being revealed. Coming up behind her, Mr Wright threw Miss Dorchester to the ground, where she struck her head on the side of Miss Kemp's headstone and died.

Mr Wright, in a panic, returned to the church grounds and, ensuring no one was around, picked up a decorative garden stone and self-inflicted a wound to the side of his head to give himself an alibi as a victim of an assault.

Detective Stone said that the state in which Mr Theodore Wright was in at the time explained his rash action, and the blow was delivered with enough force to create the ruse. Mr Wright had intended to say he fought off Father Horan's assailant and paid the price. Thus, when conscious in the hospital, Mr Wright claimed to have been assaulted and a victim worthy of sympathy.

Clever police work and public assistance led the detectives to believe Mr Wright was lying. In seeking his arrest, they found the villain in the cemetery searching for the ring he had offered Miss Dorchester and lost when abandoning the murder scene. Beset by guilt or in a state of delirium, Mr Wright was begging the deceased Miss Dorchester for forgiveness at her graveside. Theodore Wright then admitted his role in the deaths and provided a full confession.

Detective Stone said the public's assistance was much appreciated and greatly impacted the case. The confession was supported by witness sightings and blood on Mr Wright's clothing retrieved from the hospital by private investigator Mr Bennet Martin.

Mr Theodore Wright will face the magistrate in the coming weeks, but we can satisfactorily conclude that justice has been served.

Lilly Lewis put down the newspaper and smiled at her writing partner, Fergus Griffiths.

'That is it then, another case concluded,' she said and exhaled.

'And an intriguing one at that,' Fergus added, running a hand through the mop of dark hair he sported. 'I cannot but feel sorry for Miss Daisy Dorchester even if she was not the nicest young lady.'

'She was dastardly from all that I was told, but to be cut down before one truly begins in life is cruel.'

'The private investigator will be happy with his mention,' Fergus said, and Lilly felt him studying her. 'Is he a potential suitor?'

Lilly did not hurry to dismiss his question, knowing she could trust Fergus and he had become a friend, genuinely concerned for her happiness.

'It is good to keep him on side, and he did find a few helpful clues with this case. My mention of him will also help him get his fee paid. As for being a suitor, with Phoebe's brother not interested in me—'

'What is wrong with the man?' Fergus cut her off, teasing.

'I can't imagine,' she said with a grin, 'except that the lady he likes is extraordinarily lovely and has become a friend of mine – Miss Violet Forrester – so I cannot begrudge him that. But thank you for your loyalty, dear Fergus.'

'So, Mr Bennet Martin, has he prospects?'

'Well, he did surprise me, I confess. I thought him to be quite vacuous.'

Fergus laughed. 'Goodness, poor man.'

Lilly waved her hand around casually. 'He is arty and pretty; I am sure that is how my brothers will see him – they are all quite rough and tumble. But Mr Martin is also quite witty and spirited. I think he likes to compete wits against me, and he is quite liberal in his views of women and their place in the world. I am not averse to a handsome man; he might keep me on my toes.'

'There might be hope for him yet,' Fergus agreed with a smile and a nod.

They both paused on hearing their editor, Mr Cowan, loudly berating two journalists. The front page had been held for their story, and they had rushed to make the late edition deadline, finding themselves in good stead with the editor.

'Thank goodness that is not us receiving his tongue lashing,' Fergus said, packing to leave for the day with the afternoon edition tucked under his arm to show his wife his name on the front page.

'Well, not today, it isn't. There is always tomorrow,' Lilly said jokingly.

On the other side of town, Detectives Harland Stone and Gilbert Payne had spent the day concluding their case and report writing. As Harland delivered the report and returned from his superior's office – thanking those he passed who congratulated him on closing the case – his thoughts went to Miss Phoebe Astin. She had been his priority at the cemetery yesterday. He would not make the mistake again of being so absorbed in his work he did not see to her comfort. While all he could offer her yesterday was his jacket, Harland had wanted to offer his protection, but her brothers were on hand, and Julius, as always, had taken care of his family. She had clung to Julius, who had placed his arm around his sister protectively, and Harland felt jealous – ridiculous, raw, green envy. He could not find an act of gallantry to do despite his desperation to be of service.

His first thought in the morning and his last thought at night was that if providence smiled upon him, Miss Astin would be his to care for and love. Now that he was established in his role and settled in his accommodation, his mind wandered to the future, and Harland imagined collecting Phoebe from her place of work and returning home together at the end of each day. Or perhaps she might be at home waiting for him, the lamps lit, dinner underway. He even indulged in the thought of finding her at home with their children. It was the first time such thoughts had entered his mind with any lady, but somehow, it could be no one else.

Harland packed the thought away as he entered the office to find an open box on Gilbert's desk filled with case notes and the young man cleaning the board.

'Our superiors are happy, Gilbert, a job well done.'

Gilbert turned to smile at him. 'That is good news, Sir. I wonder what challenge we shall be given next.'

'Well, let us hope it is held over until tomorrow. Leave while you can, Detective, and thank you.'

'I will, Sir. There is a poetry gathering tonight, and I might get along to it,' Gilbert said, standing straighter and looking pleased at the thought.

'Then I shall see you in the morning, inspired and ready for work.'

A short time later, alone, Harland's thoughts returned to departing, but instead, he decided to pay a visit to *The Economic Undertaker* and ask after Julius and Miss Astin's health. It was, after all, on the way home. He grabbed his jacket, straightened his tie and undertook some grooming before departing with purpose in his step.

Bennet Martin played down the mention of his name in the late edition of *The Courier* when his clerk, Daniel, returned from retrieving a copy and, with Mrs Clarke, fussed over it. But secretly, he was delighted and grateful to Miss Lilly Lewis.

'I shall prepare your account for Mrs Stewart immediately, and we shall all be paid this month,' Daniel said in jest, enjoying his employer's wry expression.

'If no other cases are pending, I might spend the last hours of the day painting while the light is good,' Bennet said. 'Shall we all call it a day?'

'An early mark, excellent! I shall prepare the invoice before departing,' Daniel said. 'I have also drafted you a report detailing your interviews, location searches, and meetings with the detectives and the coroner. You can fill in the bones in the morning if that is convenient, and we shall send it to Mrs Stewart with the invoice?'

Bennet nodded. 'Well done, thank you, Daniel. I did not do a great deal, but for what Mrs Stewart is paying, I am satisfied I earned my keep, especially undertaking the interviews with the debutants and their hovering mothers.'

Mrs Clarke removed her apron. 'You would be a good catch, Mr Martin; you cannot blame the ladies for wanting to see their daughters well matched.'

'Haven't I always said you are a good catch?' Daniel teased him.

'No cheek from you, young man,' Mrs Clarke told her nephew. 'Dedicating yourself to finding a lovely young lady would not hurt you. Lord knows your mother is despairing for a grandchild.'

'Yes, Daniel, your aunt has a very good point. Why are you not courting? You have good employment and prospects,' Bennet said, enjoying, giving as good as he got.

'I shall see you both in the morning,' Mrs Clarke said, giving them a fond look.

As Bennet climbed the stairs to his studio, he decided to visit Julius tonight and perhaps persuade him to come out for a tipple since his friend was on the mend. He was more confident he could withstand the mention of Phoebe's name should it come up; Bennet's mind was drifting elsewhere from the lovely Miss Astin.

As he opened the door, he saw her. On the canvas near the window was the beginning of a new portrait of a fair maiden with brunette locks, the bluest eyes and a mouth that could be quite sassy. He felt a frisson of excitement and hurriedly removed his jacket and got to work.

Julius felt at ease for the first time in days as he looked at the faces around the table. Ambrose was doing a spirited recount of the whole sorry tale at the cemetery over a late afternoon cup of tea in the office of *The Economic Undertaker* – the first time they had been client-free all day. Miss Violet Forrester from the mourning wear store next door was present with the family, as was Mrs Dobbs, who had baked and served her speciality apple tea cake. Randolph shook his head after hearing the tale.

'I don't know what madness has befallen this place of late,' his grandfather said and sighed, adding in jest, 'Ambrose has been the most responsible; the shock is not good for me.'

Ambrose laughed and nudged Julius. 'And you thought the day would never come, brother,' a smug look adorned his face. Julius resumed his usual expression of patience.

'If only the day would come when you stop vexing me.'

'That much change is not good for anyone,' Ambrose assured him.

Randolph continued, 'My eldest grandson has been most uncharacteristically reckless, throwing himself in the way of knife-wielding youths and striking men to the ground.'

Julius winced at the description. He did not like any reminders that he was capable of being out of control as he was as a youth, but his burning wound and bruised hand reminded him of his actions.

'And my granddaughter, who cares little for being amongst people, has immersed herself in too many of late, causing us all great anxiety.'

'I am sorry, Grandpa,' Phoebe said, taking his hand. 'I completely forgot there was a killer on the loose when I went to the cemetery to farewell my dear friend, Hyde.' She refrained from dwelling on Daisy's warning as Mrs Dobbs was likely to bless herself numerous times at the mention of the afterlife.

'Forgiven, my dear,' Randolph assured her. 'And your excuse, Julius?'

'I will endeavour to avoid knives and not chase criminals for a few days at least, Grandpa,' Julius promised.

'Good. In all earnestness, we could not bear to be without you, lad,' Randolph said soberly, and all heads nodded.

Julius felt himself the subject of everyone's attention and found the presence of Violet particularly distracting, even though he spent many hours contemplating ways to be in her company. On this occasion, she read his discomfort, her eyes full of compassion, and she turned the attention to herself.

'I am not sure I can take the excitement either, Mr Astin,' she agreed with the senior Astin. 'I have slept very little, consumed too much tea, and paced the floor until it shines. Poor young Mary has worn out her rosary beads, and Mrs Shaw had made us all fortifying broths... several times. And if I may add without offence, Mrs Shaw is correct, the hours spent in her steamy kitchen does make her hair unruly.'

Everyone around the table laughed, picturing poor Mrs Nellie Shaw's springy hair. Violet looked to Julius and said in jest, 'If you persist in such reckless behaviour, I may need to find a quieter position of employment.'

A quick smile changed his countenance, making him appear younger. 'With hand on heart, Violet, Grandpa, I promise you there will be nothing more unexpected from now on... calm waters only.'

They heard the door swing open. Miss Kate Kirby had arrived, all flustered and excited, the hansom driver helping with her cameras and tripod, the afternoon light perfect for their agreed photographic session of both businesses. The gentlemen rose from their seats.

'Good afternoon! Photographic time then?' she asked, seeing the group all turn to look at her loud entrance and giving a special smile to Ambrose as he leapt up to assist.

'I will help you set up,' he said enthusiastically, 'Just remember to get my best side. Oh, what am I saying? They are both good.'

Julius rolled his eyes, Kate laughed and returned outdoors, Ambrose in pursuit.

'I best straighten up,' Mrs Dobbs fussed, tidying her hair as she departed.

'Our jackets will need to be brushed down once the horses and hearse are in place,' Randolph said, rising to grab the grooming brush.

'I shall tell the stable lads and get the hearse around the front,' Phoebe said.

'Tell them to put their jackets on,' Randolph called after her as she headed down the hallway.

'I will prepare the ladies next door,' Violet said, getting to her feet, 'and ensure our work area is clean.'

'Perhaps we will start with the calm tomorrow then,' Julius said and was rewarded with a smile from Violet as his grandfather handed him his hat and began to lecture him on where best to stand to avoid the afternoon traffic.

THE END (but not for long...)

# Author's notes:

I HOPE YOU ENJOYED this story as much as I enjoyed writing and researching it. I was inspired to include a photographic opportunity for *The Economic Undertaker* after coming across the images taken by John Hislop Funeral Directors in Brisbane circa 1892,[i] just two years after my novel is set. The hearse is pictured outside the building with plumes on the horses for those wanting to spend a little more on their funeral. Three men stand by the window, another is in the driver's seat of the hearse, and one man is in front of the hearse. A bystander seems to have been caught in the shot on the far left. While my fictitious Astin family do not feature in this photograph, you can imagine Julius, Ambrose and Randolph standing out front of the business, Will and Claude on hand, and Miss Kate Kirby taking the photograph and capturing them forever more.

I based the sad murder of Miss Constance Kemp on the real-life tragedy of Miss Susannah Stacey – a story discovered for my non-fiction book *'Grave Tales: Tasmania'*, and never forgotten. Susannah, 18, was brutally murdered by her intended, Richard Copping, with an axe after he saw her in the company of another man. There was a huge outpouring of grief for the young lady and sympathy for Richard, as the families were well respected, and the young couple was to be married. Richard sat on the fence waiting to be taken away; he was hanged. A journalist from the *Tasmanian Evening Herald* blamed Richard's actions on "the frenzy of love in an evil moment."[ii]

There was a comet that visited for a time and a learned astronomer discovered it. Thus, Julius, Ambrose, and Phoebe's father may have used the cosmic visit to woo their mother.

The Great Comet of 1861 was visible to the naked eye for approximately three months from May to August 1861 and then visible in telescopes until May 1862.[ix]

The newspaper article about the competitiveness and pressure on debutantes, as read by Lilly to her *Vexed Vixens* friends, was based on a real article written in 1890 and featured in the *Australian Town and Country Journal*. The link is below should you wish to read this article and consider the pressure put on young girls to make a good match. As the writer said of debutantes, "It is therefore a rather serious matter to see if they have the necessary capacity, the air, and the balance for the great future awaiting them."[x]

Violet's recipe came from a real cookbook of the era, Mrs Lance Rawson's titled *The Queensland Cookery and Poultry Book*. From Rockhampton, North Queensland, Mrs Rawson's book was first published in 1878 and is considered a "a time-capsule of colonial Australian culinary lore".[xi] Quite a few of the native favourites went into the pot!

While it is fiction, I do try to be as accurate to the era and facts as I can and sincerely praise and thank Trove (the National Library of Australia) and the State Libraries for providing such wonderful sources of information about days gone by. Thank you to Karri Klawiter, Art by Karri, for the beautiful cover and thank you for reading the *Dastardly Debutante*; I hope you enjoyed it.

**References:**

[i] Horse-drawn carriage used for funerals outside J. & J. Hislop Undertakers in Brisbane, ca. 1892. (2010). John Oxley Library, State Library of Queensland. Retrieved 11 September 2023 from URL: https://collections.slq.qld.gov.au/viewer/IE1193006

[ii] The Execution of Richard Copping. (1878, October 22). *Tasmanian Evening Herald (Launceston, Tas.: 1878)*, p. 3. Retrieved March 31, 2022, from http://nla.gov.au/nla.news-article232957111

[iii] Shocking Tragedy near Sorell. (1878, May 14). *Tribune (Hobart, Tas.: 1876 - 1879)*, p. 2. Retrieved March 31, 2022, from http://nla.gov.au/nla.news-article201731697

[iv] The Bream Creek Tragedy. (1878, May 16). *The Mercury (Hobart, Tas.: 1860 - 1954)*, p. 2. Retrieved March 31, 2022, from http://nla.gov.au/nla.news-article8963244

[v] Op.cit. Shocking Tragedy near Sorell. (1878, May 14). *Tribune.*

[vi] Execution of Copping. (1878, October 23). *The Cornwall Chronicle (Launceston, Tas.: 1835 - 1880)*, p. 3. Retrieved March 31, 2022, from http://nla.gov.au/nla.news-article66501400

[vii] Ibid.

[viii] Shocking Tragedy near Sorell. (1878, May 14). *Tribune (Hobart, Tas.: 1876 - 1879)*, p. 2. Retrieved March 31, 2022, from http://nla.gov.au/nla.news-article201731697

[ix] The Great Comet of 1861 - C/1861 J1. (2023, August 30). In *Wikipedia*. https://en.wikipedia.org/wiki/C/1861_J1

[x] Bringing Out the Buds. (1890, March 29). Australian Town and Country Journal (Sydney, NSW: 1870 - 1919), p. 34. Retrieved May 10, 2023, from http://nla.gov.au/nla.news-article71109480

[xi] Mrs Lance Rawson's *The Queensland Cookery and Poultry Book* – https://www.amazon.com.au/Queensland-Cookery-Poultry-Book-1890/dp/1975938801

# About the Author

Helen is a hybrid-published and Amazon best-selling author.

After studying English Literature, Media, and Communications at universities in Queensland, Australia, and obtaining a Counselling Diploma, Helen has worked as a journalist, producer and marketer in print, TV, radio and public relations. Born in Toowoomba she has made her home in Logan Village, Australia with her journalist husband, Chris, and Boxer dog, Baxter.

**Connect with Helen:**
Website: www.helengoltz.com
BookBub:www.bookbub.com/authors/helen-goltz
Facebook: www.facebook.com/HelenGoltz.Author

# Also By Helen

**Miss Hayward & the Detective Series (historical mystery/ romance set in Australia):**

*Murder at the Carnival*

*The Artist's Missing Muse*

*Mystery at the Asylum*

*The Mortician's Clue*

*Murder in Bridal Lane*

**The Clairvoyant's Glasses series** (paranormal/romance)

*Volume 1 – A vision unexpected*

*Volume 2 – Time has a shadow*

*Volume 3 – Love has no bounds*

*Volume 4 – Fate comes to call*

**The Jesse Clarke series** (cosy mystery):

*Death by Sugar*

*Death by Disguise*

*Death by Reunion*


**The Mitchell Parker series** (crime thriller):

*Mastermind*

*Graveyard of the Atlantic*

*The Fourth Reich*


**Writing as Jack Adams** (mystery suspense):

*Poster Girl* (stand-alone)

**The Delaney and Murphy** childhood friends' thrillers:

*Asylum*

*Stalker*

*Cult*

*Hitched (coming early 2024).*

Printed in the USA
CPSIA information can be obtained
at www.ICGtesting.com
CBHW021500290124
3824CB00031B/134